Table of Contents

CHAPTER ONE

The Mandan Villages, 1810

First, Baptiste heard muffled gunfire, then furious drumming. It meant the boats were finally arriving, bringing the Mandan chief back home from Washington City, where he had met the Great White Father. Soon Baptiste and his parents would board one of those boats and it would take them away from the Mandan Villages and down the river. His mother had told him over and over that it would happen. He had begged her to tell him what it would be like in St. Louis. But Sakakawea had no stories of the future. All she would say was that Captain Clark would raise him.

A weak sun hung low in the sky. The autumn wind howled, sweeping in and around the clay mounds along the shore, bending bare trees toward the ground. Baptiste ran all the way from the top bluffs, where he liked to stand, his arms spread wide, and pretend he could fly, swooping zigzag down the steep slopes to where the flotilla spread nearly the breadth of the frigid river. Almost everyone in the Mandan and Hidatsa villages was streaming down to the shore. Those who didn't were perched on the domed roofs of their lodges to watch from afar.

Baptiste found his mother in the crowd. She was shaking her head. "Our neighbors are peaceful people. They think they live at the heart of the world and strangers will come to trade in peace, as before. But the world is changing." She held him close. He breathed in the familiar smell of her leather tunic and the beaver castor perfume she wore.

Ever since he could remember, Baptiste's mother had told him that he would go to live with Captain Clark, who chose him because he was special. She said that Clark had called him a promising boy. It meant that one day he might do important things in his life. Clark had asked to prepare him for this future. "Destiny" was a blurry thing, though. Sakakawea said he must be patient. *Only with time will you understand who you are meant to be.*

BAPTISTE AND HIS parents, Sakakawea and Toussaint—a Shoshone woman and a French interpreter—boarded the lead boat. Baptiste studied his mother's broad face. This was another uprooting for her. She had been just a child when she was stolen away from her people by the Hidatsa, then sold to Baptiste's father, the French Canadian Toussaint Charbonneau. Baptiste and his parents had gone all the way to the great western ocean with Captains Lewis and Clark! There, at Fort Clatsop, one of them, Captain Clark, had grown so fond of Baptiste that he asked to raise him as his son.

For weeks, Toussaint bragged about how he had gone to St. Louis years ago, when it was Spanish. But when Baptiste peppered him with questions, he said only "Wait and see" or "Some of their houses are made of stone. They're made to stay put."

Men with stern faces and long rifles lined the decks of the boats. Baptiste met one man's eyes. Their blue depths were cold. No one had given him such a look in his life. Everyone in the villages knew him and liked him. He didn't flinch from the man's stare.

His mother beckoned and he scampered to her side. She was wearing her fine antelope shift, embellished with elk teeth and intricately woven dyed quills, a beaded belt, and leggings. She had folded the top of her buffalo robe to show her long hair with its daubing of red clay. She was beautiful!

At last, they were on their way! His friends on the shore waggled their fingers and made sad faces. His puppy ran in circles around them, yipping with confused excitement. When the boats were launched, the boys trotted alongside until they could no longer keep up. Their cries were snatched by the cutting wind.

CHAPTER TWO

Chouteau

When he could no longer see the figures on the shore, Baptiste felt
a stab of sorrow. All the ball games he had played with his friends,
the times they pretended they were warriors, sneaking behind their
strutting elders, his little brown puppy, who had just tracked a
rabbit for the first time—all gone! He'd left his bow and arrows
and his slingshot behind. Wouldn't he need them? He had always
known he would go to Captain Clark one day, but it suddenly felt
like a kidnapping. What was wrong with his old life? He had
been happy. The way ahead, his mother had made clear, would be
full of tests. He glanced at her. She nodded. *You will be all right.*

When they had drifted a few miles, Toussaint sidled up to a
group of growling men with the motley look of fur traders. After a
moment, Toussaint's raspy voice rang out. "Baptiste!"

"This is my boy," he brayed, brandishing a familiar worn piece
of paper. "Captain Clark begs me to let him raise this 'beautiful
and promising child' as his own son!" He poked at the marks on
the paper and licked his lips. "He calls me friend and gives me a tract
of land in return for my valuable service to the United States."

Baptiste had heard the story of Clark's letter many times.
When it was delivered to the Mandan Villages three years earlier,
a visiting Englishman had to read it to him. *But I'll soon learn how to*

read, Baptiste thought to himself. *I'll be able to understand any letter.* Thanks to Clark, he would acquire a power that his father didn't have.

Bored with Toussaint and his letter, Baptiste noticed a trim figure who strode up and down the deck with a walking stick in one hand and a book in the other. This fellow was a different sort of Frenchman. The skin of his clean-shaven face was paler than Toussaint's; his military suit clung to his body, and his boots gleamed. The man's superior air struck Baptiste as funny. His mother said that Clark had laughed with delight at her son's antics when they'd spent the winter at Fort Clatsop. Baptiste now began to strut along in the Frenchman's wake, pantomiming preoccupation with a book.

Then he glimpsed his mother's face and stopped. Why was she frowning?

But the men sitting around Toussaint guffawed. One called out, "*Eh bien*, M. Pierre. You have yourself a shadow." The man suddenly whirled, dropped his stick and book, and swooped Baptiste into the air.

"You do as I do, eh?" he said, suspending the boy just above his glowering face. Baptiste, holding his breath, didn't blink. A long moment passed.

"Then you will do well, my boy!"

He set Baptiste down, patted his head, and picked up his book. Baptiste was thrilled by those words. *You will do well.*

Toussaint hurried over, bowing to the Frenchman, who ignored him. He grabbed Baptiste and backed away.

"That's Pierre Chouteau," Toussaint muttered, his fingers digging into Baptiste's shoulder. "He is commander of this fleet. All these traders and mercenaries are his. They are here to protect us on our journey. Chouteaus are the men you want to know in St. Louis. They are not to be laughed at." His fingers relaxed their grip. Baptiste rubbed the spot.

The boy trotted back to his mother.

"Baptiste, you don't know these men," she said softly. "Not all men are alike. Captain Clark loved to watch you strut and dance. Another man might not." Then she smiled and touched Baptiste's face. He blinked at her. He would have to hold himself in check while he learned how to conduct himself.

They could hear Toussaint boasting to the traders. "Did you see him favoring my boy?" He began barking out his notions about the weather or the snags that might catch them up in the fast-moving river or the chances they'd be attacked by hostile tribes. Soon he was playing cards most of the day. Sakakawea sat calmly mending her deerskin skirt.

Toward evening, someone started playing a fiddle. Music always made Baptiste's feet dance. He began to step high and twirl about. The fiddler noticed and picked up the tempo, making him go faster and faster. Everyone laughed; even Sakakawea smiled. Baptiste loved to amuse his mother.

As the hours passed, Sakakawea hummed to herself while she sewed. Baptiste stared into the dark water. Chunks of ice still floated there. Once in a while, he glimpsed figures on the shore who quickly vanished. Buffalo moved unhurriedly, indifferent to the passing boats, even when music and laughter exploded from them. Sometimes he spotted a drowned carcass. Baptiste had seen the beasts venture out on the ice and fall through. Months later, their fermented meat was a great delicacy, but he thought the odor was horrible.

His friends would be playing now with their dogs and ponies. Would they remember him after many moons had come and gone? If his was the great destiny his mother promised, would he ever hunt with them again? And yet, a moment later, he let go of the past and was bursting with eagerness to see Captain Clark. His mother promised that Clark was kind and wise. He was tall and strong. Baptiste remembered nothing but the man's bright red hair. Excitement and fear were the same rattling feeling. How strange it was that his mother could sit, placid as ever, when such a great adventure lay before them! But then, her life had already been so full of adventure. And so had his! She had told him the stories over and over. His mother had carried him all through the long journey to the western coast. She had found food for the men when the supply they brought was exhausted. She had saved their papers and instruments when their boat nearly sank. He and his mother had both fallen very ill. But the captains had brought potions that cured them. On the edge of the ocean he had seen a huge fish lying dead—his mother had insisted that they be allowed to go to it. Then, on their way back to the Mandans, Captain Clark had carved Baptiste's nickname, Pompey, on a gigantic rock. All that, he and his mother had done together, and he knew because she had told him.

THE TRIP LASTED three months and there were no attacks on the fleet. Soldiers had entered the largest Arikara village on the way north and obtained a promise of safe passage. Then, one morning, as layers of mist gradually burned away, cries rang out from the leading pirogues: "Land ahoy!" "Look!" "St. Louis!"

Baptiste hustled to the prow of their boat, craning to see. Thickly sprinkled, steep-roofed, smoke-spewing buildings sat as if strewn by a mighty hand above the water. As they drew near, everything came into focus, but was no less strange. This was St. Louis! Baptiste had never seen a city before!

The fleet bumped and pushed its way into a maze of boats crowding the wharves like puppies at their mothers' teats. This was very different from the little trader settlements they'd passed along the way, different even from the big wooden fort the Corps of Discovery had erected next to the Mandan Villages. Baptiste had been born in that fort.

Men onshore fired their muskets in welcome, sang, passed whiskey from mouth to mouth, pounded one another's backs, grinning like wolves. There was a rush to get off. Baptiste had to fight to stay on his feet as bodies pressed against him. His mother had never failed him. He kept checking her eyes. *Keep moving*, they said. *Stay close!* He gaped at men and women dancing frantically together on the porch of a shack. Boxes, crates, trunks were piled everywhere, just coming off boats or waiting to be loaded onto them. Bustle and enterprise, sharp voices that grated on his ears. He squeezed his eyes shut for an instant, to banish the fear that had suddenly pierced his gut.

Toussaint grabbed a man's sleeve, spoke urgently to him, listened, then squinted toward the town. Men were tossing packs of beaver pelts into mule carts, teeth clamped on fat cigars. A few horses pranced and skittered in circles, their riders shouting. A man flailed at a mule that wouldn't budge.

They walked along a muddy street lined with houses built of upright log posts and timber. Each had a plot of ground alongside, barren in the winter cold. Up close, the arrangement was orderly, the streets crossing to form squares. Here, Baptiste was amazed by houses built of gray stone blocks. They had the permanence of mountains. He skittered along, swiveling his head this way and that. Music poured from a building and he wanted to go in to listen, but Toussaint gave him a shove—*Keep going!*

Somber men with bright blankets draped around their shoulders passed them in single file. One, a giant, wore a vivid blue American Army jacket, his bare legs poking out below, and shaded himself with a scarlet umbrella. They seemed quite at home in this place. So did hunters who might have been Indian, or might not—Baptiste couldn't tell. They dressed in greasy buckskins and there were women unlike any Baptiste had ever seen, clothed in fabrics of every color, their cheeks red and their eyes outlined in black. They walked arm in arm with men, not behind them as Mandan women would. They were in a great rush and chattered brightly in French, his father's language. Baptiste was confused. His mother had said he was going to live among white men. But there were few white faces. Most were every shade of red, brown, and tan. A sharp burst of laughter from a window made him look up.

"Allons!" Toussaint barked, yanking him by the wrist. More stone houses glowed with whitewash. Here and there, a man or woman glanced at them, but most did not. The streets they were now on were not crowded. Lodges in the villages had teemed, inside and out, with people related by blood or custom, some working, others busy lounging and gossiping. It made him feel safe to remember their easy routines. He checked his mother's face to see what she thought of their new surroundings. She stared unwaveringly ahead, but he knew she was gathering facts and impressions. She had been

his teacher and guide all his life, always ready to explain. But for the moment, they both had to depend on Toussaint.

His father veered into a dooryard and confronted several men before he seemed satisfied by a response. They set off again along narrow, walled streets. Baptiste's ears rang with the sawing, cursing, hammering, scraping, singing, yelling from every side. A sharp clink came from a corner doorway. He saw men pushing balls around a table with sticks. Hands clapped, glass struck wood. One of the men, seeing Baptiste, leaned out and beckoned. "Have a drink on me, little fellow," he called in French, laughing. His mates joined in. Baptiste laughed too. "*Allons!*" barked his father.

Toussaint vanished through another doorway. He reemerged, frowning. "Finally some news of Clark," he said grimly. "But it is not good news. The captain has left the city. He's gone to the East to see Mr. Jefferson." He wiped his lips. "They say there is extreme land hunger in the Louisiana Territory that he must attend to. If they mean to give it over to farmers..." He shook his head and made a noise of disgust. "Americans are coming. Watch out!" Baptiste felt his mother's body tense. Did their long journey, leaving the old life for a new one, mean so little to Captain Clark that he wasn't even there to meet them?

But it turned out that Clark had arranged lodging for them in a squat house whose dirt yard was bounded by a high, rickety fence. They arrived there as the sun was setting. "When Captain Clark returns, he will tell us what to do," Toussaint told his family, before disappearing.

Their landlord was a portly Frenchman with gleaming eyes and a cunning smile. He catered eagerly to Sakakawea, bowing and calling her madame, and promised to bring them some apples from his cellar. Would she like pecans as well? She bent her head and put her palms together. "*Merci, merci.*"

The next day, Toussaint told them Baptiste needed new clothes. They all went to a shop, where his father picked out a shirt, vest, pants, and shoes for Baptiste, holding them up to his body to estimate the proper size. Sakakawea occupied herself in another part of the shop, where clothing for women was displayed.

"Come, woman!" Toussaint called to her when he had paid the shopkeeper.

She didn't move, and when he glanced at her, she held up a garment.

"What? You want to wear that?" he barked, and she nodded. He hesitated, then relented. "All right. Let them see who we are." Baptiste was amazed, both by his mother, who was trading away her best clothes, and his father, who never indulged her.

Back at their lodgings, Sakakawea urged her son to put on his new outfit. She did the same, smiling shyly. In the trim blue jacket, long patterned skirt, cobbler's shoes, and, most strikingly, a colorful turban, she was transformed. Mother and son looked each other up and down and burst out laughing.

That night, they joined the parade that circled the central plaza every evening. People were showing off their finery, she told him. "And so will we." Baptiste pushed his arm through hers. They were a lopsided pair, linked elbow to elbow. She pointed to a tall Frenchman. "See how he carries himself." Baptiste puffed himself up like the Frenchman. He would be a man before long, and he would take care of his mother—better than Toussaint ever had.

The Frenchman abruptly turned and stared at them. After a moment, he strode to them. "Madame," he said, "I am certain that you are Sakakawea. My friend Cruzette has sung your praises many a time. I will tell him that I have seen you." He bent low. Sakakawea nodded to him. He bowed again, and when she said nothing, he turned and walked away.

Sakakawea's eyes sparkled and she dipped her head. Baptiste clung to her arm. He felt prouder than ever of his mother. He felt protective, too. His father never showed her such respect. They resumed their perambulation. No one else approached them, but even so, St. Louis now seemed more welcoming.

WHEN THEY HAD been in town for a few weeks, and Captain Clark still had not sent for them, Baptiste decided to find where he lived. He would keep an eye on the place and be the first to know when his benefactor returned. He set off on his quest without telling his parents. Toussaint, he felt sure, would tell him to stay put and wait to be summoned.

This was a landscape of sharp angles. But he'd never been lost and he had no fear of it anyway. He turned two corners and ducked through a doorway to a dark room piled high with cloth sacks. A single shaft of light from a small, high window pierced the dusty air. A man stood muttering to himself while he marked papers at a wooden stand. Baptiste asked him in French, his father's tongue, where Captain Clark lived.

Without glancing at Baptiste, the man asked, "Why do you want to know?"

Baptiste was relieved. "He has sent for me," he replied.

The man looked at him and guffawed loudly. "I'd like to know what for!" he said. "Corner of Main and Vine. See if you're expected!"

Baptiste could hear him chortling halfway down the block. Clearly, people here had not been told of Clark's plan for him. In the Mandan Villages, many people knew about it.

The names Main and Vine were of little use until he could find someone else to ask how to find them. He approached a woman who smiled and pointed up the street they were on, indicated a right turn and after that a left.

He found a large, low-slung building, a stone wall on one side of it, a few apple trees, and three other log structures, one of them attached to the house. He waited a long time, hunkered down in front of the main house, but there was no one around.

After a few minutes, he set off to explore the rest of the city. In just an hour, he heard what sounded like half a dozen different languages spoken. He saw French men and women in fine clothes, a chief attended by half a dozen warriors, a man in a leather apron apparently driving a hard bargain with a pair of dusky voyageurs.

The streets were barely wide enough for laden wagons pulled by teams of oxen. Some were bordered by narrow sidewalks. He passed little shops with windows displaying blankets and kettles, others edibles, but beautiful, unlike any food he'd ever seen. He stilled his appetite. Without the necessary currency, there was no chance of tasting any of it. But he would, someday! He would buy and taste and touch! He would have whatever he fancied!

Away from the center and the shops, dark-skinned men and women swept and chopped wood. When he reached the harbor, he saw others loading freight. They woke a dim memory of Clark's tall, muscular servant standing in the firelight at Fort Clatsop, where Toussaint had had to do "women's work" while he and his mother went to see the great beached fish. She had loved that man, York. The captains had told Indians that he was the only one with that skin color. But here Baptiste saw many.

AT THE END of the street was a paved open place. He watched a woman fill a bucket at a pump and then he tipped his face under the stream so that the cool water washed into his mouth and down his cheek. No one paid him any attention. Among the Mandan and Hidatsa, he was surrounded by playmates and kindly adults. It hurt to go unnoticed. There was plenty to see in the town, but he missed his friends, missed running with their puppies, shooting their bows and pretending to be grown up. Feeling homesick, he found his way back to their room. His mother was preparing supper.

Toussaint came home very late and didn't say where he had been. He could explode in a temper at times like this, so Baptiste was careful not to draw his attention. His father had found a good soft stone and was carving a pipe. Toussaint's wandering glance fell on the boy nevertheless, and he narrowed his eyes, as if searching out some secret his son harbored. He grunted and said, "Come closer." He cupped a hand over Baptiste's head and kept it there, a trap. "Clark's dancing boy," he muttered. Baptiste managed to slide out from his father's grip.

He looked back at Toussaint: Was he angry? Bitter? Sarcastic? But his father's face was slack and unreadable. "A son of mine has to be baptized," Toussaint suddenly announced. "Even I was, back in Montreal." Toussaint slapped his bony thigh. "Smaller than you, I was then. No memory of it, but that's usual."

Baptized. What could that be? It sounded like his name: Baptiste.

"We won't wait for Captain Clark," Toussaint said. "The priest is coming from Cahokia. He can stay only until the new year." He turned to Sakakawea. "I know why Captain Clark is so long away. Are you listening? Captain Lewis is dead in Tennessee—by his own hand, they are saying." He muttered an oath. "Lewis had no use for me. He would not have invited us to St. Louis."

Sakakawea pulled Baptiste close. Tears had sprung in her eyes. "Captain Lewis gave me the herb that brought you out of my womb," she said softly. "We must ask the Great Spirit to ease his journey."

Toussaint glared at her. "You will have the most important man in St. Louis as your godfather," he declared, poking Baptiste's shoulder. "It's all arranged. M. Auguste Chouteau will stand for Captain Clark. When he was a boy, just a few years older than you are now, he and his father founded this town. Think of that!"

Baptiste had no idea what to think of it.

"What is a godfather?"

"He vouches for you. The bigger the man, the better your chances in life."

Toussaint explained that Auguste had grown up to be a merchant, trader, landowner, and head of a huge family. He was the most powerful citizen in St. Louis. The man with the book on the boat was his brother, Pierre. All the Chouteaus had long traded with the Osage. "Their Osage wives give them sons and they bring their sons here to be baptized and go to school, like you will," Toussaint said. "Their French wives live here in lofty comfort."

"But I'm to be Captain's Clark's son."

Toussaint's face reddened. "You ignorant whelp," he yelled. "We go to this trouble and you don't have the sense to see why."

Sakakawea said, "He doesn't understand why he must be baptized. We never see you honor this god."

"*Woman,*" he said witheringly, "French boys, Indian boys with French fathers, they are all baptized in the cathedral. It doesn't mean he has to go to Mass. Frenchmen rule this town. If the boy is considered a heathen, he can't look the Chouteaus in the eye." He turned on Baptiste. "Are you agreed, then?" he asked sarcastically. "Clark and the Chouteaus do business together. One is the right hand and the other the left. Your baptism will satisfy both."

Baptiste nodded. His father must be obeyed. Not for much longer, though. Soon, it would be Captain Clark he must obey.

When he and Sakakawea were alone, he asked, "What does this god want from me?"

"It is your father's wish that you be named in the French church." She pulled him close. Then, as if to reward him for accepting this arbitrary desire, "Soon, you will read and write. You will see great distances, even into the future. "

Baptiste sat pondering these things. For now, Clark was no more real than a puff of smoke. The Frenchman Chouteau, on the other hand, was coming to his baptism. He wondered what the great man would look like. Chouteau had *started* St. Louis when he was just a little older than himself. Baptiste could hardly wait to see this hero.

☆　　☆　　☆

ON THE DAY of the baptism, Sakakawea gave Baptiste a scrubbing and dressed him in a new shirt and trousers. Baptiste asked
his father what was going to happen. Would it be an ordeal, like
the Okipa ceremony of the Mandans? Would he be hung by his
skin to see if he was man enough not to cry out? "Where did you
get that idea? You'll be dipped in holy water. All your sins will be
washed away."

As they headed to the church, they were trailed through the
streets by a few stray dogs. At the open square called the Place
d'Armes, their little procession attracted some attention and
Baptiste heard "Chouteau" whispered in the crowd. The church, a
small log building with a wooden cross on its roof, sat behind
a stockade. A little shed containing a big silver bell was attached.

Inside, there was murky candlelight. A man in a hood stood by
a chest covered with a white cloth and a gleaming cross, beside it a
stone basin. An Osage boy of about fifteen, dressed in white,
stood behind him.

Voices from the street grew louder, and a little clutch of people
burst through the doorway, led by a tall man in a black cloak
trimmed in fur, who paused to dip his knee and cross himself.
Chouteau! A young girl followed, in a lush cape, fur hat, and rustling
skirts. Never had he seen a child of either sex in such finery. She
glanced at Baptiste, tossed her head, and stood close to Chouteau.
What was a girl doing here? Baptiste wondered. She must be his
daughter. Two men in buckskins scuttled in behind her.

The monk made the cross sign on his forehead and chest.
Toussaint snatched his hat from his head and held it sheepishly in
front of him.

"This is the child?" asked Chouteau. Baptiste steadied himself and met the man's black stare. "A fine-looking boy," Chouteau murmured, and turned to Sakakawea with a bow. "Madame." Something passed between them and she lowered her eyes. Baptiste thought, *This man understands who she is.*

"*Merci, merci,* M. Chouteau," muttered Toussaint, grinning foolishly. The young girl looked at Baptiste and rolled her eyes. He looked at the floor, his cheeks stinging with shame. Girls had teased him, back in the villages. But this was his day!

The monk had begun to read from a thick book in a language Baptiste had never heard. The monk drew his fingers across Baptiste's head and chest. He spoke some more, then gestured to Baptiste to open his mouth. He did and tasted salt.

Baptiste sneaked a peek at the girl. Just then, the monk reached over and laid fingers on his eyes and ears.

He droned some more.

Toussaint jabbed him and Baptiste said yes.

The monk told him to bend over the font. He did, and suddenly, his head was drenched with freezing water. He recoiled and Chouteau's firm hand restrained him. The monk spoke some more in the strange tongue. He handed candles to Chouteau and Toussaint. Baptiste felt the icy water drip down his neck. He saw the priest's white-clad Osage assistant suck in his cheeks to suppress a smile. After a long spell of talk, Chouteau clapped Toussaint's back. Chouteau's daughter kissed Baptiste on both cheeks. "Felicitations," she murmured, fussing with her gloves.

It was over, then. Chouteau saluted Sakakawea and led his party out of the church. He was baptized. The only pain had been the shock of ice water. The rest was a lot of mumbo jumbo. He didn't feel changed. He had acquired a godfather. But the man had walked away without promising a thing.

As if mocking his thought, Toussaint barked, "Now you'll go to heaven when it's all over." He cuffed Baptiste on the head. "Be grateful to your old father for saving your soul."

BAPTISTE MADE A daily check of Captain Clark's house, but saw no sign of him. So he kept moving, from one end of town to the other. Once he ventured inside one of the corner establishments devoted to the game with the stick and the table. Men laughed and teased him. "You want to try?" One fellow lifted him up to the table, showed him how to use the stick to send balls careening into holes along the edge. They cheered when he missed and again when he got the knack of it. "Keen little man, aren't you!" "A born billiards player!" But it was boring after a while, so he continued his ramble.

He followed the stone sentry posts along the town's periphery, past the garrison barracks and the long, narrow field plots that were laid side by side from river to prairie. People grew vegetables there. He roamed from Broadway to Jefferson, to the south commons where cattle grazed near sparkling springs and women pounded their laundry. He peered into sinkholes in limestone caves.

On the waterfront, workers unloading peltries from pirogues bellowed colorful songs. The sharp aromas of buffalo robes and horse blankets, human sweat and whiskey, stung his nostrils. Traders shot craps and traded insults and stories that made them roar with laughter. Once he saw Toussaint playing cards and bragging. This was his father's life, separate from his own and Sakakawea's. He was making a separate life too, he realized.

But he got tired of exploring all by himself. Hearing boyish shouts and laughter coming from a yard behind a tavern, he peeked around the building to see who was there. A scruffy gang of boys was taking turns flipping a knife in the air so that it landed point down in the dirt. He watched for a while, then called a hello. They all looked over at him, but without any change of expression. He went closer.

"Will you let me?" he asked, indicating the knife.

The boys exchanged glances. Finally, a blond boy about ten years old pulled a corncob pipe out of his mouth.

"You want a throw of the knife, little one?"

Baptiste nodded.

"Then place your bet," said the boy.

"Bet?"

"Your wager. Money."

"I have no money."

"You have to pay something for a turn in the game."

He was good at contests, footraces, pony races, archery. He wanted a turn. He could win! The boys smirked at him.

"How can I?"

"What are you called?"

"Baptiste."

"See those persimmons yonder, B'tiste? Can you snatch us a one?" asked the boy, indicating a stall at the far end of the market.

This was a surprise. He peered at the stand of persimmons.

Someone snickered. "He's scared, Cyrus," another said.

"Looks like he wants to disappoint us," agreed Cyrus.

Baptiste blurted, "I'll do it," and the ring opened for him.

He set off across the square, taking deliberate steps, feeling their eyes on his back and hoping no one else would notice him. After all, he was as good as invisible in this town. The persimmon seller had turned away to tie a bag of feed to his horse's bridle. This was going to be easy! Quick as lightning, Baptiste palmed a persimmon and pivoted to make his getaway.

But the boys had vanished. What about the bet? Baptiste broke into a run, rounded a corner, and there they were.

"Well done, little one. All shake hands with B'tiste," said their leader. They solemnly shook hands.

"You said I could pitch the knife," Baptiste said.

"Oh, I reckon I did." The boy drew on his pipe and sent smoke into Baptiste's face. "Find us tomorrow."

He'd been cheated! He was used to believing what people said to him. He must learn to be careful. The next day, he was waiting at the spot when the pack trudged down the street.

"I want my turn," he said.

Cyrus looked amused. "Come on, then," he said.

They traced a ring in the dirt behind a tavern. Four boys took turns pitching the knife. None of them hit the mark.

"Your turn, little B'tiste," said Cyrus. Baptiste took the knife and tossed it. The knife landed squarely on the target. He glanced at the boys' surprised faces, keeping his own expression neutral. It was no surprise. He had always been a marksman.

"I reckoned you could do that," Cyrus said airily. "Here's a picayune. Keep it in your pocket." Baptiste took the little coin. A man's head was carved on it and a garland of letters. He stuck it in his shoe. He would find out what to do with this token.

"You're in the gang," Cyrus said. Baptiste grinned. He had been accepted. It brought back the good feeling of being blessed and belonging.

"WHY DON'T YOU fellows have to go to school?" he asked.

"There's no school," Cyrus said.

"But the French boys go," Baptiste said. "Even the girls do."

Cyrus snorted. "Well, their papas pay, don't they? Ours can't pay. Anyhow, why would we want to? We do whatever we want."

"Whatever we want" meant mostly hunting, fishing, and trapping, when they weren't competing to see who was fastest or strongest or could tolerate the most pain. Baptiste was the smallest, but he held his own, and often won whatever contest was waged. He got used to life in St. Louis. It was good.

THEN, ONE DAY, as spring began to warm the city and the ice on the river was gone, Baptiste came home to find Sakakawea and Toussaint gathering up their scant belongings.

"Prepare to bid your mother farewell," Toussaint said gruffly. "We are leaving town."

"What?"

"Mr. Manuel Lisa offers me the post of interpreter at his new trading fort near the Villages."

Baptiste was stunned. "What about the land Captain Clark gave you?" he asked.

Toussaint snorted. "I'm no farmer!"

Baptiste stared helplessly. "What about me?"

"You'll go to Captain Clark," Toussaint told him. "You'll do whatever he says."

"But he's not here!"

"He'll come. He sent word."

Baptiste threw himself on his mother.

"Don't go," he begged. "I'm sorry I left you here! I can take care of you!"

She kissed his face. "If your father goes, I must go with him."

Baptiste whimpered, "You don't belong to him. You belong to me!" The pathetic sound of his voice shamed him. But he was desperate to make her stay.

She seized his ears, compelling him to look into her eyes. "I am not free to choose where I can go."

He stared back at her. Could that be true? Then a new idea came to him: She *wants* to go. *A force is pulling her.* He imagined it, a malevolent spirit drawing her out of the town and into the wild reaches. Was there nothing he could do to stop it? He slumped to his knees.

She lifted a lock of his hair and pressed her lips to his forehead. "You will have a different life. It is only beginning here, in this city. White men are spreading their ways everywhere. Do you understand what that means? *Learn!*"

"Please don't go," he whispered.

"You don't need your mother now. We have traveled a long way to bring you to Captain Clark," she said. "He chose you." A picture flew into his head: Clark as an eagle hovering above, Baptiste's destiny clutched like a rabbit in his claws.

Her eyes were fixed on him, demanding an answer.

"Yes, Mother."

"You are my promising boy," she said, smiling. "You are the bravest, the smartest, the fastest. Do as the captain says. They are making a new world for you."

"Yes," he repeated.

He knew that she loved him. And he knew that her spirit would stay with him, even after she was gone. But she left him with a terrible emptiness. He had only words to hold on to now. What was going to happen to him? Why hadn't his father told him he had heard from Captain Clark?

SAKAKAWEA AND TOUSSAINT boarded one of Manuel Lisa's boats. Lisa intended to dominate the Upper Missouri fur trade. Toussaint said Clark had invested in the expedition as well. A rival flotilla, belonging to John Jacob Astor, the New York fur king, had already departed for the rich trapping country, and Lisa wanted to overtake it. Baptiste watched men scurrying to load provisions onto dozens of keelboats that had been rigged with sails. But sails were of little help now. A trip upstream required muscle power: burly men poling and pulling the boats.

A teamster standing next to Baptiste muttered, "It will be a long time before we see them again . . . if any manage to return." Baptiste quickly counted the big guns on the nearest boats. There were enough—there must be enough—to protect from an attack!

Lost in his troubled thoughts, he didn't see the boats cast off. Men were already pulling with all their might against the heavy current.

He scanned the fleet and found his parents. They were looking back at him. Toussaint nodded gravely, as if to say, *You're on your own; make the best of it.* Sakakawea lifted her arms high and wide, her eyes blazing, and never moved until the string of boats was just a tiny dot on the horizon. Baptiste felt her fierce faith in him like a knife in his heart. He needed her as he never had. For a moment, he was tempted to find Cyrus and the boys. But the thought alone made him unbearably guilty.

He heard himself emit a little cry of misery. Why had she not been able to stay? Who would tell him spirit stories now? Who would believe in him as she did?

CHAPTER THREE

School

A voice said in French, "Are you ready, young fellow?" For a moment, Baptiste thought he was being asked to board another boat! The tall, slender man didn't wait for an answer, but steered him firmly toward the town.

"I am Cadet Chouteau. My uncle is your godfather and you came to St. Louis on a boat with my father, do you remember?"

Of course he remembered!

"Do you know where I am taking you now?"

"No, sir." A gusty wind was blowing. Sailcloth snapped with a sound like gunfire. A man raced after his hat.

"To a house where you will live with other boys like yourself. You will learn to read and to write letters. They are important. Business decisions are made from letters. You will make your manners, get a bit of history, be able to move about in our world."

Baptiste stared. What did he mean?

"What's the matter, boy? Don't you want to be in school?"

"Where is Captain Clark?" Baptiste blurted.

"He is in the East, with his family, on business. He asked me to deliver you to your school."

His family. Baptiste puzzled over that. His mother had not spoken of a family.

＊　＊　＊

BAPTISTE HAD TO trot to keep up with Cadet's long strides. After a few minutes, they came to a wooden building on a side street. Cadet knocked on the door.

It was opened by a man with a sallow face and sunken eyes, one eye staring sharply at Baptiste, the other milkily at Cadet.

"The general's child," said Cadet.

"Ah. Has he been saved?" the man asked, now casting his good eye on Cadet.

"He was baptized in the cathedral."

This drew a snort. "We'll see that he learns to fear the Lord." The man's seeing eye swiveled back to Baptiste. "Do you know what you are to do here?" he asked.

"Read and write," Baptiste said.

"Huh. Thank you, M. Chouteau. You, boy, come in."

Several small brown faces ogled him curiously from a doorway. The man pulled Baptiste inside, and as he turned, the faces vanished.

Down a hall, he was handed over to a dark-skinned woman.

"He wants a scrubbing, Priscilla," said the man.

"Hands up," said Priscilla. She pulled off his shirt and leggings and rubbed him all over with a rough piece of rag that she wrung out in a bucket of cold water. He heard a scraping of wood on wood from another room and children's voices speaking in unison.

Priscilla pulled a new shirt over him and had him step into breeches that hung comically to his shins. He had not eaten or drunk any water all day, but he didn't dare ask for any. "Be good. Make General Clark proud," said the woman.

"Captain Clark," Baptiste blurted. He stared at her, trembling.

"He's a general now." She gave him a push down the hall. In a square room, a dozen boys were lined up by size. One or two of them were nearly men. They were all bigger than Baptiste. Most had skin as tawny as his. "Mixed bloods," like himself. But not picked by Captain Clark!

"Eyes ahead!" the man commanded. "Take your seat, Master Jean Baptiste." He indicated a small wooden chair. Baptiste had never sat in one. Toussaint hadn't bothered to buy furniture, treating their little room like a lodge. Gingerly, Baptiste turned and dipped his backside. The chair toppled over. The boys all laughed. Their laughter cut through his fear, thrusting him back in time. At the Villages, he'd been a comedian. Without thinking, he pantomimed trying to master the chair.

"Quiet! Enough of that, Master Jean Baptiste!"

A stinging blow landed on the back of his neck. He whirled to face the raised rod that quivered in the man's hand. "Sit down!"

He had never been hit. He did as he was told.

A boy handed him a slate and a piece of chalk. The teacher pointed to a paper hung on the front wall and told them to copy the marks on it.

Was this school, then? He had drawn all his life, in the dirt with a stick or on an animal hide. But he drew because he felt like drawing, never because someone told him to. He learned new skills by trying them out on his own or following an older boy. All his friends had done that.

"Jean Baptiste, you have felt the rod. Must I also take the lash to you?" asked the man. The boy stared back. The man shook his head and told him to stay behind when the class was dismissed.

Baptiste rose with his head high. He would not be broken! Pain
was easily endured. He had known that for as long as he could
remember. No one had ever complained of pain in the Villages.
Some had even sought it.

"Savage blood runs in your veins," his tormentor was snarling.
"It renders you fickle and destitute of steady purpose. We will
teach you to overcome these defects, but first, you must submit."

Baptiste could hear the boys talking in low voices, with spurts
of laughter. He felt the cold sweat of fury. No man was going
to beat that out of him. His uncle had been a brave Shoshone
chief. That was his "savage blood." He didn't belong in this place
where such things were not understood. He would wait for the
right moment and follow his mother up the river. No one could
stop him!

"Hold out your hands."

He did and was struck three times with the rod. He didn't
flinch. The schoolmaster shook his head as if at a particularly
stupid case and sent him away.

PRISCILLA LADLED THEIR dinners from a big kettle. Each
boy got a sour, colorless mush of pounded corn, softened with
water, along with a hunk of hog fat and a piece of rock-hard
bread. The schoolmaster recited something while the boys lowered
their eyes, put their hands together over their plates, and tonelessly
repeated his words.

"Eat your supper. And you will be silent."

They all shoveled food into their mouths with their knives.
Baptiste had fingers designed to do the job, he thought, but he
knew how to use a knife and so he followed suit. The food tasted

spoiled, but he forced it down, figuring that not eating would lead to more punishment. What if the schoolmaster tied him up for the night? He drank something bitter from a tin cup. The boys seemed used to their fare and kept their heads down, though several kept staring at him from under their brows. He wondered if he could find an ally or even a friend among them. Not yet.

An hour later, the boys were herded into another room to listen while the master read droningly from the same thick volume. Baptiste's stomach began to cramp. Its gurglings were loud enough to make the boys around him snicker. A black man stood at the doorway behind them. When Baptiste couldn't tolerate it any longer, he got up and lurched back, pointing to his gut. The man seemed to understand his frantic expression and led him to a privy in the yard. The pain subsided with the explosive contractions, but he was too weak to move. He lingered as long as he dared, the stench being less awful than the room he'd left.

Back there, an older boy was reading aloud. The master gave Baptiste a menacing look, but he said nothing. Afterward, they all climbed to an airless attic. Baptiste lay down on a lumpy, prickly mattress. His first bed. The other occupant, François, weighed down the middle and Baptiste rolled into him.

In the morning, the boys splashed cold water on their faces from a bucket. Suddenly, two of them picked the bucket up and dumped it over Baptiste's head. It sent the others into gales of witless laughter. Baptiste made fists. "Pretty boy is a fighter!" said a boy they called Big Louis. They held Baptiste's arms behind his back while Louis strutted and pointed. Struggling to free himself, Baptiste managed to get one arm loose. At that point, the schoolmaster appeared.

"Baptiste! Fighting is forbidden! You are not among savages here."

Baptiste gaped. Couldn't the man see what had happened? How could he blame him? He searched the boys' blank faces. Someone would take his side! Never in his life had he faced a hostile gang like this one. He had done nothing to harm any of them!

The schoolmaster took hold of his ear. "You will spend the day in the storeroom," he snapped. "You will repent of your actions."

It was a relief to sit alone in the storeroom, dusty and airless though it was. He had been brought here by mistake! There was some mix-up between the Chouteaus and Clark. It was probably Toussaint's fault. Baptiste spent the long day planning his escape.

That night, he carefully slipped from his shared bed and out of the building without being seen—at least no one came after him. He took off down the street, clutching his waistband to keep his new trousers from falling, past a house where men were hoarsely singing, past shuttered stores and mechanics' shops. His legs, his lungs, his pumping arms, took him farther and farther from the school. He had a purpose now and it quieted his mind.

He turned north and followed the river along the bluff, crossing the narrow strips of common land. Miles from town, he checked: There was no one behind him. His heart was still racing. Shivering in the chilly air, he gathered branches and grasses to make a bed and some cover for himself. He dared not risk a fire. Lying down, he heard a wolf's mournful howl. He wondered if bobcats would sniff him out.

He managed a fitful sleep, waking from time to time to the mournful sound of a whip-poor-will. First light found him

hungry, damp, and itching all over. He scanned the horizon for
trees that would mark a spring or a stream. A flock of gaudy parrots flew past, trailing their piercing cries. As he walked, he kept
an eye out for signs of humans. Whose country was this—Sauk,
Osage? Would they kill him? Would they consider him one of
them or a white boy? Any tribe might be at war and take him as
a hostage to be bartered, like his mother was when she was a
girl. He'd give anything for a pony.

He'd lost his awful dinner and eaten nothing since. He had to
find food. Birds wheeled above, cawing.

He clambered down a steep slope, clutching at branches and
irritating a flock of turkeys that clumsily fled. Butterflies of many
colors swirled in the sultry air, lifting his heart for a moment.

He crept through a small grove, hoping to find a spring. But
there was none and instead he came to a little open plain. Smack
in the middle was a plot of ground that appeared to have been
planted. Hardly believing his eyes, he ran toward it.

"Hands up!"

Baptiste froze. A shock-headed man was pointing a musket,
none too steadily. "What are you doing, young varmint," he said.
It wasn't a question.

"I'm hungry," Baptiste said simply. He was too tired to lie.

"Where in tarnation did you come from?" the man asked.

Baptiste kept silent.

"Upriver? Cote Sans Dessein?" demanded the man. "Are you
kin to Dorians? Tibeaus? Chouteaus?"

Baptiste said, "Yes." The man wouldn't shoot a Chouteau,
would he?

The man hee-hawed, displaying a few yellow stumps of teeth. "I'll be damned," he said. "Did they lose you? Huh? Did you run off?"

Baptiste said nothing.

He was led to a rickety cabin made of rough black pine. No one had bothered to fill the crevices between the logs. A worn-out-looking woman in a bonnet and sack dress was smoking her pipe in the slanting doorway. "Lo, you've snagged a wee 'blood," she observed. "Can we put him to work?"

"Chouteau, he is. They let him escape," said the man.

"Do you reckon he's worth anything to them?" asked the woman. A boar ambled around the corner of the cabin and rubbed its hairy flank against her skirt.

Baptiste looked wildly around for a way to escape. The man and the woman discussed the options at length and decided to take their chances on demanding a ransom for him. The man tied Baptiste's wrists and they set off for a trading post. The woman drew thoughtfully on her pipe, watching them go.

When they had walked a long way, the man untied him and shared bits of the bread and jerky the woman had packed. Baptiste wolfed them down, but they only teased his hunger. So weary he could hardly drag one foot after the other, he felt utterly beaten. He stumbled along a broken trail. Finally, they came to a river. A keelboat was tied up on its bank. A cabin stood a short distance away. Men and women were piling beaver pelts on a rack outside it. He looked at their skin, their clothes. They looked more like Baptiste than his captor, but they showed no friendliness to the white man. And they made no move to help Baptiste either.

The man tied Baptiste to a tree while he bargained with them. Apparently there was no satisfactory outcome. He swore, and came back to plop down in the shade. "I'm not going without just deserts," he grumbled.

There they sat until sundown. The peltry sorters roasted meat on sticks over a fire, talking in low voices. Baptiste's stomach wrung itself painfully. He was hungrier than he'd ever been. Maybe his captor would fall asleep. He would signal the trappers and they'd release him. He had no idea what he would do then, but the plan kept him alert. It had been crazy to think he could find his mother.

Shadows had lengthened and the air was turning blue when they heard hoofbeats. A rider entered the clearing, tied up at the cabin, and exchanged words with the trappers. He threw a surprised look toward Baptiste and his captor.

"I'll be damned!" he cried, striding over to them. Baptiste gasped. It was Cadet Chouteau. "I have been looking for you," he said. "For a mere chit you have caused considerable worry."

Chouteau was stern, but he didn't sound angry. Baptiste felt a flood of relief.

The old man put up a fuss when Cadet said he wasn't about to pay ransom for a runaway schoolboy. But he clearly knew better than to try to outmaneuver a Chouteau and agreed to accept a tin of coffee. Cadet got one at the little post cabin and the old man trudged off toward home, grumbling to himself.

Baptiste perched behind Cadet on the fine big horse.

"We don't need to tell the general you were so restless," Cadet said.

Baptiste murmured, "*Merci.*"

"Your schoolmaster won't tell him either. He would be judged rather careless, I think, to have lost track of you so easily."

Baptiste was silent. He longed to ask how Clark could be told anything when he was nowhere to be found.

"Did you think Indians would take you in?" Cadet inquired.

"Yes," he admitted.

It started to rain. Cadet went on casually talking. "We see the way they live, without cities or laws—or schools. We think they are happier than we are and we want to run away to live the way they do. . . ." He paused. Baptiste said nothing. "Are you listening, cub?"

"Yes, sir." Cadet certainly had a limited idea of how his people lived. But Baptiste wasn't about to say anything. He could hardly keep his eyes open.

"You are with us now. You can't run away from the world as it is." He sighed. "You must apply yourself, little Baptiste. Study hard and learn what the master teaches." His words echoed Sakakawea's. *Learn everything.* It was her wish—her command. He would have to submit to school. He had promised her he would.

"Such an opportunity will come only once." Cadet spurred his horse and they sped toward St. Louis.

CHAPTER FOUR

_____◆————◆————◆_____

Clark at Last

Baptiste held his tongue and did as he was told. Finding him cooperative, the schoolmaster began to show a gruff kindness. Baptiste surveyed the faces of his classmates, seeking friendly signs. He didn't find them. François understood the situation and gave him advice. "You'll have to show you can fight," he said. "Every new boy has to."

The chance quickly came. A crew of boys was put to work chopping firewood in the yard. Baptiste was told to stack it. He picked up a few logs, cradling them in his arms, and started for the pile. Someone stuck out a foot and tripped him. He tried to get up and was pushed down again. Big Louis's sneering face loomed over him.

"What you doing there?" the cook yelled. She came out and slapped the kicker's face. "You leave him be!"

Baptiste warily gathered up the logs and started again to pile them. The woman went back into the house. Suddenly, he was shoved hard from behind. He rolled forward and sprang up, fists balled. He faced a crescent of glowering boys. "Who wants to fight?" he taunted. No one took up his challenge.

"Clark's pet," he heard someone mutter. So that was it.

Whenever the schoolmaster or Priscilla was otherwise occupied, one or two boys seized the chance to torment Baptiste. He fought back, but he was smaller than most of them. He often went to bed with bruises. As he lay trying to find a position that didn't hurt, Baptiste vowed to make himself into a fighter. Clark was a soldier. He would expect his son to be a fighter too.

COPYING THE MARKS in class was easy and it was fun to get them right. After some weeks, their meaning was suddenly revealed to him, as when clouds parted before the sun. Letters became words. Words were sentences that conveyed thoughts. *"The duck has a wide, flat bill; the moon is smaller than the sun; the man who drinks rum may soon want a loaf of bread,"* he read happily from their book. He remembered watching Toussaint stare uncomprehendingly at Clark's letter. He had already advanced beyond his father. And this was only the beginning.

It was the same with figures. He learned to put them together and take them apart, rising promptly when called upon to state the correct answer in a clear voice. Sums were the way to figure amounts of flour, sugar, peltries, and their worth. He learned to add and subtract in his head, even though the classroom buzzed with distracting voices reciting figures and sentences.

Once a week, the boys were served a jerk of beef or a chicken leg. Sometimes there were potatoes, and a small garden plot yielded some carrots and onions. There was still mush on most days, but his stomach learned to accept it. Food was his main comfort.

One day, passing a crumbling wall, he heard a mewling sound. Reaching into the cleft between stones, he touched something soft and, to his delight, pulled out a tiny kitten. He looked all around. There was no sign of a mother cat or any other little ones. He carefully put the kitten inside his shirt, where it lay quiet and warm. How was he going to keep it at the school? He couldn't worry about that. It needed food. He got some milk from the icehouse in the school's yard and sat watching the kitten lap hungrily. He carried it to the attic and lay cuddling it, whispering comfortingly. It had been a long time since he'd had an animal to take care of.

When the supper bell rang, he put the kitten under the quilt, told it to stay put, and went downstairs. The boys wolfed down their meal, and the schoolmaster dismissed them until Bible-reading time. Baptiste waited until they had gone outside, and crept back to the attic. The kitten was right where he'd left it, asleep. He knelt and touched his cheek to its soft fur.

He fed it again. Before the boys came up the stairs, he folded his second shirt and pair of pants under the bed and set the kitten down. And in the morning, it was there blinking up at him. He managed to take milk to it during the day without anyone noticing. When school was over, the master sent him to the store for a bag of cornmeal. He came back to find François waiting for him with an odd look on his face. He seemed almost friendly, and Baptiste felt his spirits lift. "Go out to the alley," François said. "Louis has something for you." Downstairs, Louis was hiding something behind his back. A few boys hovered, smirking.

"Look what I found!" Louis cried. He had the kitten by its tail. "Let's have some fun with B'tiste's cat!"

"Put it down!" Baptiste leapt toward him. Louis danced out of reach, the kitten squeaking with fright. He dangled it over a rain barrel. "Down the well it goes," he chortled, and his friends whooped.

Baptiste threw himself at Louis. It was like running into a tree, but he managed to stomp on one of Louis's feet. That made the bigger boy howl and let go of the kitten. Baptiste took a wide swing and landed a blow on the side of Louis's head. They were encircled now, all of the boys cheering and dancing excitedly. Some were shouting, "Hit him, B'tiste!" He hauled back his right arm and let it fly.

Louis grunted and fell back, but his long arms caught Baptiste in a bear hug. The boys went down together, rolling and kicking. Baptiste was up, then Louis. Baptiste jabbed his knee between Louis's legs, pushed at the older boy's chin, and levered him to his back. Then he pressed his lower arm onto Louis's neck. Louis had hold of Baptiste's hair. It felt as if he'd pull it all out, but gradually his grip loosened. His face had turned bright red. Baptiste kept pushing on his neck.

"Nuff?"

Louis exhaled, coughed violently, and gasped, "Nuff." Baptiste released him.

"Well done, B'tiste," said François. The others muttered agreement. His back was patted by several hands. They were with him now. He had beaten more than just one bully.

But the kitten was nowhere to be found. He guessed it had found a new place to live.

A FEW WEEKS later, the master ordered the scholars to line up in the yard.

"Smallpox is ravaging parts of the East and Europe. It may come here next. Dr. Saugrain finds that an injection of cowpox will prevent the infection. He has offered to vaccinate all of you. Pray show your gratitude."

The good doctor, standing nearby, laughed. "Bare your arms in turn," he said mildly. "And you do not have to enjoy it."

The schoolmaster had to hold some of the boys down while the Frenchman inserted his lancet in their arms. He worked his way down the line to Baptiste and, when he saw him, cried, "You must be Baptiste! I know your mother, Sakakawea. What a fine woman! You'll be glad I've pricked you if the pox ever comes your way."

His mother! Baptiste asked, "Did you see her at Lisa's fort?"

"No, my boy. I saw her a year ago, when you all came here. You must miss her."

Baptiste nodded. Hearing her name made him miss her acutely. He shut his eyes while Saugrain cut into his skin and it hardly hurt at all. It was his heart that hurt.

THE BOYS HAD to stay inside the school, and a sign on the door warned visitors to stay away while they underwent the course of the disease. For a day or so, Baptiste felt no symptoms. Then his head ached terribly and his arms began to itch. Scratching brought no relief. He was horrified to realize that a bright red rash had crept over his body. Priscilla told him to lay cold, wet cloths on his skin. It helped a little.

Cyprien had already been exposed, in his mother's village. "It don't last," he told them confidently. But Baptiste knew that the smallpox had nearly wiped out the Mandan, leaving only a remnant of the great tribe. He had heard it from grandmothers who saw it happen when they were children. He anxiously observed his symptoms, hoping they wouldn't get any worse. It might be a matter of luck, who lived and who died.

To his horror, the rash turned to blisters and filled with pus that ran yellow when they broke. Then the fever flattened him. Baptiste's armpits swelled; he ached all over and was so weak he couldn't get out of bed. François wasn't sick and let him have the bed to himself. Baptiste's teeth rattled with chills. He tried to remember having fever before, but no sickness had ever been as bad as this.

"Am I dying?" he whispered to François. "Tell me!" He knew he was pathetic, but he wasn't ashamed. He thought it was François he was beseeching, but the shape hovering by his bed had become a masked spirit that started to pluck at him! He moaned and the sound echoed back at him from the walls. The air throbbed with his misery. He was so cold! He wanted his mother's arms around him, her voice cooing in his ear. But a bigger masked shape, some new demon, barred her way. It spoke in the master's voice.

"Wrap him, keep him warm," it said, sounding like distant, rumbling thunder. But he wasn't warm. He called out again for his mother. He was dying—he had left his body already and was gazing down at it from beyond the world.

He tasted water. He tried to sit up, to drink, but the demon snatched it away. He was so thirsty! And achingly hot, then numbingly cold. Every inch of him hurt. He was willing to die.

Then, suddenly, his head cleared. He beheld François's serious, kind eyes staring at him as if trying to pierce his depths. "B'tiste," he said. "You're better! We feared you were a goner!"

He sat up. "I didn't die."

François laughed. "No."

Baptiste looked down at his body. The pustules were covered with thick black scabs. "François, do you look like this?"

"No. Thankfully, you don't have them on your face. You're as ugly as ever, but not hideous. They'll fall off now. You suffered the worst of any of us. I was scared. But the doctor came. He said you'd recover and be all the stronger for it. I stayed by you to be sure."

Baptiste's eyes welled up and he blinked. Then he punched François. He was so weak, his fist glanced off the other boy's arm.

"You'd do the same," François said simply. And Baptiste knew that he would.

THEY WERE THE two best students. They'd been put in the same bed before anyone could tell they were so suited. It was a great piece of luck. At night they compared experiences, spun tales, predicted the future, and discussed weighty matters, such as who could run faster or shoot more arrows into the air. They were both growing weary of their lessons. The master possessed only one primer, and they'd been through it so many times, Baptiste could recite it half asleep. Most of the time, the master reverted to Bible readings and other Christian lessons.

"I wouldn't mind if he had some books we could read," François said. Baptiste grunted agreement. "Ones not supposed to make heathens repent." After a few moments, he whispered, "Are you glad you're here, François?"

The other boy clasped his hands behind his head. "I don't think about that," he said. "I *am* here."

"But do you wish you were back with your mother?"

"I miss my mother. But I wouldn't want to live as she does. Or my sisters."

"But you wouldn't work like a woman!" Baptiste said. "You would hunt."

François laughed. "And count coup. No. I'll stay in school until my pa puts me to work. I'll run express for the fur company. I'll visit the village sometimes, but I won't live there. I don't want to be tied down. That's what school has taught me."

He rolled over and gave Baptiste a cuff on the ear. "What about you? You wish you were back with the Mandan?"

"Sometimes. My mother is at Lisa's fort. I have no place to go back to. And I like being schooled." He was a chair sitter now. But he wished Captain Clark would come and tell him what it was all preparation for.

ONE OCTOBER EVENING, a strange light appeared low in the sky like an eerie lantern trailing a tail that pointed up. No one had ever seen anything like it.

"It is an omen," one of the boys said.

"Omen of what?"

No one had an answer.

The schoolmaster had no natural explanation. He prayed and read scripture with more than his usual ferocity.

Weeks passed and the weird light didn't budge. It seemed to cast more than a glow—it cast a spell. It drew Baptiste outdoors, pulled him through the narrow streets. The city felt different because of the glow. Through open windows, he heard people arguing about it, their voices shrill with worry. But the mystery of the fireball excited him.

That night, François had a new theory for them. "They say Tecumseh conjured it to take revenge for the defeat at Tippecanoe."

"Conjured it? It's something nature has made. No man has the power."

"Well, he twice predicted an eclipse of the sun. Everyone knows that."

"We should ask Dr. Saugrain what it is."

The fireball was telling them something. He wondered if his mother and father could see it. He walked to the edge of town, checking every few blocks to see how it appeared from a new vantage point. Indians were streaming from their encampments toward the river. Was the fireball Tecumseh's doing after all? Did they know? Most wore expressions of alarm. He trotted alongside an Osage who was carrying a big parfleche painted with geometric designs.

"Why do you flee?" he asked the man.

"To find safety with our people" was the gruff reply. He added, "Or we prepare to die with them." Baptiste watched from the bank as canoes covered the river from shore to shore.

In town, he saw heads poking from doors and windows to see that the fireball still hung over them. Men embraced despairingly in the middle of the street. The weird light was brighter than the moon and changed the surface look of roofs and walls, peoples' faces, paving stones, trees—everything. Would the world be lit by it 'til the end of days? Baptiste tried to behave as if life hadn't changed. But it had. The light was brighter and brighter, until night was the same as day. And it struck the same fear in the hearts of everyone, no matter the color of their skin.

ONE DAY, THE schoolmaster handed Baptiste an envelope.

"Take this to General Clark. It's your report."

He nearly cried out. The hero had returned!

He raced for the door. Priscilla grabbed him by the collar and gave his face a violent scrubbing. "That important man be shamed if you're covered with dirt," she said. "Why, look at you shake!" and she hugged him close, which calmed him a little.

Clark's office was in a building behind the house. Baptiste stared fixedly at the door. It wouldn't do to tremble. He straightened up, breathed in, and steeled himself to knock. He had never in his life felt so disordered. A deep, muffled voice told him to enter. He found himself in a long, high-ceilinged room. Tall portraits of men in splendid uniforms hung on the walls, alongside a profusion of buffalo robes, wampum, flags, porcupine quills, skins, horns, claws, saddles, spears, powder horns, blankets, and more. There was too much to look at! He forgot himself for a moment.

"Well, well, Pompey," Clark said in a warm, carrying voice. He sat at a desk at the far end of the chamber. "Come!" Baptiste ran to him. He was a man, not a phantom! His ruddy face wore a broad smile. His hair was as red as Baptiste remembered. A long-buried memory of being held by those strong arms nearly made him throw himself on Clark's breast. But he stopped and stuck out his hand to be shaken, as he had been taught. Clark smiled approvingly. His buckskins gave off a pleasantly familiar odor.

"Our celestial intruder causes consternation in the town," he said. "Have you been worried?"

"Yes, sir," he said. "I heard it is Tecumseh's doing."

"Well, he would like us to think so. It is a comet," Clark said. "They fly across the heavens often, but are so visible only a few times in a century. It won't strike us. They almost never do."

"It isn't a signal of doom?" Baptiste asked.

"Superstitious people say they portend trouble. Others think they are a good omen." He smiled. "That can lead to some awful miscalculations. Apparently this one moved Napoleon to invade Russia, with disastrous result."

Baptiste brightened. This was interesting!

"Let science reveal the wonders of the world to you," Clark added. "Beware superstitions."

He looked Baptiste over, from head to toe. "You seem strong and well nourished," he said. "Are you content at your school?" Baptiste wasn't ready for the question. He would not have used the word *content* to describe his feeling. When he didn't reply, Clark made a face of mock surprise.

"What, you don't know? Are you attending to your studies? You were such a bright little fellow, Pomp."

Baptiste quickly said he liked to read and could write sentences and do figures.

Clark reached out and gave him a pat. "Good. Let me show you something," he said, suddenly rising, his hand on Baptiste's arm. At his full height, with massive shoulders and torso and easy carriage, he was the model of an invincible warrior. Baptiste followed him back down the room, past armaments, beds, shields, tunics, various ornaments, pipes, pots, and warbonnets, to a dugout canoe that was suspended from the ceiling between a pair of enormous chandeliers.

"Do you remember this? I tell all of my visitors that it was Baptiste's cradle."

They regarded the canoe, Clark with a faraway expression that took years off his face. Baptiste didn't remember the canoe. He had been just a baby. He waited silently for Clark to say something more.

"Janey is a good woman" were his next words. This was another riddle, until Baptiste remembered that Clark had called his mother that name. "She never faltered in all those strenuous months. She had you to care for and yet found countless ways to serve us. Has she told you?"

Baptiste nodded. But he wanted Clark to tell the stories.

The general seemed to understand, and continued. "She showed us how to find her people and the horses we required. She even protected us from hostiles. She ought to have been rewarded for all she did." He shook his head over the injustice. After a few moments of reflection he said, "But I do make sure that your father is steadily employed."

Was it Clark who had arranged for Manuel Lisa to hire Toussaint?

"Did you send my mother away?" he blurted.

Clark's eyes widened. "No, I did not. Your father was vexed by the exigencies of farming. He resolved to return to the Upper Missouri. And your mother, I am told, was pining for the wild lands too." His expression softened and he laid an arm around Baptiste's shoulders. "But you miss her, don't you?"

Baptiste blinked away a few tears. "She said I would be your son."

"Well, you are, in a way. I saw that you were promising. I wanted you in school, nearby." He pulled Baptiste closer. "That was before I found my dear wife. And before she gave me our son. But it remains true."

Baptiste pulled away. *Our son.* Suddenly, he felt as if he were on the edge of an abyss with nothing to grab hold of. He would never be Clark's favorite.

Clark looked tenderly at him. "Buck up! You must do well," he said loudly. "I expect much of you." His tone suggested that was the end of the matter. "What have you brought me, boy?"

Startled, Baptiste remembered the school report he'd been clutching. Clark examined it, humming softly. "Well," he said, smiling. "You are an accomplished scholar. I am satisfied. These years are your ladder to manhood."

Baptiste stood at attention, his face frozen. "How like your mother you are!" Clark said softly. "You have her calm spirit and I believe you will show the same courage."

"Do you have news from Señor Lisa's fort? Is she well?"

"Oh, yes. And she is much beloved by the traders." Baptiste felt his throat catch and swallowed hard. Was there more? Apparently not, and he didn't know what to ask. They were both silent. After a moment, Clark snatched an object from one of the shelves, closed his fist, and then opened it.

"Can you guess what it is?"

Baptiste shook his head. "It's the tooth of an elephant!" Clark said merrily. "No one ever guesses." His eyes twinkled. "I have two of them." Then his tone shifted again. "I must attend to my work," he said. "Here in my office I correspond with the government in Washington and draw up my reports. Here I receive delegations of tribal leaders and reason with them. The Indian agency, which I lead, is the largest department in the United States government. Do you understand?"

"Yes, sir. That is your work."

"Well, it is a bit more than just work. I am trying to keep the peace. A great many interests clamor for my attention and all want to have their way. There is only one way. Many are left disappointed."

Baptiste nodded, although he didn't know what all that meant.

"I am very glad to have seen you, Pomp. I will send for you again soon."

From his commanding height, Clark nodded toward the door. The interview was over.

Outside again, Baptiste wondered what lay waiting at the top of his ladder to manhood.

There was a knot of people in the street, gazing silently up at the house. Music drifted down to them. "That's Mrs. Clark playing her pianoforte," a woman whispered to her companion. "They bought it in New York." He listened to the pleasing sounds. He was bursting with a strange kind of elation. He was more on his own than he had ever thought. But Clark was still guiding him with a firm hand, even if not as a parent. Baptiste made a vow to himself—as soon as he was big enough, he would make himself useful to Clark!

ONE DAY, THE boys all realized that the comet, which had been fading, had vanished entirely. François reckoned the number of days that it had shone: two hundred and sixty. Nothing really terrible had happened because of it. That fear was only superstition, just as Clark had said.

But less than a month later, his certainty was called into question. The boys were in class when the building suddenly convulsed. Two boys fell out of their chairs. There was massive, ominous rolling thunder. First, animals began screaming and then citizens did too. The boys and their master all looked at one another, mouths gaping, eyes affright with the same question. Was it the calamity the comet portended? When nothing more happened, the master sent Baptiste and Antoine outside to see what they could find.

A chimney lay in pieces in the alley next door. They found

doors hanging on their hinges and a shed tilted off its plumb. The faces of frightened citizens peered anxiously from broken windows at the blackened sky.

"It's an earthquake!" a man yelled. *"Earthquake"* echoed through the streets.

There were only a few aftershocks. The boys were put to work helping with repairs to the damage. Weeks later, the master told them New Madrid, the epicenter of the quake, was no more. He had learned that President and Mrs. Madison felt the tremors all the way in Washington City. For a time, the Mississippi River had run backward! Lakes had been formed, whole villages had drowned. Waterfalls appeared in the shallow muddy river, and fissures five miles long opened in the ground. Eerie lights flashed from out of the earth itself. It had been a wondrous catastrophe, one for the ages.

The quake spared St. Louis serious harm. Gradually, all realized the rest of the world would survive too. But Baptiste heard nothing from Lisa's fort. That must mean his mother was all right, he told himself. . . .

MORE WEEKS PASSED, until one day the schoolmaster called them to attention in a tone befitting another emergency. The boys ceased working their sums.

"The city is under threat." This set the boys to chattering. "Quiet!" the master went on. "The governor has ordered a stockade to be built."

"Sir, are we at war?" one boy asked.

"If war has not been declared, it will be soon."

"Sir, who is expected to attack us?" another boy asked.

"Our enemy are the British. As you have learned, we seized our liberty from their king and his laws some thirty years ago. But they have not given up their zeal to claim parts of our country. Today they occupy Detroit. Tomorrow they may invade Missouri."

There were exclamations of surprise. No one had ever seen a British soldier. They couldn't picture the enemy.

"The British fur company has made willing allies nearby. Chief Tecumseh of the Shawnee pledges to halt the westward advance of Americans and even to drive us out of the country. He claims to be bulletproof, which murderously emboldens his followers."

The schoolmaster paused to let his pupils couple this information to what they already knew of politics and commerce. They all owed their presence at the school to their French fathers, who were at pains to keep the peace with Indian tribes so that they could do business together. The British intended to replace this peace with war and drive Americans from the fur trade.

"We have been spared violent intrusions in the town for many years. But the British led one thousand warriors against us some thirty years ago. Today we can command only two hundred and sixty armed men to defend us," the master continued. "It is not sufficient."

This was sobering to hear. Later, the boys huddled to talk over the new developments. Cyprien said, "What will we do if the Sac attack?"

"We offer you up as a hostage," François told him with a straight face.

"Aren't you scared?"

"Tecumseh is a great man. He is defending what belongs to his people."

Benoit snorted. "You're mad if you think the Americans will ever let his people survive."

"He'll trick them. He's clever."

"He thinks he is."

"Why isn't there enough land for everyone?" Baptiste said. "It stretches all the way to the western ocean." They all looked at him.

"Men always want what other men have," François said. "It's their nature."

One day, they heard that scalped white bodies were floating in the turbid river. A wave of dreadful excitement passed through the boys. No one had ever seen a scalping or anyone who had been scalped.

The Indians must be desperate, Baptiste thought. The Mandan didn't attack white settlers; they were more apt to be attacked themselves by the Sioux. But other tribes sometimes rampaged against the white invaders, especially if provoked by the British fur traders. It was a war between British and Americans—the Indians were being used by both sides. What if the British won?

Outside the French tavern at Second and Myrtle, he heard a frantic conversation among a group of Americans.

"Washington City has been set afire by the redcoats!"

"They're winning in the East and on the Lakes."

"They say respectable families are selling out, moving back to Kentucky come spring," added one man.

"If that keeps up, the Louisiana Purchase will be nullified. We're in a fragile place if there are too few settlers to keep the

Indians away," another responded. These were the men who wanted to till the wild land.

One of them noticed Baptiste and shot him a squinty look of warning: *What are you doing here?* Baptiste hurried away.

He kept his worries to himself for a few hours. Finally, in bed, he whispered, "François, the Americans are planning to leave the Missouri Territory. We're to be ruled by the British, the way things are going."

"The British lost," François muttered sleepily. "Long time past."

"But they never went away. What will they do with us if they come?"

"I don't know. Make us bow to the king. Go to sleep."

But Baptiste stayed awake a long time. It was a war between two nations of white men, enemies using Indian proxies. His schoolmate—who had relatives on both sides—seemed to think it had nothing to do with him. But no one could escape the consequences, whichever side won. His mother hadn't seen this war coming.

BAPTISTE WAS APPROACHING the Indian agency one day, when he saw Clark, his wife, and their sons climb into a coach laden with trunks and cases. He dashed over and peered into a window to catch Clark's eye. But if Clark saw him, he chose not to acknowledge it.

"Where are they going?" Baptiste asked a man he recognized as one of Clark's slaves.

"Virginia" was the reply.

Virginia? Was Clark fleeing with his wife and children because he expected St. Louis to fall to the enemy? That couldn't be!

Clark wouldn't run off. He wasn't a coward! But Baptiste felt helpless, watching the carriage vanish into the distance. If the city fell, where would *he* hide?

THERE WAS NO invasion, but the tension gripping the town was displayed in newspaper headlines. The *Gazette* screamed: *"The blood of our citizens cries aloud for VENGEANCE. The general cry is to let the north as well as the south be JACKSONIZED."*

General Andrew Jackson's brutality toward Indians was a favored topic everywhere Baptiste went. Jackson was the hero they yearned for. One day, he heard a dry goods merchant haranguing a crowd outside his store on Second Street.

"Let our policy be the slaying of every Indian from here to the Rocky Mountains!" he shouted. His listeners blared approval. Baptiste felt sick. He worried about his mother all the time. It couldn't be safe at the fort. White people like that merchant spoke of violence. And the British had bribed tribes on the Upper Missouri to go on the warpath.

A FEW WEEKS into the new year, Priscilla pulled Baptiste out of class. A man had come asking for "Toussaint Charbonneau's boy." Baptiste had seen him before—he'd been a passenger on the boat that took his parents to Manuel Lisa's fort. Baptiste's heart jumped. Had he brought news of his mother? The man led Baptiste out to the street before he said a word. He said he was John Luttig, clerk of the Missouri Fur Company. Then, puzzlingly, he took off his hat and held it over his heart. An oxcart piled high with goods approached and they flattened themselves against the wall of the building so it could pass. Baptiste strained to make out what Luttig was saying.

"...come from Señor Lisa's fort... your mother was the best woman residing there"—Luttig was stopped by a fit of coughing—"succumbed... to the putrid fever."

Succumbed? Baptiste struggled to think what that meant. *Dead!* His mother dead! It couldn't be—he paid tribute to her every day. Her spirit was always with him. Yet he had not expected ever to see her again. In his mind, she was already gone from his life. But *dead*...?

It meant she would never know when he found his destiny. She would never be at peace. Death was a great stone and he couldn't move it. He blinked at this melancholy man with his long, greasy hair and willed himself not to cry.

"I can't account for your father," Luttig went on, avoiding Baptiste's eye. "He recently went out to the Mandan, and afterward Sioux attacked the fort. Some time elapsed and I recorded him deceased. Today, I signed the court register as your guardian." More grating coughs. "Your tuition is paid by the Indian agency, as arranged by General Clark." He glanced up the narrow street, as if the great man himself might verify it, then peeked sideways at Baptiste. "So that's all right, then." With a half salute and a parting tap to Baptiste's shoulder, Luttig turned on his heel and walked away.

Baptiste stared after him. He was this stranger's boy now? Why did Luttig sign the court register, whatever that was?

"Because he is a man of conscience," the schoolmaster explained later. "You are a lucky boy, Baptiste, that he has looked out for you."

"Lucky?" Baptiste cried. "General Clark said he'd raise me as his own son! He took me from my mother and now she's dead!"

The schoolmaster frowned. "She fell sick," he said. "There was nothing the general could do."

Baptiste didn't believe that. General Clark was all-powerful. The full force of his mother's death sent him reeling. She would not have understood the school or its lessons. But she had loved him. She believed he would learn from white men and not fear them. But learn for what? *She is gone. She is gone. I am alone.*

He had to stay in school. There was nowhere else to go. Someone told the other boys about his mother and they avoided him. Even the schoolmaster tolerated his funk and didn't call on him in class. Baptiste was only eight years old. One thought took hold of his mind. It was more important than ever to do what his mother would have wanted. But he wasn't sure how to choose. . . .

ST. LOUIS WAS not attacked, neither by Indians nor British. Plans for the stockade were abandoned. When the ice melted on the river in the spring of 1813, the schoolmaster told Baptiste that General Clark was back in St. Louis, after an absence of six months.

"He has asked me to send him a report on your studies," the master said.

"He's not my guardian!"

"Of course he is. He continues to pay your way."

Eventually, Clark sent a boy to fetch Baptiste.

"He says for you to come over now."

Baptiste stared blankly at the boy for a moment. Then he dashed out to the pump to splash cold water on his face.

Outside Clark's house, a child in a miniature officer's jacket and tall cockaded hat was marching up and down, beating on a drum. "Who goes there?" he chirped, holding up his hand. "No business of yours," muttered Baptiste's escort. The soldier boy stuck out his tongue.

Baptiste and his escort went around to the back of the house. Another servant let them in. Clark was sitting at a table in the brick-floored kitchen. He awarded Baptiste a look of fond concern.

"Pomp, we are saddened by your mother's death. She was a good woman."

"Thank you, sir, but—"

"It has made me want to inspect you in the flesh. How are you faring?"

"I am grieving."

"Of course you are."

Two dark-skinned women were cutting up fruit at a long table, and a white woman stirred a pot at the stove. Sweet aromas filled the room. Baptiste opened his mouth again to speak, but Clark went on, "I think we had better get you some new clothes. Your present wardrobe doesn't complement your present size. . . ."

The young woman at the stove turned to look at him then, her pale face flushed and damp.

Baptiste drew a deep breath, to calm himself. He hadn't expected to confront Clark in front of other people. "Sir, I learned of my mother's death from a stranger. . . ." He heard his voice rise, swallowed hard, then hurtled on. "He said he had signed the book and was my guardian."

Clark interrupted. "I was away in Washington City, Pomp. It was only temporary. . . ."

"You never told me. You have left me to fend for myself. You told my mother you would raise me as your son—" He looked away, to master his distress.

"Pomp, your journey to St. Louis was delayed by the Arikara, who blockaded the river. When you finally came, I had married. I had a son. You knew that." Clark turned to bestow a smile on Mrs. Clark. She was much younger than her strapping husband, and looked quite wispy in her pale flowered gown. She must weigh no more than a bundle of straw.

Clark continued in his unruffled tone. "There has been much difficult business to conduct. I have not been able to attend to you as I hoped. You must trust in my affection."

"My mother said that you would have a plan for me."

Clark lifted a hand, the only sign that his patience was tried. "Pomp, my plan has always been the one you know. I feel a moral obligation, not only to you but to all Indian and half-blood boys whose lives are disrupted by great change. You will be educated. Then we will see. For now, you must devote yourself to what lies before you: your studies."

Baptiste blinked at his patron. All boys? But he was Pompey, the "promising" one. . . .

Clark and his wife exchanged another tender glance. She turned to Baptiste then and left the stove to bring him a cup of cider and a biscuit.

"You were so small to have taken that long journey," she said softly, wrinkling her nose. "Your poor mother endured so much. The expedition could not have succeeded without her. . . ." She cast a glance at Clark, who nodded affirmation. "He has told me that often. I couldn't have done what she did! Our trip from Virginia was very nearly the death of me! I don't know if I have the strength ever to go again. . . ."

Baptiste wolfed down the delicious biscuit in spite of himself and was given another. The warmth and comfort of the room and the affection in Clark's eyes soothed him. He wanted to believe that Clark cared for him, *especially* for him.

"I admire your spunk, confronting me as you have. You must always speak up for yourself," the general said, smiling.

The boy with the drum burst noisily in. "Be quiet, Lewis, you are in the house," said Clark. The miniature militiaman ignored him and began to beat a deafening tattoo. The slave women rolled their eyes. "Oh, Lew," said Mrs. Clark. But she laughed as she said it.

"He is a spirited boy," said Clark fondly, "always up to something."

Baptiste found himself staring at Mrs. Clark's pretty, animated face. When she caught him at it, he hastily averted his eyes. Lewis ran out of the room, colliding with a pair of young men who picked him up and shook him before plopping down at the table, quite at home. One of them also wore a militia uniform. Baptiste admired its trim cut and braid. The fellow was splendid-looking, and knew it.

"You can see, there is a full household here under my management," Clark said, stretching his arms wide. "My three children, my nephews who are like sons . . ." The O'Fallon nephews sprawled on their chairs, legs splayed carelessly. Neither acknowledged Baptiste.

Clark went on. "Your school report pleases me very much. You are at the top of your class in rhetoric, spelling—I envy you that!—all excellent marks. Your mother would be proud of you."

Baptiste felt wonderfully relieved. This was the idea that always guided him: to live up to his mother's dreams for him. And Clark was telling him those dreams could continue to guide him, even though she was dead.

After a moment, Baptiste said, "Sir, the master gives us the same exercises we have done for the past year now. I don't think he has any further knowledge to impart to us."

Clark chuckled. "I wouldn't be surprised if you do know more than he does." He leaned forward. "You know, Pomp, two missionaries from the East have applied to open a school just across the street. Their students will be the sons of our important men and I think you should join them. Much can be gained from the whip of competition. And you have had little of that in your present situation."

Baptiste grinned. "I welcome a contest, sir."

"You are turning into a scholar. The reward for that is a more rigorous course of study!"

Mrs. Clark interjected: "Pomp, let me give you a basket of biscuits to take back for the boys." Another woman, dark-skinned and serious-looking, appeared, carrying a wailing baby. She handed it over to its mother. "I am very glad to know you, Baptiste," Mrs. Clark said, as the infant's cries subsided, and he understood that his visit was over. The general smiled. "You will hear from me when the school is ready to receive you," he said.

Hurrying to leave, Baptiste was stopped short by a face staring from a mirror. It took a second to realize it was his own and not his mother's! The same round, deep black eyes, small straight nose, grave mouth, dusting of pink on his brown cheeks gazed back at him. For an instant, he imagined that her spirit had entered him, saying she was proud of what he had done. Clark did believe in him. The proof lay in this new challenge. An American school, with students from the leading families. He must perform with the best of them—or better. He grinned at himself.

The lanky slave boy with the big hands who had escorted him earlier was waiting outside.

When they got to the school, Priscilla was at the door. "B'tiste, get yourself upstairs," she said, and pulled the other boy into the kitchen. Baptiste left the room but lingered in the hall to listen. The two acted like spies. What could be going on?

"How are they doing over there, Gilbert?" Priscilla asked in a low voice.

"Juba ran off. Scipio and Ruby have been sold down the river," said Gilbert.

"Oh, lord, no," Priscilla said. There was a pause.

Gilbert added, "He gave Venus fifty lashes. Says she's good now."

Baptiste poked his head around the doorframe. "Who did?"

The slaves regarded him disdainfully.

"Master General Clark brought us to this wild frontier, split us from our families back in Kentucky," said Priscilla softly, "snatched us from our old home, our old ways. None of us want to live here in the rough." She heaved a sigh.

"Priscilla, do you belong to him too?"

"I do. He hired me out to the schoolmaster. I bring Master Clark some extra income. He's always looking for that."

Baptiste felt disgust for the arrangement and pity for the slaves. His mother had been a Hidatsa slave, but she wasn't mistreated until she belonged to Toussaint. The practice in St. Louis seemed very different. Was it the color of their skin that made master and servant alien to each other?

THAT SPRING, BAPTISTE stood in a little crowd of citizens on the bluff as one hundred and fifty-five Sauk and Fox canoes swept down the river. These tribes, according to rumor, were being armed and relocated by Clark, to serve as buffers against other tribes allied with the British.

He and his schoolmates also watched excitedly as the new territorial militia practiced maneuvers on the parade ground. Every leading citizen was issued a gun. Outside of town, two of the Boone boys were leading Ranger outfits. A few families in the countryside built their own forts.

Baptiste stopped at the Green Tavern once a week to check the front page of the *Gazette*, which was posted outside. The agitated remarks of the men who came for the news were as interesting as the headlines. The Sac and Fox, led by Chief Black Hawk, had turned on the Americans. They had even prevented Manuel Lisa, who got along famously with most of the Indian Nations, from going to his fort. He heard them say that the Indians took horses and cattle from several white settlements and killed two men. No place was safe from the conflicts, it seemed. Would St. Louis be next? The angry crowd demanded that General Clark do something.

EVERY BOY IN St. Louis had always hunted, fished, and trapped. Now they played war. Baptiste and his friends could find a mock battle on the edge of town any day. They took turns as the "enemy" and "the militia," and everyone seemed to relish their roles in equal degree. Baptiste sometimes wondered who he resembled more in their eyes.

Clark's little navy was back in St. Louis only a month later. Baptiste went aboard a gunboat and asked a Ranger what had happened. His ruddy face shone with victory.

"We fired on Sac and Fox and captured a good many. They were persuaded to withdraw their support for the British. When we landed at Prairie du Chien, the redcoats ran like rabbits. I tell you, it was decisive!"

CHAPTER FIVE

A Superior Education

But as the *Gazette* angrily reported, Clark's success was short-lived. When he sent a second fleet up the river, one thousand Sac, Fox, Kickapoo, Potawatomi, Ioway, Santee Sioux, and Winnebago routed it with their own big artillery. The United States was not prevailing against the British-backed Indians in Missouri. People were calling 1814 the Bloody Year.

Then General Andy Jackson trounced the British in the Battle of New Orleans and the war was over. Only thirteen American men died, while Jackson killed more than two thousand British. A high Mass to give thanks was said in the cathedral. The night sky was ablaze with roman candles, rockets, pinwheels, and torpedoes, and echoed with the sound of exploding firecrackers and gunpowder.

Baptiste and his friends followed a gang of whooping and hollering voyageurs, stevedores, and lead miners prancing through the streets. The revelers kept up their carousing all night long. No one told the boys to go home; men even passed them their canteens to drink from—bitter, stinging liquid Baptiste didn't swallow. Candles flickered in the windows of every house they passed. He stopped to stare into bonfires while disheveled patriots sang. Men lifted women into the air and twirled them until they tumbled, shrieking, into the shrubbery. The joy was contagious. Baptiste was giddy. The republic was triumphant and he was part of it!

But triumph left him feeling uncertain. The war was between a European country and the one whose capital was in Washington City. Both sides had used Indian tribes to do some of the fighting and now relations between them would never be the same, would they?

Then, as if he were to be personally rewarded for his country's victory, General Clark sent for him. He had a request. "Ah, Pompey. I need you to do me a service." Baptiste's heart jumped. Clark stamped his seal on a paper tube. "Here is a document from Washington that must go to M. Chouteau. You are to give it to him and only to him. Stop nowhere and speak to no one else."

"Yes, sir." Baptiste immediately turned on his heel and made for the door.

"Wait!" Clark snapped. "Tell him the peace council will be held at Portage des Sioux. Runners have been sent to notify the tribes. However, the man we dispatched to the Sac was killed." He shook his head. "The Sac are trouble. But they will no longer have the British to back them up. We will keep them in check now."

Clark motioned impatiently for Baptiste to make tracks.

Outside, he had to stop himself from letting out a whoop. He was Clark's chosen messenger! He dashed through the streets to the vast stone Chouteau mansion, which gleamed with a coat of lime. The house and lawns covered a full block and were protected by a thick, high wall pierced at intervals with gun holes. Spacious galleries stretched along both its stories on all sides.

"What is your business, cub?" the watchman asked. Baptiste showed him Clark's seal on the message and was allowed to enter the gate and climb the steps to the front door. Once admitted, he ran a gauntlet of servants. "I am to give it directly to M. Auguste," he repeated to each of them in turn. The clatter of utensils on plates and the murmur of conversation grew louder as he approached the dining room. Chouteau sat at one end of a table lit by flickering candles. There were at least a dozen companions. All fell silent when Baptiste entered.

"A message from General Clark, sir," he said in a clear, carrying voice that he thought befitted his position. Chouteau extended his hand. Baptiste approached him and delivered the message with a bow.

Chouteau didn't look at it. "Are you his aide-de-camp now?" he drawled.

Baptiste felt his scalp tighten. "I am his ward, Baptiste Charbonneau. You—"

"I remember. Will you come with us to Portage des Sioux and run express there?"

"I would do that, sir!"

"You are a good boy. He was right to bring you to St. Louis. Albert"—he gestured to one of the waiters—"give the boy a slice of tarte to take."

Then Baptiste found himself on the street, wolfing down a delicious pastry, hardly knowing how he'd gotten there.

THE AMERICAN DELEGATION and their counterparts assembled in St. Louis. Convoys of pirogues with warriors and their women arrived in advance of the council. The canoes of Sac and Fox lashed together spanned the broad width of the river. The men paddled up and down past the harbor, standing tall in their boats, singing and chanting. All of St. Louis took notice. They were trying to intimidate Clark, some people said, adding contemptuously that they would probably succeed.

Some chiefs took refreshment that night in the great houses of their old friends the French traders. Baptiste posted himself outside Chouteau's mansion, half hoping to be invited inside. He spoke to a tall, magnificent Osage draped in a buffalo robe with bloodred hands and red and black stripes painted on it. Baptiste asked him what it meant and the chief told him, "It depicts the Missouri from its mouth to my village, with the blood that will soon run in all of its waters."

Baptiste sucked in a breath. He felt sick. Violence wasn't the answer to the problem of land. Did the Osage know how many more white people there were?

During the days that followed, he made sure he was outside Clark's office as often as possible. "Why do you hang around there so much?" François asked him.

"It's not to be repeated to anyone," Baptiste answered. "But he will probably ask me to serve him as messenger at the peace council."

François snorted. "Why would he do that? He has a host of men to choose from."

Baptiste smiled condescendingly. "He trusts me." François snorted again and went away.

But when Clark left for Portage des Sioux, he was holding the hand of a small boy in a militia uniform. This was the child Baptiste had already seen, beating his drum, Clark's son, Meriwether Lewis.

Clark waved to Baptiste, who felt drained of life as he stood watching.

"He is barely old enough to understand," Clark said cheerfully, "but he will never forget what he sees."

"No, sir," Baptiste muttered.

François gave him no quarter when he heard about Baptiste's disappointment. "You were dreaming," he said. "Clark had no cause to take you." Baptiste was hurt. His friend seemed to take satisfaction from his disappointment.

BUT FINALLY HE shook it off. Summer brought blanketing heat and the usual clouds of mosquitoes. Most of the other boys went back to their mothers' villages. The schoolmaster put Baptiste to work helping Priscilla scrub the building from top to bottom. She was in a talkative mood, telling him stories of life back in Kentucky. General Clark had been a country squire, managing a fine estate called Mulberry Hill and playing host to many other rich, white gentlemen. His four sisters all married officers in George Washington's army. Clark had gone with York to Virginia and fallen in love with Julia Hancock. Priscilla had all the facts at her fingertips, naming the family connections and describing the great houses people inhabited in excluciating detail, until Baptiste nearly cried out with boredom.

He didn't have to work all the time. Peace was bringing great activity to town. Wagonloads of strangers poured in from the East, now that the Indians were no longer attacking and their British allies had been dispatched. Baptiste heard English spoken everywhere. Stores opened to serve the needs of these newcomers, who were staking claims and founding towns overnight. Traders began

to resurrect the fur business too. Fur companies currying favor
with visiting Indian traders even ferried them out to the forest on
hunting parties. The city had been violently roused from sleep
and was shaking off its torpor.

One June day, a written message came for Baptiste. *Your father
wants you to come to Lisa's fort*, it said. *He wishes to witness your progress.
I will escort you to Indian country in one week's time.* It was signed *Bijou
Bissonet, engagé.*

Baptiste was so stunned he laughed. So the old man wasn't dead!
Few favorable thoughts of his father ever occurred to him, and yet
it was unnatural to feel no tender tie. Now it seemed that Toussaint
wanted him after all. A sojourn in Indian country was very appeal-
ing. And if his mother was buried at Lisa's fort, he would visit her
grave and lay flowers on it, as the Americans did at cemeteries.

But Bijou explained that they were going to a new fort, near
Council Bluffs. They carried a cargo of blankets, lead, tobacco,
knives, guns, and beads for trading with the Sioux. As the boatmen
labored to move them along, Bijou pointed out settlements, sometimes of French and Indian families living side by side in peace.

In places, the banks had collapsed into the water where settlers
had felled all the bordering timber. Bijou remarked that the river
above Council Bluffs had even more snags, sand bars, and knotted
trees that made the currents swirl violently. Boats couldn't navigate
it. Consequently, the Upper Missouri would always belong to the
Indians. Baptiste wondered if that could possibly be true. If so, he
rejoiced. The Mandan would be left alone, as long as the Sioux and
the Arikara confined their fighting to each other.

One of the other passengers was a man from Missouri who
had lived many years near the Platte, trading with tribes. But he had

found himself longing for home and so had returned to St. Louis not long before, vowing never to go back to Indian country.

Yet there he was, on board the boat. Baptiste asked him why he had changed his mind. "There is so much deceit and selfishness among white men that I have already tired of them. I have a painful arrow wound that keeps me from chopping wood. Whiskey I can't drink and bread and salt I don't care about. So I will go again among the Indians."

Bijou laughed and said he understood. Baptiste decided such sentiments must explain his father's attachment to that life. To his surprise, he felt a little jolt of affection for the old man.

As they neared their portage, meadows bloomed bright colors on every side. The scene was so tranquil the fortified stockade looked out of place. As soon as he stepped on land, children swarmed around him, their dogs and puppies yipping and leaping, spilling from an encampment of Potawatomi.

Baptiste laughingly shook off the children and entered the fort. He asked a trader for his father.

"He's busy wagering" was the ready reply. Baptiste smiled to himself. "Tell him I have come," he said.

Toussaint didn't seek him out until it was past time to dine with Señor Lisa. He greeted his son impatiently: "Here you are! Come along! We don't keep Lisa waiting, boy!"

His father presented him to Lisa. "This is my boy, that I gave over to Captain Clark." He added vaguely, "He's about nine years. . . ."

Lisa waggled his thick eyebrows. "You go to school, then? Read about the great men of history?"

"Yes, sir."

Lisa brusquely motioned to Baptiste to sit next to him. Toussaint found a spot down the table and sat with a sullen expression. A hodgepodge of men ladling food into their mouths paid no attention.

There was another guest on Lisa's other side, a traveler from Boston, about thirty, dressed conspicuously in yellow corduroy pants and a brown velvet jacket. Lisa said the fellow would memorialize them all in a forthcoming book describing his western journey. "And you'll be able to read it," he said to Baptiste.

"It won't get written if he goes home in a box," Toussaint muttered.

The future author heard him. "You've been lately at war," he said nervously. "So that danger persists?"

"On the contrary," Lisa snapped. "We have kept most tribes of the Upper Missouri from going to the British. I urged the Ponca and the Omaha to attack the Ioway, which kept them from attacking Missouri settlements. Then I called a council of Teton Sioux that made them agreeable. The Indians of the Missouri trade in peace on their own grounds and we trade in security with them. It is only the tribes of the Upper Mississippi that require a military force. You have seen the numbers of horses, cattle, pigs, and fowl we keep. Not one is ever touched by an Indian."

"It is said you are the king of trade on the Missouri, and get more furs than anyone else," the visitor gushed.

Lisa licked his lips and spread his hands wide. "And men ask how I get so much rich fur. Do I cheat the Indians?" He waggled his dark eyebrows. "No! Never! I put into my operation much activity. I go a great distance while my opponents are considering whether they will start today or tomorrow. Ten months of the year I am buried in the depths of the forest. I am their benefactor, not their pillager! I give them superior seeds for their pumpkins. I have my blacksmiths work for them for free. I lend them traps. Here at the fort, I take in their aged and sick, any who can no longer follow their lodges. THAT is how I get so many furs!" He sat back, black eyes blazing. "Of course, I also keep the tribes occupied by provoking their mutual wars." Then he laughed. All the men at the table laughed with him. Baptiste could hear the arrogance of Lisa's pronouncements. But he kept quiet.

"Drink up, gentlemen," Lisa said. "The wines are all French, and so is the brandy."

Their meal was a rich one of roasted bison rump, boiled bison tongues, sausages of minced tenderloin and fat, and fresh bread made out of wheat flour. It surpassed anything Baptiste had ever eaten. "We beg your pardon for the lack of vegetables," Lisa said. "But it is early in the season."

Over the following days, Baptiste saw him huddling with French, American, and Spanish traders, issuing orders to guides and hunters—half white, half Indian, like himself—meeting with a visiting Omaha chief, and, surprisingly, sitting alone, engrossed in a book.

The dignified chief had come to air a grievance. After he and Lisa had smoked a pipe, the old chief quietly confided through an interpreter that the fort was bringing calamity to his small village. Its hunters were depleting game in the vicinity. And young braves, seeing the treasure the white men harbored in their fort, began cultivating wants. They couldn't satisfy the wants and so became unhappy. It was a pitiable destiny for his people, was it not?

Lisa said, "I'll do what I can to ease your difficulties. I cannot suspend our hunting. But I can give you a portion of our game." He also gave the chief some vermillion, a collection of beads, a few metal tools, and a mantilla for his wife.

Baptiste was sorry for the chief. He considered for a moment whether he was part of the trouble. Was it wrong to benefit from the white man's way of life while others suffered from it? He didn't think it was. But he couldn't entirely banish the idea.

Watching the Potawatomi boys at their games and contests made Baptiste long for a saddle horse. So many had been stolen during the war that only the very rich in St. Louis owned one. In the country, people were hitching plows to their milk cows.

But here there were plenty of riding horses. He'd even heard Lisa say a good mousing cat was more valuable than a horse because of the plague of rats in the grain stores. Baptiste began hanging around the paddock, positioning himself so that when a hunting or trading party came in, their mounts winded and running rivers of sweat, Baptiste was right there, ready to take the reins, walk the animals to cool them off, water them at the hole nearby, give them apple treats, and wipe them down, talking calmly all the while. Pretty soon, he was acquainted with all the horses, knew which ones had tempers, which were obedient, which frisky, which affectionate, and they knew him. They were mostly misused, in his opinion, ridden too hard and too long, whipped and kicked. He soothed them as well as he could.

One night at dinner, Lisa gazed piercingly at him through the smoke of his black cigar. Presently, he said, "Ba'tiste, I've seen you with the horses." Baptiste stiffened. Had he done wrong? But Lisa went on. "I remember your mother. She was never perturbed, and neither are you. It's important not to be skittish around horseflesh."

Baptiste tried to keep a straight face. He was mightily pleased.

"Louis Legère has an ornery pony he wants to put down," Lisa continued. "Pony's been whipped until he's no use to anyone. But if you can calm him enough to stay on his back, he may be redeemed."

"I can do it, sir!" Baptiste cried.

Lisa laughed. "You may and you may not. But if you do, he'll be yours to keep."

Baptiste shot to his feet and danced. This was more happiness than he could hold!

Toussaint horned in. "Señor Lisa, we thank you for your generosity. But my boy has been sitting in a schoolroom these past years—"

"Hold your tongue, Toussaint," Lisa snapped. "This is a capable boy, by some miracle. I can't see that he takes after you at all."

The pony, a paint, with patches like skipping stones all over his body, was certainly skittish. Baptiste approached him quietly from the side so the animal could track him every inch of the way. He talked continuously in a low tone, with reassuring words. When he was close enough, he extended a chunk of apple, but the pony shook his head violently and backed away, whinnying and snorting.

Baptiste, unhurried, patient, kept trying. Finally, the pony took the apple, baring his teeth. He seemed to be laughing. "What's your name?" Baptiste asked. "Are you Skipping Stone? I like that! I'll call you Skip."

"He's got the devil in his disposition," said a trader who was saddling his mount. "But he seems to like you."

Every day after that, Baptiste had only to come to the paddock fence and Skip would separate from the twitchy horses clumped together and trot over, nosing at him until he produced an apple. That was a big first step. After three weeks of trying, he was able to clap a bridle on Skip and then to climb onto his back.

Skip threw him right off. That was good. It showed spirit. Baptiste landed on his backside, the air whooshing out of him and his teeth slamming together. When he caught his breath, he got back on a few times, to be thrown repeatedly, but with less and less conviction. Some Potawatomi boys were watching his efforts, and when he was finally secure on Skip's back, they tendered their congratulations by whooping. Skip swung his head at the sound, nearly knocking Baptiste off again. There were more delighted yiyis from the Indians, which Baptiste acknowledged with a bow.

The next day, Baptiste was riding Skip at last. The pony never bucked again. Baptiste could tell him to turn, speed up, or slow down by squeezing his thighs against Skip's sides. The connection to an animal—especially one so strong and willing—went deep, deeper than any Baptiste had.

He wasn't supposed to leave the fort because of the danger of being kidnapped. But one clear day, he and Skip set out over bright carpets of snake herb, milkweed, and borage, and Skip raced as fast as his heart would let him. On the way back, marveling at the fair wind and bright weather, Baptiste noticed a moccasin tied to an oak branch. On Skip's back, he was just the right height to reach it. There was a note from a trader inside. He had been robbed of his horse by Omaha and could be found on foot, heading to his cache. He included a hand-drawn map.

"We'll go after him, Skip."

He kept his eyes peeled, and before long, there was the man peeking out of a ravine.

"I wasn't sure if you was friend or foe 'til you came near," he said. "Two days ago, I was a man of some wealth. All of it has been stripped away. My horses are gone and my cache is emptied. I've been tortured by wasps, to boot."

"Climb aboard," Baptiste said.

The trader talked into Baptiste's ear of good luck and bad, and of knaves and their victims. What a vast gap lay between the fortunes of Lisa, master of the fur company, and this itinerant trader who also wanted to get rich, Baptiste thought, as they trotted along. His schoolmaster said the love of money was the root of all evil, yet it seemed to be the greatest driver of men.

LISA KNEW BAPTISTE'S passenger and invited him to stay as long as he liked, so he joined the mixed gathering of traders, interpreters, and guides. At dinner, the men gossiped about people they knew, narrow escapes they'd had, and the prospects for a decent haul in pelts. Lisa presided with a monarchal air, sometimes raising his voice, at others lowering it so that everyone had to lean forward to hear. He was a consummate manager of men, Baptiste thought.

Mostly he thought about Skip and how he'd ride him around St. Louis. Stabling him would be a problem. Maybe he could do chores for someone with a yard. He'd figure out something.

THE POTAWATOMI ENCAMPMENT lured him. He laughed at a group of girls shrieking with delight as they tossed one of their number in the air on a blanket. Boys were racing their ponies in contests of speed and agility, hanging off their animals' sides and shooting arrows through a rolling hoop. He bet Skip was a match for these ponies. "Let's try," he said to his pony.

It was easy enough to communicate using sign and the words he already knew. Baptiste lined up with eight other boys on their ponies. Another on the sidelines gave the signal to start. Baptiste kicked with his heels and Skip bolted. He wanted to catch the others and was galloping at full speed, but he wasn't the fastest. And Baptiste wasn't the most foolhardy either. They finished in the middle of the pack. "Good boy," Baptiste said, stroking his neck. "We'll do better next time."

And they did. But the contests kept getting harder. They shot arrows from horseback and bent to pick them off the ground without breaking stride. They leapt from one speeding pony to another. When the races were over, they danced to drums. Baptiste didn't much care if he won anything or not. That wasn't the point for him. His father liked to sneer at going to school, claiming it made him soft. He wasn't soft any longer—he was holding his own.

Would he ever have this experience again? Not knowing made every day more precious.

He didn't see much of Toussaint, who led hunting parties by day and played at cards or dice through the night. Baptiste had questions about his mother. He wanted to know how she had died and if she had spoken his name. But he never asked Toussaint. Whatever the old man might say could only reopen the wound of Sakakawea's death. Why wasn't his father there to help her?

One night, Toussaint was amusing himself by bothering a young recruit with tales of Indian attacks. The company clerk overheard him.

"That's enough, Charbonneau," he snapped. He added, under his breath, "He ought to be hanged." Baptiste heard that and cringed.

"I do the greenhorn a service," Toussaint drawled.

"Do the company a service, then! Pay your liquor tab! It's as long as the river and months overdue," the clerk said.

"I serve the company well," Toussaint protested. "There's no need to hound me over trifles."

"You'll get no more drink, then," the clerk retorted. "That's the end."

"Whoa," said Toussaint, looking bug-eyed.

"You heard right. Pay up or go thirsty," the clerk said, and turned to leave.

Toussaint blinked. "All right," he muttered. "You'll be paid before sunup."

The next morning, Baptiste went with his morning treat to the paddock. He called and called. Skipping Stone never came trotting over. Toussaint had gambled him away.

BAPTISTE RETURNED TO St. Louis vowing never to see his father again. His only comfort was that he probably couldn't have kept Skip in St. Louis. But how he missed his pony! Was he being taken care of? White men and Indians alike were so hard on their horses!

But he couldn't go on whining forever. He just had to steer clear of Toussaint Charbonneau. And now he had a new school, where the other boys came from the best families. Clark expected him to do well. He was going to have to put his heart into his studies, not into a lost pony.

✳   ✳   ✳

THE BAPTIST MISSIONARIES set up their school in a warehouse belonging to the fur-trading Robidoux brothers, cater-corner from Clark's house. On the first day, Baptiste reported with a ditty bag containing a spare shirt, two gorgeous parrot feathers he had found, and a folding knife.

Mrs. Clark was playing her pianoforte when he passed their house, providing an anthem for this new chapter of his life. He was done with the old school, its brittle master, and its horrible food. Señor Lisa's superior mess had shown him he should not have gotten used to it. He wouldn't miss most of his fellow students. Even François, his closest friend, didn't understand him. He would go back and see Priscilla from time to time. She was kind. He would have to make new friends now. But if he failed, he would survive. It was safest to be self-reliant.

The two young missionaries wore identical long, rusty black frock coats with gray collars and cuffs. Tall, ungainly Mr. Welch, whose nose and face were long and his brows permanently set at an imploring slant, told them he would teach them mathematics, botany, and zoology. Mr. Peck was tall and well proportioned. His mouth was narrow and his eyes piercing under his broad brow. His courses were reading, writing, Latin, and metaphysics, which allowed him to expound on his various philosophical ideas.

Baptiste sat next to James Haley, who cracked his knuckles and released woebegone sighs. Clark's son Jeff sat quietly in the row behind, a pair of Chouteau cousins next to him. The room held twenty scholars altogether. In contrast to most of his former classmates, they wore clean, well-tailored clothes, and spoke in grammatical sentences. When the Reverend Welch took his place at the lectern, everyone quieted at once. This was a serious school.

Baptiste sat with his hands folded on his desk, eager for what these masters would throw at him.

"It is our aim to awaken your minds and arm your souls for a treacherous world," Welch began. "Your reading will range widely, from Cicero to Diderot. Mr. Peck and I are your guides, but you are not our blind followers. . . ." He looked piercingly into each pair of eyes in turn. His lopsided mouth gave him a look of permanent rue until it suddenly adopted a crooked smile. "Some of you will discover a capacity for *thought*."

Baptiste's first task was to decipher Latin passages by comparing them to their English translations, which were printed on adjoining pages in his book. "You will learn them by heart and be able to recite them in a week," Peck said. The names of the Roman emperors and the kings of England back to John also had to be memorized. Baptiste's English tense conjugations were shaky at first, but before long he was at ease with the pluperfect. He wrote notes on all subjects in copybooks, using quills Mr. Peck cut with a special knife. Baptiste imagined his brain swelling impressively as it absorbed knowledge. Was it possible to stock it with all he would ever need to navigate the world?

The other boys went home to their families every evening. Baptiste was the sole boarder, sharing living quarters with Mr. Peck. The Reverend Welch, who had a wife and child, had taken rooms in a house on Pear Tree Street. Baptiste was assigned some of the upkeep of his new bachelors' quarters.

Peck dispatched him, with careful instructions, to the market. He was to haggle for a chicken, a pound of cornmeal, and vegetables, if there were any to be found. Peck knew that butter was

forty cents a pound, inferior flour twelve dollars a barrel, corn on
the ear (suitable for Peck's horse only) one dollar a bushel, chickens
thirty-seven cents apiece, and eggs about forty cents a dozen. If
Baptiste's expenditures didn't match these figures, Peck made a great
show of disappointment, but he never accused him of being taken
advantage of—although that he may have been, sometimes. Peck
cooked, Baptiste assisting, and their simple meals were eaten
together in silence, to demonstrate gratitude for their nourishment.

Peck had favorite rules. "Cleanliness must be one of your virtues," for instance. Every day Baptiste was to "comb your head and
wash your face, hands, and mouth in cold water; not hastily and
slightly, but thoroughly." Baptiste also began bathing every week,
stepping into the lukewarm tub Reverend Peck had recently vacated.

THE SCHOOL'S LIBRARY consisted of a suitcase of books the
missionaries had carried with them from the East. After they had
been in session for a few weeks, the Reverend Welch announced that
the vast library of M. Auguste Chouteau, which he had purchased
from Jesuits during St. Louis's Spanish years, was open to anyone
who wished to read more widely. "It sits little used, as our citizens
are too occupied with making their fortunes to partake of learning,"
said Welch with a frown. Baptiste went to see it that afternoon.

He entered the grand front hall, where four servants on their
hands and knees were waxing and polishing the floors to a mir-
rored blackness. A dignified Indian woman dressed elegantly in
the French style suddenly appeared and asked what his business
was. Before he could answer, a bony old woman he took to be
Madame Chouteau called from a doorway, "Let him pass, Therese.

Monsieur Peck, the schoolmaster, has sent him over to borrow books." She giggled. "I wouldn't take you for a scholar," she added, squinting at Baptiste. "What do you think, Therese?"

The other woman didn't reply.

"Therese is my concierge," Madame explained. "I can't do without her. She has managed this household for fifty years." She laughed.

Baptiste was too flustered to say anything.

"All right, young Baptiste Charbonneau, come along."

He followed her into the room where the books were kept. He thanked her with a bow and she took a seat, watching him with narrowed eyes and restless fingers, giggling occasionally, for no reason he could see. A tall clock ticked. It was crowned by a bust of a long-nosed man wearing a sardonic expression. Baptiste took off his cap and turned his attention to the glass-covered shelves.

"You're from the Baptist school. Protestant boys don't read stories," she remarked. "The clergy don't trust them to resist romantic notions." She let out a cackle. "But maybe you're more independent. Do you like novels?" She shuffled to one of the cases and pulled out a slender volume. It was called *Candide* by Voltaire. "This one concerns a young man like yourself," she said, "an innocent young fellow who learns about life through adventures wilder than any he could have dreamed. And," she added archly, "it has a fine moral." She examined him for a moment, before pressing it into his hand. "It made the priests in France so angry they banned it." She cackled again. "We have sixty books by M. Voltaire. He was a friend of my uncle's. This one is a rare volume." She cocked her head at the clock. "See him there? He stands watch over our books."

Baptiste promised sincerely to read it. She nodded approvingly while he picked out more volumes. "Return them whenever you like. I will remember every one," she called cheerily when he left with half a dozen in his arms. He went down the street, grinning. She was a fine character and had obviously liked him! The French were so carefree, seeking pleasures and forgiving sins. He considered that a virtue, even if Reverend Peck might not.

The school curriculum emphasized manual labor, as a practical as well as a moral matter. The missionaries pitched in to work alongside their charges. "Whatever purifies the body fortifies also the heart," Reverend Peck would testify, spading earth for a garden. He often asked them to thank their maker for placing them in the Missouri Territory at just that time.

"The West is the instrument of salvation for mankind, the stepping-off place for Zion," he told them. "On the frontier, we convert to freedom!" Baptiste was touched by his passion, though he was pretty sure "conversion" would not always be welcome. Peck, sensing that, seized the chance to uplift a willing disciple. "We will ever hew to the possibilities of success," he would tell Baptiste, reinforcing his feeling that a clear path lay before him. He needed only to hold course until its purpose was revealed.

In the late afternoon, Baptiste often saw Peck riding his horse, Catullus, his face in a book, trusting his mount to take him where he wanted to go. He was conspicuous, and not just for the book. Saddle horses were still objects of envy. It gave Baptiste a powerful pang to see Catullus every day and be reminded of Skip.

One Sabbath, Peck returned from a remote settlement where he had preached his message of evangelism. Baptiste heard him and got out of bed to help.

"I am weary, but from the Lord's work," Peck said, smiling.

"May I get you some water?" Baptiste asked.

"That would be ambrosial, my boy."

Baptiste produced a tin of fresh cold water and stood by while Peck drank it. The near-full moon emerged from behind a cloud. Peck's face looked worn in its milky light. But he was cheerful.

"The backwoodsmen I met have renewed my faith," he said. "Their rough, sturdy habits are laying the foundation for individualism and democracy, because these men must ever begin anew with each settlement as they move west. They cannot take freedom for granted."

Baptiste listened sleepily. He wasn't expected to respond. The preacher continued. "It is not true of many hunters and trappers. They become so enamored of their wandering as to lose all desire to return to civilization. I expect them to remain for the rest of their lives in the deserts. It is a melancholy example of the tendencies of human nature toward the degraded state of savages." He looked up then and fixed Baptiste with his bright, kindly eyes. "The improvement of the species is a slow process—and so is the improvement of the individual. That is why you must cleave to your books, my boy!"

"My father proves the truth of your idea about wanderers," Baptiste said. "He was here for a while, but soon fled city life. And my mother longed for her homeland as well. But you must not call her a savage."

"I mean no ill, my boy. I use it as merely a Christian's word for those not yet civilized."

"Indians suffer when they try to live among whites. You see that with the few here in town. They are not accepted and their skills are ill-suited to most jobs here."

Peck's eyes burned with a furious light. Then his expression abruptly softened. "You are right. We have doomed their way of life, and yet they resist ours. But their souls are ripe for salvation. It is my Christian duty to save their souls."

That was to be Peck's last word of the day. Baptiste followed him inside, where they prepared for bed. As he lay waiting for sleep, he could hear the minister praying. Peck was a good man, he thought, possibly the model for what a good man could be. But goodness and its works could seem futile, even foolish. Praying and converting weren't going to solve the problem.

BAPTISTE READ HIS history and Latin texts in his room, but he liked to take storybooks and poetry to a secluded spot overlooking the river, away from town. His imagination, freed from the rigors of everyday obligations, opened completely to a tale, transporting him to wherever it was set. It was in this refuge that he read *Candide*. He decided to keep the book a secret from Peck, out of consideration for the preacher's feelings. He would think the story too Catholic and therefore cynical. Peck said papists absolved themselves of sins merely by confessing them.

There would be no danger of Mme Chouteau finding him too cynical. He went to return his books in the late afternoon, hoping to encounter her again. A slave fetched her and she went with him to the library, hooking a scrawny arm through his.

"Well, what did you make of it?" she asked.

"Candide? I agree he's a bit like me," he said.

"*Oh là là!* You're in for it, then," she replied.

He laughed. "All those calamities, you mean," he said. "But Candide survives them. I believe we live in the best of all possible worlds."

Mme Chouteau sat herself in a thronelike chair that made her look like a wizened doll queen. "My boy, I don't think M. Voltaire meant for you to be so accepting of the world."

He thought for a moment. He didn't want her to decide he was stupid. But maybe she was being playful. "I know that he poked fun at sinful men and corrupt works. But in the end, Candide and his Cunegonde do the sensible thing. They cultivate their garden."

"I hope you will sow seeds over wilder ground before you settle in a garden," she said slyly, and tapped his arm. "Hmm. What shall I propose for you next?" She mimed searching her mental inventory, but he could tell that she already had a book in mind.

"*Don Quixote!* Our worthy friend Señor Lisa is never without his copy. He carries it into the wilderness and there reads it over and over. It clearly profits him to do so!"

"I think I saw him with it!"

"If you have met him, that is not surprising. It is Spanish. The hero is no youth, like Candide; he's a skinny old man maddened by chivalry. But there are similarities. The Don is not innocent, he's a fool. His odyssey shows that the world cannot be understood by a closed mind. I usually laugh when I read it, but I'm not sure I shouldn't be weeping. One doesn't know at all what to make of this book. And so it is great art."

Mulling this paradoxical remark, Baptiste took *Don Quixote* away with him. But his mind was still on *Candide.* Had he just revealed to her how innocent he was? The book was meant to amuse, he could see, but had a serious purpose. Since no possible good came of the Lisbon earthquake, it proved that nature operated independent of God's will. Voltaire also seemed to say that reason was no guarantee of progress. Faith and reason, equally useless? Baptiste wondered which side Voltaire would have chosen in the debate between "civilization" and "savagery." Perhaps a simple life in the wilderness didn't have to be a savage one.

St. Louis didn't suffer from the ills Voltaire was mocking—an all-powerful church hunting down heretics, desperate poverty, an army on the march. The New Madrid earthquake hadn't left St. Louis in ruins, as Lisbon was. Not even the recent war had touched the city directly. On the contrary, it grew more prosperous every year. Baptiste smiled to himself. Didn't Americans think their nation was the best of all possible worlds?

He was happy enough at the new school, but as he had expected, it wasn't easy to make friends. Every Missouri boy honed his wilderness skills by hunting, shooting, riding, and tracking, and so did he. But he was usually alone. The Clark boys, O'Fallons, and Kennerleys didn't shut him out on purpose, but they were so used to being together, they had a way of vanishing when the school day ended. The Chouteaus and their French friends, on the other hand, went to lessons in fencing or music or to watch their fathers conduct business in their offices.

One afternoon, he was wandering along a street, when he heard sudden collective gasps followed by suspenseful silences and more gasps from the Place d'Armes. He trotted over to see what was happening. A rope dancer in striped tights was scampering back and forth about twenty feet above the ground.

A diverse crowd had collected to watch: Sioux in western clothes looking on somberly, French women in bright dresses and mantillas, leaning together, men in beaver hats, boys and girls jostling even as they gaped at the show. Their exclamations were timed to the rope dancer's steps. When he paused and teetered, people loudly sucked in their breaths; then, when he recovered himself, they turned laughingly to their neighbors and clapped for him. Baptiste glanced around the square. People were watching from the market gallery too.

A moment later, a tall, scruffy, strawheaded boy had materialized at his side. As the dancer accelerated his trips along his rope, throwing a pair of ninepins in the air and catching them, the boy whistled through his rabbity teeth. When the performer had finished and taken his bows, the crowd melted away, but Baptiste stayed put. So did his neighbor. The boy wheeled and gave Baptiste a poke.

"How long you reckon it takes to learn that?" he asked in English.

"It could be a person is born to it," Baptiste said.

"That would be peculiar," said the boy. "From what I have seen, babies can't hardly do anything."

"I meant it might be an inborn talent, like a fellow who can make music or paint a likeness," Baptiste said, laughing. Baptiste liked this boy's frank, curious nature. He wanted to know him and see what might come of it.

He blurted, "We could try it! It shouldn't take long to see if we're born to it or must try to learn."

"I'm game," said the boy.

"I'm Baptiste."

"I'm Jim Bridger."

They bounded off, laughing and caroming off each other.

There was a rope lying behind a dry goods store and they stretched it from a tree to a shed roof in the tinsmith's yard, which Jim said wouldn't bother anyone. Baptiste climbed onto the roof and gingerly put his foot on the rope. It dipped, but held fast. He added his other foot, and the first one slid. He toppled to the ground with a wild pinwheeling of his arms. They both thought it was hilarious.

"You try it, Jim." It was the same with Jim. They laughed until they hurt, tried it again and again, but neither one ever got any farther along the rope.

"I guess whatever looks easy you can be sure isn't," Jim said.

"I conclude the same thing."

"Well, say. I know where we can find us some nice black Cuban cigars."

After a brief negotiation behind a house on rue Principal, they sat smoking, while fur traders and their women hooted and danced by firelight on the porch.

Baptiste didn't get back to the school until long after midnight. He reeked of smoke and didn't feel quite right in his stomach. He was sure he'd get a tongue-lashing. But if so, it was all worth it. He liked Jim so much, felt completely at ease with him. What did they have in common? A taste for trying things out, for adventure.

A lone candle flickered where Mr. Peck was reading in his room with the door open. Baptiste tried to tiptoe past, but the missionary called softly to him. He presented himself, hanging his head penitently.

"Have you been sinning, Baptiste?" Peck asked, his slender form casting a long shadow like an accusing finger. Baptiste told him where he had been—most of it.

"You drank no whiskey?"

"No, sir."

"There are nightly orgies, scenes of drunkenness and profane revelry in this town." Peck sighed mournfully. "Even if you were not tempted this evening, you opened the door to sin. We must ask God for mercy." He told Baptiste to kneel alongside him.

"Lord, give us gratitude and humility that we may rise above temptation, yet never be proud or vain. Amen. . . . Ask your friend Jim if he wouldn't like to come to school. We turn no one away, even if he cannot pay."

"I will, sir."

"What I oppose most vigorously is ignorance, Baptiste. At least half the Anglo-American population are infidels of a low and indecent grade who lack learning or sense and are utterly worthless for any useful purposes of society. But we can save your friend Jim, if he is willing."

ALTHOUGH JIM COULDN'T even write his name, he was aghast at the idea of school.

"I couldn't be stuck in a chair, squeezed up to a desk while the daylight hours creep uselessly by."

"There's a lot that's interesting in books," Baptiste said. "If you can read." But Jim shook his head and reared back in mock horror.

Then, one day, seeing Baptiste carrying his book of Roman history, Jim asked to hear it read aloud. While reading to Jim, Baptiste discovered that the nickname Clark had given him, Pompey, was the name of a Roman general.

"Can you beat that!" Jim said. "He pegged you for a warrior!"

Baptiste laughed. "I was pretty small. He saved my life when my mother and I were washed over a falls." He hesitated, then decided he would confide everything. "He said he wanted to raise me as his son."

Jim stared at him for a long moment. "Is he doing that?"

"He pays my tuition at school. He says he has a plan for me." The words sounded hollow.

"A plan," Jim repeated in a flat voice. "I don't know, B'tiste. He seems to leave you fairly on your own."

Baptiste was stung. It was painful to hear his doubts come from someone else's mouth. "He's a busy man. He's the most important man in the Missouri Territory. He's the governor."

"Well, I guess I do enjoy it when you read to me!" said Jim. "Thanks, General Clark."

BAPTISTE TOOK TO choosing books he thought Jim would enjoy. Jim always listened intently. "Mighty intriguing!" he would say, at regular intervals. *The Pilgrim's Progress* became his favorite. "What's going to become of Christian?" he kept asking, and cheered when the fellow got himself out of the Slough of Despond, only to be tempted at Vanity Fair. That brought a groan. The story, all about Christian's journey to celestial salvation, reminded Baptiste of *Candide*, except it wasn't at all funny and he grew tired of reading it. To divert Jim from the endless allegory, he showed him a tattered volume the boys had furtively passed around at school: *Aristotle's Masterpiece*, all about how men and women made babies. It had pictures.

Jim glanced at it and laughed. "I don't need a book for that," he said.

Baptiste felt his cheeks flush. He had never seen a woman naked.

"What are you looking at?" Jim asked after a moment. Baptiste realized he'd been staring while trying to work up a question.

"Have you?" he said.

"Have I what?"

"Seen a naked woman."

"Well, I guess, living with a sister in one room, I have," Jim said dismissively.

JIM WAS INTERESTED in events and politics and wanted Baptiste to read from the *Missouri Gazette* every week. Old copies stayed tacked to a board outside a Second Street tavern until they dissolved in the elements. One story was about Napoleon's final exile to the tiny island of St. Helena.

"I wager he'll try to make another escape," Jim said, drawing on his cigar.

"They'll never let him get away again," Baptiste protested. "It is a cruel thing to confine an emperor and make him helpless!"

"According to this, he's still living like a royal," Baptiste said, "waited on hand and foot." They agreed that Napoleon had forfeited his place in history and would be soon forgotten.

BAPTISTE NO LONGER visited Mme Chouteau in her library. He didn't dare take one of those precious books on a ramble with Jim. It made him feel just slightly guilty, that being with Jim meant not being somewhere he was expected to be. It raised the question of whether Clark would approve of his friend. He told himself he might not be studying, but he was learning plenty from Jim that he couldn't get from books.

They visited the crumbling stone forts left by the Spanish.

"Our forts are built of wood," Jim observed. "They'll be gone long before these are."

"I was born in one made of wood, way upriver," Baptiste told him. "It was dead winter."

As it grew warmer, they swam below the milldam in Chouteau's pond, with the laughter of washerwomen pealing over the crashing water.

They climbed the mysterious Cahokia Big Mound, said to have been built, like the Pyramids, by ancient peoples. A community of monks lived on the top now. Mr. Peck had told his class that Mr. Jefferson had taken an interest in mounds.

"He says this was once the seat of a great Indian civilization," Baptiste said.

"Balderdash! Can you see any Indians you know running a great civilization?"

This was an Anglo attitude that Baptiste had encountered before. "Indians have their own civilization, Jim," he retorted. But arguing over civilizations was a losing proposition. You had to concentrate on what lay ahead, not what lay behind. Otherwise, he might dwell on what would have happened to him if he had never come down the river with his parents, but stayed in the Villages. He would have followed in his father's footsteps, probably. The thought made him shiver.

Instead, his best friend in the world was this Anglo boy, as different from himself as he could be. But they loved to do things together. They made traps for squirrels and muskrats out of branches and leather thongs. They turned bones into fishhooks and brought down airborne ducks with a stone. Jim was still practicing the skill.

One day they ambled along the high riverbank, following a faint deer track through scrub hazelnut toward a stand of cottonwoods garlanded with vines. Baptiste stopped to imitate a deer calling its mate, throwing his voice so that it seemed to come from the thicket. Sure enough, a deer came out from the brush, froze when it saw who had called, and hastened back to cover.

Beyond the grove was a pond. Birdsong filled their ears and Baptiste felt a wonderful calm. Freedom! He stopped to watch some ducks descend toward the water.

Suddenly, the peace was shattered by the blast of a gun. Too close!

"*Merde!*" Baptiste exclaimed. A mop of greasy mouse-colored hair popped up from brush a few yards away.

"Didn't see you," called the shooter. His voice cracked. He looked to be about thirteen and wore an old militia shirt and hat. He ignored Baptiste and spoke to Jim. "I seen you at the market."

Jim nodded.

"What are you doin' with him?" asked the boy, tipping his head toward Baptiste.

Jim shrugged.

"He's a 'breed," the other boy muttered.

Jim gave him an incredulous look. "I'd rather be with him in a hard spot than anyone."

Baptiste kept his face blank. When the moment came, he'd take a swing.

"My friend is well known," Jim added. "Tell him, B'tiste."

Baptiste hesitated. He had told his story only a few times and he didn't want to waste it on an Anglo who thought he was superior to everyone with darker skin.

He considered for a moment, while Jim waited eagerly. A story that told who you were was precious. It had to be truly heard. But he decided he owed it to Jim, who wanted him to be important, so he turned to the boy and said: "I am the child saved from drowning by General Clark at the Great Falls of the Missouri. He brought me to St. Louis."

"*Clark*," the boy said scornfully. "He's an Indian lover, ain't he? My pa says he should be ousted and Andy Jackson brought in to rid us of the aborigine menace!"

Baptiste stared back. Should he lick this ignorant oaf or teach him a lesson? He was smaller, but he was strong and quick.

"Look," Jim said, whipping around. Another pair of fat ducks flapped over toward the pond.

The boy hastily raised his gun and cocked it. He took his shot, sending a puff of smoke into the air. The ducks flew on.

Jim chuckled. "Your aim ain't so good," he said. "Bet you my friend B'tiste can bag you a duck without firing a shot."

Baptiste sent him a warning look.

The boy cursed quietly as he reloaded his gun. "What are you talking about?"

"You really should see it," Jim said mildly.

"I ain't a fool."

"I'll lay you a wager," Jim persisted, which was something Baptiste had heard him say in a variety of situations. Jim collected quite a few French and Spanish coins that way. "What have you got?"

"Nuthin'," said the boy. "How can he do that without firing a shot?"

"Jim," said Baptiste under his breath, "I can't do it every time."

"Well, he'll show you!" said Jim, ignoring the whispered protest.

The boy looked them both over as if he hadn't quite taken them in before. "I got some tobaccy," he said finally.

"That'll do," said Jim.

"Follow me," said Baptiste. It had to be done now. Either he would succeed or he wouldn't.

Dozens of ducks glided on the pond's bright surface. "Both of you go in and scare them up," Baptiste said. Jim ran into the water, splashing and waving his arms. The other boy hesitated, then ran in after him. Squawking ducks flew straight up and veered off in every direction.

Baptiste folded and unleashed his arm like a spring. *Thwack!* A duck fell like a plumb weight into the water. Jim ran to collect it.

"How'd you do that?" the boy asked. Baptiste opened his hand and showed him two stones he hadn't thrown.

"I'm damned," the boy said.

"Let's have your tobaccy," said Jim. "The duck's yours. We're sorry for you that your gun is no use."

Jim and Baptiste sauntered off. "Some joke," Jim said with a dismissive laugh. "What a saphead." He was very pleased with himself.

It was a fine thing to have a friend, Baptiste thought. Wasn't that the best protection from a hostile world?

☆   ☆   ☆

SINCE ST. LOUIS was becoming the center of a vast trade network, sending goods to every corner of the world, Mr. Peck announced that he would offer lessons in map reading to the general public on Friday afternoons at four.

"You have had the benefit of Jedidiah Morse's textbooks, but many of our citizens are not as informed," he explained.

Baptiste took the notice to the newspaper editor for publication. He lingered to watch the man warm the typecase at his fire, wipe the letters clean with urine, which he called chamber lye, then arrange them by the light of a soiled window.

To Baptiste's delight, Peck asked him to serve as his assistant at the presentation. He helped Peck affix stiff backing to his maps and then spent several hours dreamily studying the continents, oceans, rivers, mountains, and great capitals. How much of the world would he see in his lifetime? He'd already been over a vast part but could hardly remember it. Maps were beautiful, but they didn't help him picture all the places he'd been as an infant. How he missed his mother's stories of their great journey. Sometimes that loss was a piercing ache that only a long walk along the bluffs would ease.

A ragtag audience filed into the classroom on the next Friday, mostly women, with a sprinkling of old men. These were the people, Baptiste realized, who had spare hours for self-improvement. Baptiste held the maps aloft and Peck indicated various locations with a long stick. He pointed first to the faraway continent of Europe and all of its major nations, then to Asia and the trade routes plied by ships from New England. "My origins are in Massachusetts. I take pride in the courage of those seafaring traders," he said.

A man asked, "What of the water route to the Pacific Ocean?"

"We are fortunate indeed that the journals kept by General Clark and the late Captain Lewis have just been published. General Clark's maps show us every river in the interior, the mountains and deserts. There is no direct waterway to the Pacific."

Beaming, Peck turned to Baptiste and gestured to him to step forward. "This young man was with them," he said, "carried all that way by his mother, Sakakawea. He has seen the Pacific, although he was an infant, and harbors no memory of it."

Baptiste blushed, made a little bow. He could hardly wait to ask Peck if he possessed the published journals of Lewis and Clark. Would he find his mother in them?

"And what of the land to the west?" someone asked.

"By all accounts, the prairie that borders us is of little use and will serve as a reserve for the aborigine nations. There is not a stick of timber to be found there. General Zebulon Pike has compared it to the sandy deserts of Africa." Peck paused and glared at his audience. "Mine is not a popular view," he said. "But if we intend for the Indians to become law-abiding farmers, we must provide them with better soil."

There was murmuring. Baptiste, uncomfortable, saw a few Christian heads nod assent.

At last, Peck concluded his presentation. Everyone filed out and Baptiste blurted: "I would like very much to read the captains' journals, sir."

Peck's eyes widened. "Of course you would. You should be acquainted with your own story as related by those brave men. And I have obtained a copy. There are not many. It is three volumes. You must treat them with the greatest tenderness."

The hour was late. "Shall you do your reading tomorrow?" Peck asked.

"I would prefer to do it now," Baptiste said. Peck kindly offered Baptiste the padded chair that always sat by the hearth in the parlor. When the good man had gone upstairs, Baptiste sat with the books closed on his lap for a few minutes. Would the experience be as momentous as he expected it to be? The idea of reading Clark's account of the journey without his knowing felt improper. But this way he could absorb information at his own pace, in complete privacy.

He read for many hours, to guttering candlelight, transfixed.

BOTH MEN'S ACCOUNTS confirmed everything his mother had told him: She had prevented disaster several times, rescued the expedition's records from a capsizing boat when Toussaint panicked and was no help at all. She had nearly died of fever, and so had Baptiste, but the explorers found medicines that cured them. Most gratifying of all, he read the story of how Clark saved his life at the Great Falls. His eyes filled with tears and he found himself unable to put into words the humble gratitude he felt. Clark had carved his name on a great rock and called it Pompey's Pillar, recording his existence for all time. He held a book in his hands that contained all of this history! No matter how much or how little he accomplished in his life from now on, he would not be forgotten by readers of this book. This thought gave him enormous comfort, but it was also a reminder of the great things his mother had expected of him.

Several passages written by Lewis upset him, and one was especially troubling. He claimed that Sakakawea (he called her the squaw) showed no emotion upon being reunited with her brother. Lewis concluded that she didn't have any feelings. "She was so loving and loyal!" Baptiste cried out loud when he read that. How could Lewis not see that she kept her deep emotions to herself, that she had as much human feeling as anyone. But Lewis had not considered Sakakawea human. She posed no threat to him, so he ignored her unless she was sick. Baptiste wished he could raise them both from the dead and force the man to acknowledge his mother's wisdom and courage. Clark had finally done that.

He fell asleep with the last volume lying open. Peck, in the morning, gently picked it off his lap.

BAPTISTE'S DAYS WERE spent in class after winter set in, and he didn't see Jim for several weeks. He learned later that Jim's life had taken a tragic turn: His parents caught a virulent fever and he stayed at their farm on Six Mile Prairie, along the Mississippi, to nurse them. But the elder Bridgers died, one after the other, in the space of days, and the land they'd been farming was seized by a bank. When Baptiste saw him next, Jim was bunking with neighbors. He looked scrawny and his mild gray eyes were careworn.

"I'm an orphan," he said matter-of-factly. "There's only me to provide for my sister." He had to find a job. Baptiste toured the taverns with him to read aloud from the public notices that papered their walls. These were the principal source of Help Wanted notices, as well as of slaves who had run off, land auctions, recruiting for trapping parties, and the arrival of new industries in town. The most jobs seemed to be on the waterfront. Laborers were needed to do the backbreaking pushing and pulling of northbound boats against the muddy current of the river. "They're always fools will do that," Jim said. "And I'm one of them."

But Jim would not be ruled by any man's will. He was fired from three boatmen's jobs, by which time he had earned a reputation for being unruly. The next thing Baptiste knew, his enterprising friend was poling a makeshift ferry of his own across the Mississippi, competing with the single horse-drawn one.

"This is no trade," he told Baptiste. "But it's worth it to be my own boss."

"I guess it is," Baptiste agreed. "I wish for that myself."

"When I turn fifteen next year, I can be apprenticed. I reckon I'll learn blacksmithing. Horses are arriving every day and will always need shoes."

"Maybe I'd like to do that," Baptiste said carelessly.

Jim turned on him. "You? You'd rather work like a sorry mule than read your books and do your sums and have the Reverend send your prayers express to heaven?" He let his mouth hang open for emphasis.

"Sorry, Jim," Baptiste said. "I'm lucky. I do know that."

Jim didn't reply. The wind was picking up. Muddy water sloshed at the shore. Baptiste gazed out over the river. He was painfully aware that the hard look had not left Jim's eyes. There was more to say, but it amounted to a confession, and he needed to work up the courage to make it. Jim finally turned his back and began coiling a length of rope.

"You know, I feel useless," Baptiste said. "School is meant to prepare me for something. But what is it?"

"Well, B'tiste. Everything around here is controlled by Clark and the Chouteaus. And it seems like they've taken you under their wings. I have heard, since we met, that you are special."

Jim's tone was clearly sarcastic. Baptiste felt his blood rise. He had been confiding, not bragging, when he told about his destiny. Didn't Jim understand that? Baptiste kicked at a stone. He guessed that, for his part, he envied Jim. How could things between them have gone so wrong so fast? It was a pretty fix.

"I don't expect they care so much about me," he said dully. "I'm in harness, while you're free."

Then Jim's expression did soften. "I know the general put you in school and makes you stay."

"I'm glad to be there. But I don't know what is to happen when I'm out."

WHEN THE DAYS lengthened, the Reverend Peck saddled his horse and left for the wilderness, leaving the Reverend Welch to preach in St. Louis. Jim apprenticed himself to a new young blacksmith who was gaining a reputation as a master workman. Baptiste, required only to keep the school building clean and its goat and chickens alive, had time on his hands for visits to the smithy's yard. Jim was still learning the ropes.

The blacksmith was a farrier, and deftly shod a few horses every day. There was a stable next door, whose horses were curried and fed by the apprentice, Jim. Sutton the smith also repaired tools, made hinges and nails and wagon parts. The carriage shop was in regular need of his services. At first, Jim was kept busy squeezing the bellows that kept the coals blazing and smoke streaming up the brick chimney. Sparks showered into the blackness that enveloped the forge. This work was quickly thickening Jim's arms and, judging from the look of the giant, sweating, red-faced blacksmith, skinny Jim would be a gladiator before long.

SUTTON MADE NO objection to his presence, so Baptiste shadowed Jim, pouring water on the grindstone while Jim turned the wheel, sweeping straw and manure, his head reeling from the smells, the wheezing bellows, and the clang of hammer on steel and iron. It was taxing. His body felt it. He admired the soot and blisters on his hands, enjoyed the aches and twinges that lasted for days after he'd been there. If he kept coming, he'd soon be stronger too.

Business was brisk when haggard farmers and their families, some of them having come with a few tools and seeds all the way from New England, streamed into town, travel-weary and clinging to hope for a new start on land the federal government put up for auction. Their exhausted horses and cracked axles kept the smithy busy.

Jim asked, "What brings you to Missouri?"

"We had to flee our home" came one reply. "We thought we'd seen the end of the world. Rivers and lakes froze over in June, crops were killed off, the icy rain never stopped falling." The man looked from one boy to the other with a blind intensity. Jim and Baptiste responded with "Gosh!" and "Say!" They were truly remarkable calamities.

"We abandoned all of our possessions but those we needed to survive," the man went on. Baptiste glanced over at the wife and children sitting dusty and forlorn in their wagon. "In Ohio, our little youngest girl took sick and perished. We buried her there and persevered. We are finally here." He sighed and looked heaven-ward. "But no bank is lending. The land agents demand bribes. If we can't take root here, I guess we'll keep going."

"Well, we wish you well," Baptiste offered when the man climbed back onto his perch.

"That's a Christian thought" was the reply. "I do thank the man who converted you."

When the pitiable family had driven away, Jim laughed. "A convert, are you? You never let on to me."

"The Easterners seem to think it," Baptiste said wearily. "A fellow who looks like an Indian and isn't hostile is presumed tamed by Christianity. After they've been here a while, they'll be accus-tomed to people who look like me."

Jim nodded. "Those ignorant Easterners will be an awful nui-sance to the fur trade, filling up the prairie and every cranny that has any water. It's not just Indians they push aside, but fur traders too. Howsomever, they do bring business to this shop."

Baptiste was remembering Indian chiefs in full regalia waiting outside Clark's office to protest treaties that took away the land they'd hunted for so long. Now farmers like the one he'd just met would plow up that land and plant crops. One man's opportu-nity was another man's misfortune, it seemed. Did anyone ever prosper without taking from somebody else?

CHAPTER SIX

Progress

Another cycle of seasons came and went. It was easy for Baptiste to keep track of activity at the Clark home from across the way. Most of the time, he saw nothing of interest. But one early spring day, he was surprised to see the general himself at work with a pruning saw among the apple trees. Baptiste watched him silently. Clark saw him and called out, "Baptiste, why do you stand there doing nothing? Lend me a hand."

He hastened over and Clark handed him a knife. Clark didn't speak, except to tell him to hold a branch or gather the cuttings. Baptiste took his silence to mark satisfaction with his work. So it turned out to be. "Well done, Pomp," Clark said. "I don't imagine you have ever pruned trees. But you're quick to learn."

"I'm very happy to help," he said.

After another quiet interval, Clark cleared his throat and asked, "I hope you do not let yourself be drawn into fisticuffs."

"No, sir." Why would he ask? Then he thought, *I mustn't seem a coward*, and added, "Unless I'm attacked."

"There are always provocations, Pomp," Clark snapped. "I heard just yesterday of a pair of youths who stabbed each other in the midst of their combat on the docks. There was no punishment, but rather approbation from the men watching. There is a rough new element among us. A violence that arises from a want of education."

Baptiste gave a little grunt of agreement.

"I am pleased by your scholarship, Pomp," he continued. "I hope it doesn't come too easily to you. Are you sufficiently engaged by your studies? You do not find yourself too often at your ease?"

It took Baptiste a moment to grasp Clark's meaning. Then he saw an opportunity. "I could find the time for work, sir."

"Humpf," said his patron. "What sort of work?"

He said aloud what flew into his mind. "Blacksmithing."

Clark widened his eyes. "I can think of many reasons to rule that out," he said. "But foremost is your size."

"Yes, sir. But I am strong. I want to work."

"More important, you are well spoken in three languages and your manners pass muster. You can reason and figure. These are your true strengths. Use them."

Baptiste was pleased. He thought for a moment. "I could ask if they need anyone at Chouteau and Berthold's in the afternoons."

"That would fit your qualifications quite well," Clark said with a smile.

Cadet Chouteau and a partner, Berthold, had opened a store where they outfitted trapping and scientific expeditions and immigrants on their way to their claims. Finally, he was on his way to being useful, if only as a clerk. It was a beginning.

CADET CHOUTEAU SAID nothing of their past encounters when Baptiste arrived to apply for a job. He merely looked amused.

"I like your determination. We can use a boy to light the morning fires, if that doesn't seem too humble."

Cadet was teasing him, but he ignored it. "I can come before school."

"What about afternoons? Can you run errands, fold blankets, stack pots, dry goods, and groceries as needed?"

"Yes, sir, indeed I can!"

He found himself alone much of the time in the back of the store, lounging against a counter, one arm draped over a pile of goods, feeling proprietary. When immigrants from Europe came in to buy supplies, he shot to attention and, following Jim's example, asked them what had driven them to leave the familiar behind and make the arduous journey to the unknown. Their answers varied—fares to cross the ocean were cheap, American taxes were absurdly low, there was no state church to collect a tithe, nor state censor nor state police. There were no laws or customs to force class distinctions. They all were glad to have left the old world behind, to start up again from scratch.

He was manning the store by himself when a bedraggled old crone brought in a bundle of fabric to exchange for goods, pound for pound. She sucked on her pipe while he weighed her stuff, which was surprisingly heavy. Her lynx eyes so disconcerted him that he fumbled with the scale and toted up what she was due twice, to be sure. She was gone in a flash with her booty.

When Cadet returned, he asked what business had been transacted.

"A woman brought in this bundle of cotton cloth for exchange," Baptiste said.

Cadet regarded it keenly for a moment, then fell to violently ripping the bundle apart. A filler of gravel and ashes spilled from the outer wrapping, which was the only usable cotton. She had tricked him!

"Dimwit!" Cadet cried, the veins in his forehead swelling. He took a deep breath and gradually recovered his usual aplomb. "This is a lesson. Don't be so credulous next time!" he said acidly.

For the rest of the day, Baptiste waited to be fired. M. Berthold would not be as tolerant. But at closing time he was still employed.

BERTHOLD AND CHOUTEAU had plenty of customers, but a scarcity of legal tender in the city meant fewer of them could pay. In its place was "shinplaster" currency, worthless scraps issued by banks with no gold to back them up. The merchants were forced to extend credit.

"We are being grievously overdrawn by liberty-loving, equality-demanding, wrangling, covetous Americans," remarked Berthold as he made elegant entries in the accounts book. "We ought to have a national bank to regulate money," he grumbled.

"There's a bank down the street," Baptiste said.

"*National* bank," Berthold repeated testily. "The First National Bank charter expired in 1811 and Congress has not seen fit to renew. The bank down the street is as reliable as that woman who gulled you the other day." It was his first mention of the incident. Baptiste said no more.

He was fascinated by Berthold's polish and grace. The merchant had fought in the Napoleonic wars before immigrating to America. He spoke five languages with ease. Curious to see the brick house Berthold had built, Baptiste hiked out from the city's center to Fifth and Pine. It was surrounded by vast gardens laid in geometric patterns, fountains that shot water high into the air, and flower beds that bloomed different colors each season. It must be a European garden. He'd never seen another like it. Cadet laughingly called it Little Versailles. Baptiste had asked what that meant and received a lecture on the late French king and the Revolution that deposed him. *"Liberté, égalité, et fraternité,"* Cadet exclaimed ironically.

"And the guillotine, a machine so efficient it produced complete terror! A pure example of equality," added his partner.

Both men carried themselves with grace. And yet neither showed a trace of the effete. They were sufficiently at ease with their manhood to allow it some poetry. Baptiste liked their elegant masculine style better than the gross, swaggering Anglo version. Of course General Clark was still his manly ideal. But Clark always seemed burdened, if unbowed. The Frenchmen let themselves laugh at life, even when bills went unpaid. Everyone liked them. They seemed to have no enemies.

In August, though, the two merchants had more reason to worry about their debts. Cadet's brother A.P. had led a daring expedition to Santa Fe to persuade the Spanish to open up trade in the Southwest to Americans. Cadet borrowed heavily to supply the party. But the Spanish authorities threw A.P. and his party into jail and confiscated their goods. Future trade with Mexico was inevitable, but for now, Cadet's investment, thirty thousand dollars, was lost.

"Our misfortune brings happier news for you, Baptiste," Cadet said. "Your father, it seems, was an interpreter with my brother. He is not dead, but lies in a Mexican dungeon."

Baptiste was preoccupied for weeks by the image of his father confined to a cold stone cell. Would Toussaint, if he got out of jail, come looking for him? The old fellow might try to drag him back down to his own crude level. But his own years of schooling made him feel strong enough to resist if he had to.

ONE DAY, BAPTISTE watched from the store's doorway as St. Louisans streamed gaily down North Main Street to the waterfront. He spotted the Irish editor of the *Gazette*. That man had done as much as anyone to drum up the day's excitement over a newfangled invention, the steamboat. The first one to make it all the way up the river to St. Louis was coming!

Cadet slipped past Baptiste and headed down the street. Then he called over his shoulder, "You may come if you like." Baptiste closed the door and hurried after him.

He and Cadet fell in beside a gaggle of French girls in colorful frocks. Cadet teased them. Did their mothers know they were out on the street without chaperones? Did they expect to take a ride on the big boat? One of them let Baptiste see a coy little smile. He wasn't sure she'd meant it for him and quickly looked behind him. This made her laugh and poke her neighbor. He grinned and shrugged. He met lots of people, working at the store, and nearly all of them liked him. Even a girl from the elite of the town dared to flirt with him.

It seemed that every kind of citizen was en route to the docks. Hearty, sunburnt voyageurs, mixed-blood trappers and interpreters, pale New England tradesmen, an Italian dancing master who sported a glossy wig and patent leather slippers, swaggering roustabouts, the portrait painter whose studio was above the store, peddlers, tinkers, elegant lawyers and doctors from the serene streets of the second town that had sprung up above the old French one, Indians in permanent residence, dressed in jackets and trousers, all paused to greet the popular Cadet Chouteau. The whole of St. Louis was out, everyone but the slaves, who weren't allowed off their masters' property without passes. Apparently, none were given out today.

He saw a group of visiting Osage in the distance. They were decked out in full paint, feathers, and bright blankets. Baptiste wondered what was in their minds. Not so long ago, all of this vast territory was theirs. He thought, as he so often did, of his mother and her appreciation of the white man's inventions. This boat that was coming was a great invention indeed. Berthold had told him steam could do the work of dozens of horses and do it much faster. "This will bring more change to St. Louis than you can imagine."

Someone gave his shoulder a hard poke. Annoyed, he whirled, prepared to object. But it was Jim! They landed a few affectionate punches and then Jim began rattling off facts about the steamboat.

"They've had to steer zick-zacks hundreds of times on that curvy old river between here and New Orleans," he said. "Sometimes whole chunks of the bank fall in with no warning. Those are hazard enough. Then there are fallen trees dragged by the currents until they're bunched and anchored in the mud. Pilots can't see them 'til they pierce a boat's bottom. Right around St, Louis, the sandbars shift and fool even the best pilot . . ."

They were at the bottom of the hill now, jostled by the crowd. All eyes were trained on the water. Jim finished his thought. ". . . fires, explosions."

A man came running along the shore, waving his hat and yelling, "It's here! It's here!"

And in a moment, there it was, right at the foot of Market Street! Cannon fired a salute and the *Zebulon M. Pike* glided into its berth as if pulled by magic, clanking, booming, and spewing hot coals. Its furnace glowed with fire and its chimney belched clouds of thick black smoke that hung over the crowd.

Dignitaries and rambunctious passengers leaned on the railings, waving their hats and calling out to the crowd. Baptiste and Jim cheered themselves hoarse.

Jim wanted to talk to one of the crew, so he and Baptiste slipped aboard amidst the general confusion. He asked a stevedore how much wood the furnace burned.

"We stop every few miles to chop trees. It took up nearly half the journey." He waved an arm. "There'll be dozens of big steamboats—much bigger than this one—on all the rivers in the next few years. It will be every man for himself, cutting down trees to feed our engines!"

The stevedore had a word for that: "Progress," he said. "It can't be stopped."

Baptiste looked at Jim. His face was bright with excitement. "Maybe I'll train to be a pilot," Jim said. It was already a storied calling. Progress in 1817 meant opportunities for a go-ahead boy like himself. When a new opportunity came up, Jim would leap right in. Baptiste felt the drag of doubt. This steamboat brought drastic change that favored a few and ruined others. Was it worth it to shear the forests to the ground so that men could get places faster?

CHAPTER SEVEN

A Democratic Election

A day later, Mr. Peck was heading out on one of his missions. Baptiste helped to carry his blanket and gear to his horse.

"Were you present, yesterday, when the *Zebulon Pike* landed?" Peck asked.

"Yes."

"Did you note the distress it caused a group of aborigines?"

Baptiste nodded.

"They are not fools," Peck said. "Such an innovation puts their way of life in ever greater peril. It makes our mission more urgent. You and I have spoken of this. They must be brought into our flock. Christian faith can comfort them."

"My mother saw the future when the captains displayed their firearms and tools at the Mandan Villages."

Peck nodded. "So she did. God has seen fit to place you amidst momentous change. He means for you to do good works one day."

Baptiste felt his cheeks redden. "I think so too, sir."

"If it is not too late," Peck added under his breath, and spurred his horse. Off he rode, to try to "save" more Indians.

Looking after him, Baptiste suddenly wondered if Peck expected him to join him. He had no desire to live among Indians and pretend he knew what was good for them because he'd been to school. Peck was making it his business to enlighten him. But surely he wasn't destined to be a missionary.

THE DAY AFTER Peck left, Baptiste was leaning on the school-yard fence so as to keep a casual eye on Clark's house, when the general emerged, stepping briskly and wearing a formal black suit, high collar, and white stock.

"Good day, Pomp."

"Good day, sir." Baptiste straightened. This was a rare thing, seeing Clark set off on foot and all alone. Could he go along?

Clark paused and turned back, with a considering look on his face.

Baptiste seized the chance. "Sir, may I keep you company?"

"You may. You will see the republic's machinery in action. Today we are voting to elect a representative to the Congress. Missouri Territory will be joining the union of states one day soon."

Baptiste sprinted to Clark's side and thrust out his chest. Anyone who saw them would have proof of his importance. But he soon had to scramble to keep up with Clark's long strides.

"Do you understand what voting is, and the Congress?" Clark asked.

"I think so, sir."

"Two candidates stand for the office. I favor Mr. Scott, who represents my interests and those of the established society here. Land seekers from the East support Scott's opponent. The citizens will decide in a secret vote which one goes to Washington City to represent us. That is democracy."

"I have heard men arguing the two sides," Baptiste said eagerly. He didn't mention the harsh criticism of Clark that was more and more common.

At the next corner, an inebriated Anglo tradesman ran unsteadily up to Clark and rasped out opposition slogans: "Remove the Indians! Put the land plots up for auction!" Clark gave no sign that he heard anything he didn't like. Other men loitering along the street let the general pass without comment, but they didn't salute him the way they had the year before. Baptiste reflected that there were people who didn't even know what William Clark and Meriwether Lewis had done. It disgusted him. Nothing true or valuable seemed fixed in this town, not even a man's hard-won reputation.

Rounding another corner, they came upon a ragged man who sat on an overturned bucket, mumbling to himself. "Scattered in his wits," Clark said quietly, and dropped a coin into the fellow's upturned cap. "Such unfortunates are more numerous in the rising economy. I hope we will find solutions to the problem."

Peck had also spoken of the numbers of beggars and the need for charity while the lucky few prospered. So this was a problem for government too.

The polling place was festooned with placards bearing the name John Scott, Clark's candidate. Armed militia, also wearing Scott tickets, swaggered around the area. Baptiste stuck close to the general. Clark's nephew John O'Fallon broke away from the crowd. "Morning, Uncle," he said, ignoring Baptiste, as usual. "We're going to beat them today."

Clark frowned when he saw men handing glasses of whiskey to voters, along with an exhortation to vote for Scott. He quickly entered the polling place. O'Fallon drew a handkerchief from his sleeve and wiped his brow. "Why did he bring you here?" he drawled.

"He said I should see the republic's machinery working. So that I will know what to do, when my own time comes, I'd guess."

"Hardly" was O'Fallon's response to that. Scanning the crowd, he added offhandedly, "You won't have the franchise, little Baptiste. The franchise is reserved for white men of property. You are not a citizen. Didn't he tell you that?"

Baptiste tried to cover his embarrassment, but this was unexpected news. He wouldn't be allowed to vote? Wasn't he in school to become an American? He mingled there with Clark's sons and the Chouteaus.

"How can that be?" he asked. "Men of every calling fought off the British to make this country, not just men of property!" He had learned that in school.

"White men of high moral standing may vote," said O'Fallon. "And this voting will decide who gets the major share of Missouri's virgin land."

Clark emerged from the polling place and announced in his most commanding voice, "I have cast my vote for John Scott."

Other important men of property quickly gathered around him. Baptiste recognized most of them. Pete Didier noticed him and said, "Is this little Baptiste?"

Clark said yes and Baptiste endured an inspection of his "littleness." Clark beamed. "He's learning how the territory is governed," he said. The men all nodded to Baptiste and they walked off in the direction of the city hall with Clark.

Baptiste stood pondering the meaning of this introduction to republican operations. Clark had invited him to see how power was apportioned—to see how whiskey influenced white men's votes, just as it persuaded Indians to sign treaties and trade furs. Clark had tried to influence them too, by telling how he had voted. He hated feeling cynical toward Clark; the man embodied virtue. But he couldn't help it!

Suddenly, John O'Fallon was upbraiding a man. "Halt, sir! You have published scurrilous pieces about my uncle!" The other man tried to ignore him, avoiding a fight. O'Fallon gave him a hard shove. "Did you take that for an insult?" he jeered.

"Not at all," said the man stiffly. He attempted to sidestep his assailant and continue on his way.

"Well, I intended it as an insult," retorted O'Fallon, blocking him. "You are a liar and a coward!"

Everyone heard him say it. The man thrust his hand into his pocket, pulled out a pistol and cocked it. The crowd gasped. He pointed the weapon at O'Fallon's face. Baptiste cringed. Would he? Yes! He pulled the trigger. There was a flash. O'Fallon's face contorted, but his body didn't flinch. The gun had misfired.

With an exclamation of rage, O'Fallon wrested the gun from the other's hand, threw it away, and began beating him with his cane. The man fled, O'Fallon crying oaths and flailing away at him.

The crowd was in an uproar. Moments later, like an actor making an entrance, Thomas Benton approached the polling place. All eyes turned to him. His beefy frame was clad in pantaloons and a double-breasted frock coat, and his black curls tossed as he cast an imperious eye over the scene. Baptiste had seen him going in and out of General Clark's office many times. Benton was famous for shooting Andy Jackson during a brawl back in Tennessee. Everyone knew it. Now Charles Lucas, the popular young son of a judge, stepped up to bar Benton's way. Baptiste held his breath. There was going to be *another* fight!

"Mr. Benton. You are not qualified to vote here today. You have not paid your tax."

Benton grinned and winked at a bystander. "You are mistaken, sir."

"Then prove it," retorted Lucas.

"I will not answer to a puppy!" sneered Benton.

"Then I challenge you to defend your honor," cried Lucas, to robust cheers from the men on his side of the square. Benton's chin shot up and he looked insolently down his nose. "All right, sir," he said mildly.

The "republic's machinery" seemed to grind out one act of aggression after another. It was almost comical, except that lives were threatened. Baptiste decided he was well out of it. What did an election mean anyway? As far as he could tell, Clark made the big decisions all by himself—the Indian treaties, the rules of the fur trade. Who profited and who did not. Money. What else mattered? Voting was an empty exercise.

As he walked away from the polling place, he heard men say the duel would not take place; that sort of thing had been outlawed ever since Burr killed Hamilton. Others believed it would happen. Baptiste went home to his books, disapproving of the ways of men.

A WEEK LATER, he was shaken from a sound sleep by Jim, who was leaning over him, whispering hoarsely. "Wake up! B'tiste!"

"Jim! What for? It's pitch-dark."

"You got to get up. They duel today at dawn!"

"Who does?"

"Benton! And Lucas!" Jim hissed. "Come on!"

"Why do I have to?"

"It's a duel! Who doesn't want to see that?"

"Jim, don't they just fire to miss?"

"It's a spectacle. Men defending their honor."

"White men."

Jim looked at him sideways and began hauling him out of bed. Baptiste sighed and pulled on his pants and jacket. He stumbled into the street after Jim. A neighbor's yellow dog opened one eye and emitted a low, deep growl.

Heavy mists shrouded Bloody Island, where duels took place, but Jim was an unerring navigator. Poling his little boat across could not be accomplished in complete silence, but no one challenged them. They tied up and hastened through the spectral trees. The fog began to lift off the muddy Mississippi.

They hunkered down some distance from the dueling ground, well hidden by brush. Six men in long coats talked in low voices. There was Lucas, there was Benton. Jim pointed out Dr. Farrar, whose voice carried over the others'. Jim whispered that he was the survivor of many prior duels, but his role today was apparently to minister to wounds. Two seconds backed up each of the two principals.

When it was fully light, Benton and Lucas strode to their positions, their seconds behind them. "They have smoothbore pistols," Jim whispered. "They aren't very accurate." The men moved into position. Jim gripped Baptiste's arm. "They're no more than ten feet apart! It will be murder by two!"

Baptiste was afraid it was true. One of the onlookers began to count: "One, two, three..." Jim and Baptiste strained to hear the word *fire!* but it didn't come. Benton looked questioningly at the counter. Then he and Lucas pulled their triggers, so close together there was a single report. But two puffs of smoke.

Lucas collapsed in a heap. Baptiste heard himself moan. Benton hovered in place for a moment. Then he strode the ten feet to his dying victim. Lucas had missed Benton completely. The two exchanged a few words, Benton bent at the waist so that he could hear the fallen man speak. Lucas lifted his hand weakly and Benton shook it. The sun was well above the horizon now and the boys could clearly see blood pouring from Lucas's chest.

"He's a dead man, sure," Jim said in an awed tone. "Everyone said Lucas was a poor shot. Benton wants to go to Congress. Now he's killed his best rival."

Baptiste's stomach heaved and he swallowed hard. "How can Benton be elected! Won't he be arrested for murder?"

Jim was inching away. "Let's make tracks," he whispered. But Baptiste couldn't take his eyes off Lucas. Why didn't Dr. Farrar save him? A man was dying, for no good reason. Jim tugged at his sleeve. Baptiste dragged himself after him. The senselessness of the occasion sickened him. To kill a man, with such absurd formality, over nothing. And this was "civilization."

In the boat, Jim said, "Lucas is well liked. This is the end of Benton in politics."

✳   ✳   ✳

BAPTISTE REGULARLY CHECKED the front page of the *Gazette*. Scott won the election. Benton was not arrested. Instead, he was expected to be elected senator from Missouri when it became a state.

ONE DAY, WHEN the prairie was brushed with frost and citizens were girding themselves for the harsh winter, a traveling panorama show set up shop on the Place d'Armes. Reverend Peck urged Baptiste to go and see the scenes depicted from history. Napoleon's defeat at the Battle of Waterloo unfurled on a long scroll. With the music playing and lights shining on the scene as it slowly progressed, Baptiste could almost imagine being there. Other scenes of ruins showed what had finally become of the mighty Roman Empire he had read about.

"Even now, when you stand among those ghostly walls, you can feel what awesome power the caesars commanded," said a man standing next to Baptiste. It was Lagonia, the dancing master, unmistakable in tight-fitting, brightly striped trousers, a scarlet neckerchief, and the dark curls of his wig peeking from under his slouch hat. He was hugging himself against the chill.

"Do you come from Rome?" Baptiste asked.

"No, I was born in Siracusa. But I took myself early to Rome. I met quite a few Americans there—a sculptor, some poets. Rome is mecca, you know, for artists. And of course for the young sons of English lords. A visit there confers on them the illusion they've been cultivated. Such is the magic of European travel." He winked. Clutching Baptiste's sleeve, he said, "Young man, I have a proposition for you. You are a handsome fellow and you move gracefully. . . . Oh, yes, I have observed you, and your manners impress me."

Baptiste made an ironical bow, to show he didn't take himself too seriously. But he was pleased.

"A surfeit of girls has enrolled in my dancing class. That is all well. But there are no partners for them! Would you help me out two afternoons a week?"

Baptiste grinned. Lately, he'd been enjoying glimpses of girls, watching them parade around the marketplace in the evening before their mothers shooed them into their houses. Dancing would allow him to hold their hands, smell their hair. . . . "I'd be delighted to, signor," he said.

Two days later, he presented himself, scrubbed and in fresh clothes, at Lagonia's studio in the ballroom of Mrs. Catrell's house on Pine.

"Ah, Baptiste," the master cried as if greeting a long-lost colleague. Baptiste was nervous, but he held his back straight and his chin high.

"This is Mrs. Shepherd, our accompanist." Baptiste bowed to a long-nosed, bespectacled woman who sat at a pianoforte—there was another, then, in St. Louis, besides Mrs. Clark's. Mrs. Shepherd acknowledged him with a raised eyebrow and a sniff.

The class began arriving. Seven girls were propelled forward by their mothers. They threw off their woolen wraps and capes, revealing brightly colored gowns and hair ribbons. One radiant maiden towered over Baptiste; the others were about his height and age. The single boy, a ten-year-old wearing an extravagant cravat, looked miserable. The huddle of French girls shot covert glances at Baptiste. His eyes kept falling on a pair of blond, freckled girls who must be sisters. Their mother caught him looking, and frowned. He bowed to her, which clearly surprised her and she responded with a dimpled smile.

Lagonia told them he would call out the steps of each dance. They would begin very slowly and master them gradually.

"Baptiste, will you and Mlle Gautier show us the quadrille," Lagonia said. "Stand a proper distance from each other as you join hands. This is requisite to the bending of the elbows as we want no ugly angles but rather a serpentine line. . . ."

The girl was about twelve. Chestnut curls tumbled over her forehead. He bowed and she curtsied, avoiding his eyes. His head barely reached hers, but surprisingly, when he took one of her little pale hands, he felt taller. Catching the mother's eye again, he assumed a role, the gallant protector, and for a moment admired the picture he and the girl must present. But instantly, he thought he'd rather die than have Jim or any of the other boys see him.

Mrs. Shepherd started to count out loud at a high volume and stamp her foot in a futile effort to keep everyone on the beat. Baptiste found that he had little trouble following the instructions, but the other children stumbled and bumped into one another and took wayward paths. Nevertheless, they learned, in addition to the quadrille, the cotillion and something called *danse écossaise* by the time dusk had fallen and the room was dark.

Lagonia called for an entr'acte so that he and Baptiste could light candles. The flames flickered wildly and the dancers cast goblin shadows around the walls. They ended class with the reel, in which two lines were formed and couples took turns scampering up and down between them, panting and giggling with relief that the lesson was over.

Mrs. Shepherd sat back, laid her agile hands in her lap, and the breathless, red-cheeked, perspiring dancers gasped and rolled their eyes at one another. "BOW! CURTSY!" cried Signor Lagonia.

"We ought to have many more dancers in the line," the master lamented, wringing his hands. "Children, tell your friends and relatives to join us."

The mothers wrapped the children in their cloaks and whisked them out the door. When they were gone, Mrs. Shepherd gathered up her music and gave Baptiste a squinty smile. "You could be dancing at any of the grand balls," she said, her tone implying he was wasting his gifts.

Lagonia gushed, "Baptiste, you met my expectations beautifully. I predict that you will make excellent use of this skill one day." He handed over a little bag of coins. Baptiste counted them when he got to the street. Enough to buy himself pastries at the confectioner's. But he decided to save them.

Lagonia stayed in St. Louis for six more weeks. In that time, he taught his pupils—and Baptiste—how to introduce themselves at parties, how to sit, how to escort and be escorted from a gathering. No girl would ever ask a man to dance, Lagonia said. Girls were helpless until approached. It was the male who initiated any activity, controlled it, and ended it, as he pleased. Baptiste learned that he needn't be tentative around girls. The conventions of society gave him power over them. But, for the moment, he had no way to apply the knowledge. Later, he encountered one of the girls on the street with her mother, and they ignored him.

CHAPTER EIGHT

✦━━━━◆━━━━✦

A Vocation

A few weeks after Lagonia left town, Gilbert came to fetch Baptiste. The general had just returned from five months in Washington City and wished to see him.

Clark was listening to an agitated French-Canadian agent's reports on conditions in the field when Baptiste let himself into the office. He quietly took a chair at a respectful distance and stared at the much augmented display of Indian clothing, weapons, and art, as well as fossils, animal skins, and stuffed birds that filled Clark's Indian Museum. The general had been given a profusion of trophies by various chiefs since Baptiste last visited. He noticed a framed letter of credit authorizing Lewis and Clark to draw on the Exchequer of the United States in any part of the world. It was another souvenir of Baptiste's own first year of life.

Suddenly, Clark's visitor cried, "The Americans' minds are warped! They kill the buffalo for tallow alone and leave the carcass to rot when it would have sustained the Indians for months!" He blew out his cheeks and raked his hand over his whiskers.

"I wish I could prevent the practice," Clark said. "I have forbidden settlement on Indian lands, but five hundred families arrive here from the East every single day. I must serve them too."

"The Grand Osage have moved six hundred miles to find game," the agent retorted, "and they are still hungry."

"I am mindful of it," Clark said wearily.

His disgruntled visitor soon left. Clark beckoned to Baptiste. His hair had been bright red when Baptiste first saw him. Now it was white. He looked careworn, but his cheeks were rosy and his eyes unclouded.

"You know, Pomp, years ago, when you were an infant, Mr. Jefferson and I thought to cultivate the Indians' love. I believe that we might have succeeded. But now, the pressure from land-hungry settlers and entrepreneurs thwarts and complicates our efforts. The land I persuade the Osage to cede is soon occupied by Cherokee who were run out of Georgia. The Sauk and Fox too were forced to move and become unwanted neighbors of the Sioux. Our policies make them compete for sustenance on a fraction of what was once their vast hunting grounds."

"I think they are without hope, sir," Baptiste said.

Clark expelled a heavy sigh. "Indians endure a wretched existence when forced to live next to whites."

"They mastered our instruments of war with lightning speed."

"That is true, Pomp. They made the horse and the gun their own in less than a generation. But warfare will end in their elimination. Commerce is the better answer. I have argued in Washington for a government-protected fur monopoly for our mutual benefit. The tribes would cooperate with us for profit, and immense quantities of the most valuable furs would come into our markets."

"And the British traders would be defeated," Baptiste said.

"That's right! What is most needed is trust between ourselves and the tribes. More than ever, we need interpreters on whom we can rely. All too many of them sow misunderstandings from which they hope to profit. Or they whisper specific demands to the Indians that are contrary to our interests."

Baptiste snapped to attention. "I am ready, sir. I think I understand the interests of both sides. As you know, I am as fluent in French as in English. I can converse in various Sioux tongues. I am well qualified!"

Clark merely looked amused. "That is not what I had in mind, Pomp," he said. "Perhaps when you finish your education."

Baptiste slumped. His request was perfectly reasonable. Clark famously placed his O'Fallon and Kennerly nephews, his brothers-in-law, and other dependents in jobs at the Indian agency. Why couldn't he do the same for him?

Clark continued. "You are at the head of your class in school. That shows me where your gifts lie. You must continue to develop them as long as you can." He cocked an eyebrow. "Here is an idea. Father Niel and Bishop DuBourg are opening a college, an academy for republican gentlemen, I suppose. The priests will not impose catechism or indeed any religion on their scholars. They will offer courses in Latin, Greek, Euclid, moral philosophy, ethics, and aesthetics. What do you think?"

"Respectfully, sir, I want to leave off my schooling at the end of this term."

Clark laughed. "You're still a pup! Education is the foundation of the republic, as Mr. Jefferson says. He is emphatic on the need to provide education to youths like you, for the good of the democracy. I envy you. I had a great taste for learning, but the army claimed me before it could be fully satisfied. The bishop envisions an academy comparable to colleges in the East, or in Europe." His face softened. "Do you know what gift I made to Mrs. Clark when young Lewis was born?"

"No, sir."

"The plays of William Shakespeare. All of them in one volume. We used to read from it nightly." He sighed. Baptiste wondered why they had stopped. Clark added, "Perhaps when the players come to town, the bishop will allow you young scholars to attend."

"Yes, sir." When *Hamlet* was playing, Cadet had smuggled him in under his long cloak, but Baptiste didn't say so now. Clark never asked what he did when he wasn't in school, as long as he stayed out of fights.

"By the way, your father has returned to the Mandan Villages. I put him on our payroll there."

Baptiste was startled. He knew that some of the party arrested by the Spanish near Santa Fe had returned to St. Louis, but no one had told him what became of Toussaint Charbonneau. So the old man was back on his former stomping grounds. Baptiste wondered if Clark had been disappointed when Toussaint declined to become a farmer in St. Louis. He must have expected Toussaint to be grateful for the land.

Clark continued. "Are we agreed that you will attend the Academy? Serving as an interpreter at some remote post would not engage your mind sufficiently. Believe me."

There was only one answer. Baptiste sighed. The new school would offer college courses. How many of his peers could rise to them? He was proud of his intellect. "Yes, sir," he said. "And I promise you that I will do my best." *Learn*, his mother had said.

She never envisioned college. A delightful image of her flashed in his mind. She was clapping her hands, all alight with pride in him.

A FEW DAYS before the term began, Baptiste packed his Roman history, ciphering book, Webster's *Compendious Dictionary*, Scott's *Lessons in Elocution*, and copybook into a leathern satchel, along with his extra pair of corduroys, smallclothes, comb, and the brush for cleaning one's teeth that Mr. Peck had recently introduced into the boys' morning routine. Wearing his good jacket and shoes, he set off on foot for his new home, a room Clark had rented for him in the home of a M. Honoré.

The pallid old gentleman who opened his door to Baptiste wore knee breeches, a vest patterned in flowers, and buckled slippers that might have been fashionable a generation before. Honoré was a longtime resident of St. Louis, he confided, and had occupied his house in the suburb for some twenty years.

"I hope that a college will enliven my remaining days." He fixed rheumy eyes on Baptiste. "Some youths make stimulating company . . . but others are merely wearying," he said coyly. "I expect you are an interesting one, though. General Clark would not recommend you to me had you not distinguished yourself. Follow me. This is my little parlor."

Baptiste acknowledged the compliment with a slight nod. His heart sank at the thought of having to spend evenings with the old fellow, struggling to make conversation. He surveyed a shelf where books were piled upon books. None of the titles was familiar. Beside the shelf stood a wing chair and a drop-leaf table with a candlestick. The walls were crowded with framed engravings of landscapes and one feminine silhouette. The shabbiness of the

simple room touched him. This elderly Frenchman had opened his
sanctuary to him—for a price, of course.

Leading Baptiste up two steep stairs to an attic, Honoré
remarked, "There have been so many changes over the years.
Americans are a covetous and quarrelsome people, is it not so?" He
glanced over his shoulder. "General Clark is an old-fashioned gentleman of great character—if only the new lot were cast in his
mold. We old men really don't know what will become of us."

They squeezed into a small chamber with a single dormer
window, a narrow bed, candlestick table, and rude chair. "This is
yours. General Clark has paid in advance for your laundry and
your firewood. And of course the tallow candle to study by."
Honoré rubbed his hands together and backed out of the doorway.
"I shall leave you to make yourself comfortable. There will be hot
chicory downstairs when you are ready."

Baptiste bent to peer out the little window. He could see the
main school building and, in the foreground, a stable Clark had
ordered built for the horses his son and his friends rode from town.
The place was truly on the edge of nowhere—beyond it was nothing but canopied forest as far as the eye could see.

He lay back on the bed and cradled his head in his hands.
"Ha!" he exclaimed aloud. This was *his* room, to be used by no one
else. Here, on the cusp of sixteen, he would have privacy for the
first time in his life. Thanks to his schooling, he knew enough
to value it. Few men enjoyed the luxury of truly being left alone.
The very idea was empowering. He felt ready to generate a future
for himself from within. Could he set boldly forth and take what
he wanted from life? What circumstance could impede him? His
mother's spirit was always there, urging him to make the most of

himself. He lay musing for an hour or so, watching the late day sun trace a golden path across the wall.

SCHOOL BEGAN WITH a convocation. Most of the boys were strangers to Baptiste. He took a seat next to a skinny youth with cup-handle ears and an amiable grin.

"Baptiste," Baptiste whispered, holding out his hand. The other boy gripped it.

"I know who you are," he murmured. "I'm Pelagie." Baptiste wondered how Pelagie knew him. When the ceremony was over, the other boy explained. "My father read the student roster. He told me General Clark's ward would be here. I reckoned it was you."

Pelagie's expression was friendly enough. Being Clark's ward seemed to ensure a welcome from these boys. Now he would have to work on presenting a self all his own.

The brand-new St. Louis Academy, with its faculty of robed priests and library of eight thousand volumes donated by Bishop DuBourg, imposed a long and hallowed monastic tradition on its students. Serious study was expected in Latin, Greek, and Hebrew as well as literature, French, German and Spanish, science and history. The method called for oral repetition of passages from the texts. The boys wrote weekly compositions and engaged in debates and contests. Learning through competition was much more fun than his former plain Protestant schooling had been. The lessons weren't dry either but often invited the boys to draw on their own experience.

Father Francis taught a class on Plato's *Ethics*. The monk was a brawny man with outsize hands, who urged the students to differ with one another and even with him. "You will learn to think for yourselves, in these rooms," he said. "It is independence of mind that will win the race in these tumultuous times." Baptiste was excited to know he wasn't constrained by a single correctness. After they'd all read the *Ethics*, Father Francis called on Georges Taillez to summarize Plato's position.

"Plato teaches that the soul must be kept separate from the pleasures of the body. Individual wishes and desires are suppressed for the good of the community," said Georges.

This brought groans from the boys. Father Francis, who had been prowling the room, made a mock show of disapproval. "My, my," he said. "Even at your age, individual desires must be suppressed if they interfere with others. The good of the community is absolute." He lifted his meaty hands in a gesture of surrender. "Is it not?"

Baptiste had already decided that good and bad were not black-and-white matters. A lie could be virtuous, for example, if it saved a life. And some wrongs, such as stealing a persimmon, as he had done, were simply petty offenses, a wrong committed against the seller but of no consequence to the community. Among the Mandan, community mattered most. But with Americans, freedom for individuals came first.

He raised his hand. At a nod from Father Francis, he stood. "Father, we have learned that Aristotle disagreed with Plato. He declared moral values to have no fixity, but are framed according to circumstance. I agree with Aristotle."

Taillez waved his arm. "Father, what about men who are spiritually weak, or lazy? How will they be governed if not by fixed rules?"

Father Francis looked to Baptiste. "What do you say to that?"

Baptiste thought about General Clark, whose goodness was compromised because he kept slaves and manipulated Indians into giving up their land. In the latter instance, he served the needs of a community that had chosen him to carry out the policy.

"I think that we are all a mixture of good and bad. We may try to work for the good of the community. But sometimes what the community desires is wrong," he said.

Father Francis clapped him on the back. "Well argued, Baptiste!" he said. "I side with Plato myself. But your position has merit. The United States rests on majority rule; it legislates according to the wishes of the community. But the Constitution protects minorities and individuals too."

Baptiste made a bow to the class. Some of them stomped their feet and others struck their desks with their books. "You have the mind of a lawyer," said the monk drily. "It is becoming a popular calling in America."

Baptiste found himself at the center of a group of smart, clamorous friends. Taillez, Wilkerson, and Pelagie all loved to read books and then argue over them. Ideas were enough to bind them. He knew nothing of their families or their prospects, only that they were all full of high spirits, though not frivolous. One afternoon the four friends were warming their feet at the hearth in the library, when Wilkerson admitted that he wrote poetry.

"Speak some to us," Baptiste said, and with a little prodding, the poet recited some verses while his friends stared dreamily into the flames. One poem seemed to refer to the death of a beloved. When Wilkerson had finished it, no one said anything for a few minutes.

Baptiste was moved by the poem. He realized that Wilkerson probably hoped to be praised. "Well done. The poem has much feeling," he said. "Your images sing with sadness. Is it about a particular someone, or just about death?"

Wilkerson blushed rather violently and Baptiste hastily apologized for his question.

"It's all right," Wilkerson said, wrapping his arms around his knees. "I haven't spoken of her to anyone. It's about my cousin. She died a year ago." His eyes watered but remained fixed steadily on Baptiste.

"And you loved her."

"Yes."

"And did she love you?"

"I don't know."

Pelagie spoke up. "Lay off him, Baptiste. You're the fellow with secrets. Have you a love you've never declared?"

Baptiste laughed. "No. Love hasn't struck me.... I wonder if it ever will."

Taillez said, "You are an odd duck!"

His voice had an unpleasant edge. Baptiste was alarmed. "What do you mean? Why am I odd?"

"Well...," said Taillez, "you have no family that we know about.... You're the best student here. Jeff Clark says his father has paid your tuition since you were six."

Baptiste felt his face redden. "He asked to raise me when I was just a baby. Jeff wasn't born yet! General Clark had no sons. He didn't even have a wife."

Taillez said, "Easy, Baptiste. You're a lucky fellow. We're glad for you."

"I am lucky. But it hasn't always been 'easy.'"

"Don't get your hackles up. We don't begrudge your good fortune."

"Taillez envies you, don't you, Taillez? He wishes he could earn your high marks," said Pelagie. "We all try as hard as we can and still, you beat us." He gave Baptiste's back a comradely slap. "No hard feelings."

Baptiste spent an uncomfortable night recalling the exchange. That Clark had chosen him as an infant had always made him proud. Now it was painted as an unfair advantage. What man would want to admit that his achievements were due not to his perseverance and abilities but to someone else's favor?

These French boys were the sons of the elite. They had advantages! How quickly they'd turned on him! The worst part was their assumption that Clark made everything possible. Exactly *what* did Clark enable, besides school? They were all put in school by their parents, after all.

He thought of his uncomplicated friendship with Jim, who already did a man's work, even though they were nearly the same age. Jim's life was a history of hardship and left him no leisure for petty grudges and complaints. He never compared himself invidiously to Baptiste. There was no envy in his heart. He didn't aspire to rise above others.

AFTER STEWING FOR a day, Baptiste decided that he gained nothing from nursing grievances. He worked hard at his studies, and his friends stopped complaining about his high marks. It was a relief. He loved learning, but not as a contest. The best part of school now was sharing his studies among equals. Of course, he wasn't a social equal to the sons of Clark and Thomas Hart Benton. He was equal in merit.

When he'd been a student at the Academy for a year, he was summoned by Bishop DuBourg himself. The bishop sat at a long table covered with papers and parchments. Light was filtered by green window curtains, giving the room an otherworldly cast. DuBourg removed his spectacles and gestured to Baptiste to take a chair. "Mr. Charbonneau, your masters tell me that you are first in most of your classes," he said in accented English.

"Yes, Excellency."

"And the work brings you satisfaction?"

"Yes, Excellency."

DuBourg gazed steadily at him. Finally, he said, "Would you say that you possess the temperament of a scholar?"

Surprised, Baptiste said, "I guess I do."

"Scholarship is the calling of our order, as you know. When our Father chooses to bestow such a gift on one of His children, we take notice."

"Thank you, Excellency," Baptiste said carefully. "I enjoy learning very much. But my studies will soon be finished. I will be going out into the world. . . ."

"Your teachers are all scholars," the bishop interjected. "Do you not find them worldly?" DuBourg didn't wait for an answer. "You must know that we Jesuits are very much of and in the world, here and everywhere that the Church sends us, which is to every continent. It is how we serve God."

"Yes, sir." Another yawning pause. But Baptiste had nothing to say. Finally, DuBourg revealed the purpose of the interview.

"I want to invite you to stay here and become one of us after your course is completed. If you agree, I will ask General Clark for his blessing."

Baptiste was stunned. Wear black robes and keep his nose in a book? Be forever celibate? It was out of the question!

DuBourg smiled. "I have surprised you. You should give serious thought to your future possibilities, Baptiste. Our order is dedicated to serving the aborigines. We make dictionaries of the native languages, for instance. There is much work that would suit you."

"I had planned to serve my country, Excellency. . . . General Clark will—"

"Jesuits already do serve it. Were you to join us, the color of your skin would never limit you," the bishop said with a narrow smile. Baptiste shifted in his chair.

"I see," he said. But he wasn't ready to surrender his freedom for a reason that was only skin-deep. He was intelligent and educated, far beyond the level of most white men. He knew how to overcome obstacles.

"You would be safe with us and secure for the rest of your life," DuBourg added.

"I don't seek safety or security, Excellency."

The bishop smiled. "You haven't seen much of the world," he said gently. "You can't properly assess its hazards."

There was no use arguing with an old Jesuit! Baptiste couldn't wait to escape the room! "I thank you for your advice, Excellency."

"Very well. This isn't my final word on the subject," DuBourg said, dismissing him with a wave of his hand. "I leave soon for Paris. Come to me in a few months and tell me how you are feeling then."

Baptiste bowed, clapped his hat on his head, and bolted from the room. The bishop had tried to frighten him. Life might be perilous for an ordinary man with mixed blood. But it would not be for him. His education was preparing him for a world with endless possibilities.

CHAPTER NINE

Statehood

One spring day, Baptiste was hailed on the street by John O'Fallon. Normally imperious toward Baptiste, Clark's nephew wore a mournful expression and limply raised a hand in greeting.

"Mrs. Clark is very ill," he said. "Dr. Farrar prescribed a sea voyage and long rest. I thought you would like to know. The family left by steamboat for New Orleans . . ."

"I'm sorry to hear it," Baptiste said. "It is kind of you to think of me."

". . . and from there they go to Virginia for an indefinite stay."

"I wish a speedy recovery for Mrs. Clark."

They tipped their hats and went their separate ways. Baptiste wondered if young Mrs. Clark had spoken about him. Was that why O'Fallon had troubled to tell him? When the *Gazette* came out, he checked it for any mention of her illness, but there was none. He did learn that the general planned to return to St. Louis and resume his duties by summertime. It seemed he was running for the office of governor of the new state of Missouri.

Another election season! Before long, every time Baptiste passed a tippling house, he heard someone ranting about Clark's policies. The newspaper called him "stiff, reserved, and unhospitable." He was "overly friendly" with Indians. Attacks on Clark made

Baptiste feel protective. But he wished the man would hurry back to town and defend himself.

One day, M. Honoré, atremble with curiosity, hovered at Baptiste's elbow while he opened an invitation that had been delivered. It was from Cadet Chouteau, bidding him to come around to his house on Quality Row for a party.

"*Ça alors!*" breathed the old man.

Baptiste explained, "I used to work for him."

"You will tell me all about the party?" Honoré pleaded.

CADET'S STONE MANSION resembled his uncle Auguste's— four rooms wide and three stories high, with an arcade on all sides, pillared balconies and dormers on the top floor, crowned by four wide chimneys. A ten-foot wall protected the house and gardens. It was pierced, every few feet, by portholes through which muskets could be fired. They had once been necessary. Now the wars were over commerce. Baptiste entered the gate, nervously bouncing on the balls of his feet. He wore a clean shirt and corduroys, barely adequate to the occasion. He hoped he could charm people into overlooking his appearance.

A dozen or so Chouteaus, distinguished by their black hair and ruddy cheeks, wearing finery imported from Paris, mingled with their guests in the great center hall and its adjacent parlors. The young women in gowns glided and posed. He imagined his witty gambits drawing delighted laughter from them. He looked for his godfather, Auguste, and Madame, who had lent him *Candide*, but they were nowhere to be seen. This was a young peoples' ball.

A long row of tables piled high with delicacies filled the central hall. There were platters of beef à la mode, terrapin, roasted reed birds, mountains of fried oysters, bowls of ripe fruits, candied oranges, blancmange—Baptiste turned away, bedazzled.

An elderly métis held out a tray. Baptiste accepted a glass of punch and drained it. Instantly, his head buzzed. He took a step, steadied himself against a wall, and looked around furtively to see if anyone had noticed. The party guests went on gesturing grandly and drawling in the languid manner affected by well-born French. Baptiste struggled to regain his self-control. This was a warning, he realized. In the days when he'd run with Cyrus's gang and with Jim, although the other boys did, he hadn't been tempted to drink, heeding the effect that alcohol had on his father. Apparently, he couldn't tolerate it either. He swallowed four cups of fruit juice in quick succession. It seemed to dilute the poison.

To buy time, he made a study of the numerous paintings and engravings of Napoleon and his battles. His eye fell on Benoit Chouteau, who had noticed him and raised his eyebrows comically. Baptiste tipped his head. Benoit was the only fellow student in evidence, an indifferent scholar who had never before spoken to Baptiste. Now he ambled over with a jovial air.

"Whatever are you doing here, Charbonneau?"

"Your uncle invited me."

"Ah, yes," Benoit responded. "I had forgotten you worked at the store for a time. It's rare for him to hire outside the family." He had a narrow little cigar and drew on it. "Will you go back to the college next term?"

Baptiste nodded. "Yes. And will you?"

Benoit expelled a puff of smoke and shook his head. "I wanted to go to West Point, you know, but Papa said the mathematics would be my undoing. A cousin of mine failed out a few years ago.

The family was mortified. They won't risk it again." He smiled ruefully. "My education will be completed at the 'Osage academy.'"

"Ha-ha," said Baptiste.

Benoit went on, gesturing grandly. "You know the story: I will join the family fur company and live like a native, with all the privileges and trials that entails. The Indians will come to know my face and trust it. I'll find a chief's daughter to marry and a French girl in town, and—voilà! I will have mastered the Chouteau enterprise." His plump face radiated complacency.

What must it be like, to have his life laid out before him, every step determined by his family and by custom? Benoit didn't have a care in the world. The wine stain on his shirtfront would be scrubbed by servants or the shirt carelessly discarded. Benoit would come to know his family business through and through. But such knowledge was narrow. Would he learn about anything else? Baptiste thought, *I want to learn more, I want to know the world. . . .*

"I may stay with the monks," Baptiste heard himself say. He had decided no such thing! Was it so important to show that he had some plan too?

"Well! A black robe!" said Benoit. "They're stout fellows, I grant you. But you have to watch your step! They definitely frown on debauchery." He gave Baptiste a conspiratorial poke.

"I may become a lay brother and not wear the black robe," Baptiste said. Then as an afterthought, "Or I might work for General Clark regulating trade with the Indians. . . ."

"Ha!" Benoit retorted. "Such as regulating whiskey. Someone has to make a show of enforcing the law. But a fur man who doesn't trade alcoholic spirits to the Indians is a fool. We French never did before the Americans came. But now no competitor will be so principled! Do you think Jacob Astor would abstain? Even your general sends alcohol to the field. He just pretends it's for the boatmen."

He took hold of Baptiste's arm and lowered his voice. "You know, Clark lost a lot of money investing in Lisa's outfit. He's had to borrow from my uncle. I expect he'll be a selective enforcer of unpopular laws. He didn't make it easy for us when he provoked Kickapoos, Ioways, Shawnees, and Sioux to attack the Osages. They are our partners. They gave up millions of acres with Clark's treaty."

Just then, Cadet's pretty wife glided up and playfully pinched Benoit's cheek. "*Viens, viens!*" She gave Baptiste a bright smile. "We are playing charades. You must come too!"

A group of young people were sprawled on the floor at one end of a side parlor. Two earnest youths enacted a scene for them, silent, save grunts and giggles. The first threw out his arms and opened his mouth wide. The second jabbed him in the ribs from behind, with a tragic grimace. This caused the first to roll his eyes upward and crumple to the floor. The audience began throwing out phrases.

"Death of General Wolfe!" someone shouted. There were more suggestions, all rejected. "Death of Caesar," Baptiste whispered to himself. The performers shook their heads and repeated the pantomime. No player hit the mark, despite the increasingly frantic efforts of the actors.

"Death of Caesar!" Baptiste shouted at last. His heart beat furiously.

"Exactly," cried one of the young men, bowing. There was applause. Cadet smiled. "Bravo, Baptiste," he said.

Baptiste made a modest bow. A clutch of pretty girls on the floor, their skirts gathered around them, turned frankly inquisitive eyes on him. He beamed.

While he indulged his dreams of glory, the game continued and a new team performed their charade. He couldn't guess it! *Next time, give me a next time*, he thought, looking around at the faces all agog. But he never got another chance. The subjects were songs or popular French novels that he hadn't read.

After midnight, pancakes were served. The revelers ate with gusto, and Baptiste filled his stomach. Colored chalk was spread over the floor of one room and the dancing began. Baptiste found that it was easy to ask one of the girls to be his partner in a reel and a jig. He had only to approach one in the line along the walls and pull her onto the dance floor. Lagonia's lessons had been useful after all! He felt marvelously dashing.

When first light appeared, the music ended and guests began to drift away. Baptiste bowed good-byes to his flushed and happy partners and to Cadet and Emilie Chouteau. Benoit was sprawled on a couch, snoring loudly. Looking at him, Baptiste thought, *I could have been dead to the world myself.* A Chouteau could afford to be seen in that debauched condition. He, Baptiste, could not! The night had been filled with pleasures—and had taught him a lesson too.

OUTSIDE OF THE shrinking French district, St. Louis was becoming a town of English speakers. On the bustling streets, Baptiste observed young men and women dressed in clothing bought in New York or Philadelphia, not Paris. New buildings were going up everywhere. The air rang with hammering and sawing. He kept close watch on the house Clark was building of red brick. It was finished just in time for the returning family to move in before Julia Clark gave birth. He happened to be in the street when they arrived. Mrs. Clark was carried into the house. She looked very pale. Baptiste was happy that she was well enough to have another child. Clark glanced over at him and gave a friendly wave. A passing stranger looked at Baptiste in surprise. He felt a surge of pride in his connection to the hero.

All summer, Indians arrived by canoe to meet with the general and sign peace treaties that ended the wars among the Quapaw, Cherokee, and Osage. Some of the chiefs stayed in Clark's new brick house, while others set up camps along the bluffs. The treaties relocated Eastern tribes to land west of the Mississippi and gave white settlers huge swaths in Missouri. Clark showed the chiefs every courtesy, Baptiste thought, while he took away all that was precious to them. The Americans who replaced the Indians were bringing their slaves along. That controversy would come to a head before long, he thought.

ONE DAY, BAPTISTE saw Gilbert sitting on an upturned bucket outside the Clark kitchen. He looked anguished.

"What's the matter, Gilbert?"

Gilbert looked around and then answered in a whisper, "Master Clark is sending Scipio off to New Orleans. Boat's ready to sail. Take away a man, turn him into cash." Gilbert shook his head and a tear dropped from one eye. "Scipio, he was an old home slave. He nursed Master Clark, back in Kentucky. He didn't want to go! So yesterday he shot himself in the head." Gilbert held his head in his hands.

"That's terrible!" Baptiste said.

Gilbert got control of his emotions and said, "Your Mr. Peck, he protests. People don't like that. I would advise Mr. Peck not to walk abroad at night alone. . . ."

Baptiste blinked at him. Threats to the Reverend Peck! His stomach lurched at that thought. He would tell Peck what Gilbert had said, but the missionary was fearless. He would never change his ways. His Christian principles were as rigid as Platonic ethics. Of course, Baptiste thought with a grimace, the slave owners considered themselves principled Christians too. Baptiste had heard one say that slavery was justified in the Bible.

NOW THAT CLARK was a candidate to be the first governor of the new state of Missouri, Baptiste followed politics more closely. He was the ward of a political leader. It was very much his business, citizen or not, especially after Clark returned to the East so that his wife's illness could be treated again. Clark published a campaign statement weekly in the *Inquirer:*

"The choice of a governor is your business, not mine, and so far as my fitness for that place may be the subject of enquiry, that matter may be discussed as well in my absence as my presence. My public service has been long, having begun under George Washington."

Baptiste pictured Clark at his wife's bedside, his long frame folded onto a chair, one hand gently holding hers, the other pressing a cloth to her brow, all of his years of public service yielding to this tender imperative. Surely the voters would honor what he had already done for them.

But the *Gazette* consistently opposed Clark, accusing him of "pocketing money" from his office and with deserting the territory during the War of 1812. The *Inquirer* took Clark's side, saying it was his duty to treat the Indians with "mildness and humanity." It praised his "dignity of character . . . suavity of manner . . . sterling integrity . . . intuitive knowledge of the human character." Reading that, Baptiste thought Clark couldn't lose. Then he kicked himself for being gullible and bending with the wind. Just because a thing was said in print didn't mean it was true!

THOUGHTS OF MME CHOUTEAU began to weigh on his mind. He imagined she had grown accustomed to his visits and was disappointed that he hadn't gone back in months.

The guilt that resulted reminded him of how he'd felt when his mother left. She abandoned him—but he had abandoned her as well. One day, he went to call and found Mme Chouteau in a parlor with an elderly gentleman. She wasn't at all put out and greeted him warmly.

"Come in! Sit with us! Doctor, see how handsome is Baptiste. They call him little Baptiste, you know. But I believe he has a big soul. And a flair for literature, which I encourage."

Her companion twisted stiffly in his chair, to take a look. Above his smiling, rheumy eyes, a noble forehead sprouted a few wispy white tendrils. "You will frighten him off, my dear madame, with your praise," he murmured. Baptiste recognized Dr. Saugrain, much the same, but older.

"How do you do, Doctor?" he said. "I am Baptiste. You gave me a dose of the pox to prevent it when I was at the Indian school."

The doctor's eyes brightened. "Sakakawea's son. I do remember you. Nearly a man now. No wonder my friend here takes such an interest." Mme Chouteau snorted. "Does Captain Clark still support you?"

"He has placed me in the Academy, sir."

"Ah. Very good. Those priests will follow a logical thought. But I am concerned about the election. General Clark's prospects don't seem good. The tide of change takes everything with it, bad and good. Our system of government obliges us to live with the whims of self-seeking men."

"He may yet prevail, sir."

"Hmmmmm. Has the bishop tried to convert you?" This unexpected question stopped Baptiste's tongue. Dr. Saugrain was amused. "He might do so without your realizing it. He is a slick fellow."

"He has asked if I would join his order. But I told him I am not interested."

Mme Chouteau giggled. "I gave the boy Voltaire," she confided.

Dr. Saugrain said, "You don't need those black coats, Baptiste! I wonder what General Clark has in mind for you."

"I do too!" Baptiste blurted.

"M. Voltaire may seem to reject society. But he really calls for keeping an open mind on all questions of human relations." Saugrain held up a small volume. "Here is an ancient work that explains the fundamental composition of the world. Have the good priests told you of it?"

Baptiste shook his head.

Saugrain handed him the book.

"*De Rerum Natura*, by Lucretius. *On the Nature of Things*," Baptiste translated aloud.

"Indeed. A remarkable work, written before Christ was born, during violent change in Rome. Lucretius believed that everything, man and nature alike, is made of atoms that are always moving. The idea came from Democritus, in 375 BC. Atoms are also capable of swerving unexpectedly. From this deviation comes our concept of free will."

Baptiste was fascinated. "How can all things, which are so different from each other, be made of the same particles?" he asked.

"Isaac Newton reached a similar conclusion," Saugrain said. "He called them corpuscular particles, whose differences account for the individual properties of things—of yourself, of this chair, of Mme Chouteau, the book, a tree, and so on."

"It is so strange to think of! And why should it be?" Baptiste exclaimed. He felt quite stupid.

"Lucretius tells us that the motion of atoms is constant, but without purpose. It is not divinely guided. 'Nature is her own mistress, accomplishing everything spontaneously and independently and free from the jurisdiction of the gods,' he says."

Baptiste realized he was nodding vigorously. The doctor smiled and continued: "We live and we die. There is no life after death. There is only life. We must embrace it fully and live as well as we can. He believed in the pursuit of pleasure."

"Pleasure?" said Baptiste, surprised.

"That which produces happiness," said the doctor.

"It is a wonderful philosophy!" Baptiste exclaimed.

Madame Chouteau clapped her hands. "The boy delights me! Tell him about your experiments."

Baptiste spent an exciting afternoon, learning about electric batteries and sparking fire with a phosphorous-tipped stick, vaccinations and theories of disease. Saugrain was a natural historian and scientist. Baptiste was fascinated. Saugrain's world opened countless other worlds. How much more there was to life than Baptiste had yet experienced! He felt as if one of Saugrain's matches had set his mind alight.

AT SCHOOL, THEY were reading Plutarch's *Parallel Lives.* The Roman writer described great men's characters rather than their military victories. Baptiste and his friends all had favorites and debated their merits during and after class. Naturally, Baptiste favored General Pompey, to whom Plutarch attributed great heart and integrity. Pompey had finally been deposed by cynical rivals.

"He was like General Clark," Baptiste asserted, to laughter from the class.

"And who do you say is our Caesar?" asked Pelagie.

"There are many candidates—Benton, perhaps."

"Do you think our republic is doomed, like Rome?" asked Taillez. It was more a taunt than a question.

"I think it must represent the interests of more of the people, if it is to endure," said Baptiste.

"He may be right," said Father Gregoire.

JOHN O'FALLON, WEARING a grim, preoccupied expression, nearly ran him down in the street one day.

"Baptiste," he muttered. "You may not have heard the terrible news. Mrs. Clark has died. My uncle is distraught."

Baptiste was stunned. He mumbled condolences. Then he asked, "Will he come home for the voting?" He immediately regretted the question—it sounded unfeeling.

"Oh, the election is lost. He has been falsely assailed by cowardly foes. Our enemies' scurrilities have succeeded. It is an outrage." With a brusque "Good day," O'Fallon strode off.

Baptiste was left with pity and concern for the general. He reviewed the exchange over and over as he walked. He wished he had pointed out that the election hadn't taken place yet. Wasn't it too soon to declare defeat?

But so many citizens hated Clark, despite his great service to the territory. It seemed that slander, when repeated often enough, could undo all the virtuous acts a man had committed in his life. It was profoundly disturbing. Poor General Clark, left widowed. Baptiste realized that in the midst of his loss, Clark was suddenly the sole caretaker of five children.

He decided to confide his feelings to Jim. His friend was feeding apples to a pair of contentedly whinnying horses in the paddock behind the smithy's forge.

"What ho, B'tiste?" Jim drawled, unemphatic as ever. He looked more muscular and a few inches taller. Baptiste was never going to be tall.

"I'm tolerable, Jim." Baptiste stroked the neck of a mare with a white blaze and flowing mane. She nibbled at his fingers. "John O'Fallon thinks the general will lose the election."

Jim shot him a queer look. "Do you know what they're saying, B'tiste?"

"That he favors the Indians."

Jim shook his head. "That's not all. They say Clark has an Indian wife and a 'half-breed' child he's put in school at public expense."

Baptiste drew in a sharp breath. "That's a lie!" he exclaimed. Then he understood the implication. "*Me?*"

Jim nodded. Baptiste was horrified. How could he stop such a slander? Would it be his fault if Clark lost the election? Would Clark blame him? His gut sank.

"I don't know, B'tiste," Jim said. "It's a sorry business. But there's nothing you can do about it."

Why should Jim care? That they seemed to be growing apart only increased Baptiste's anguish. In his mind, the rumor about him and Mrs. Clark's death were entwined. He desperately wanted to see Clark, to ask for forgiveness—but of course he hadn't done anything wrong.

CHAPTER TEN

——◆———◆——

A New Way of Trapping

Baptiste went back to work at Chouteau and Berthold's store after school. They needed him; the government forts had been closed, and its monopoly was over. It was every man for himself now. Some intrepid free agents had managed to cross the southwestern plains and enter Santa Fe, opening up a huge new market for the store.

Clark didn't come home to St. Louis—Baptiste walked past his house every day—until the election was over. He lost it in a landslide. The federals appointed him Superintendent of Indian Affairs, so he was still running the Indian agency. Baptiste waited in vain for Clark to summon him. He supposed the worst: It was because he had helped cause Clark's defeat. Of course he must also be swamped with cares, managing Indians and settlers and a passel of little Clarks. But Baptiste couldn't banish the guilt he felt.

One day at school, he was handed a note saying the bishop was back from Europe and wanted to see him.

DuBourg welcomed him warmly.

"I understand that your scholarship has only improved while I was gone. I feel very hopeful. You apply yourself as befits a man with a future."

Baptiste said, "I enjoy my studies." He declined to say anything more. *Safe and secure* were the words the bishop had used to describe his life if he became a Jesuit. Those words didn't appeal to him any more than they had a few months before.

The bishop beamed at him. "I don't dwell on the past," he said. "But you do make me long for the open mind and eagerness of youth." He glanced down at a paper and frowned. "But your attendance at Mass is spotty."

Baptiste responded honestly. "I am not a believer."

Neither the priests nor the Puritans, Peck and Welch, had convinced him that the white man's god ruled over nature. It was the other way around. No prayers could have made the comet disappear or prevent the earthquake. They were natural occurrences. It was as Dr. Saugrain had said: The atoms of existence moved randomly, without divine guidance.

"It takes time to find faith," DuBourg was saying unconcernedly. "We continually examine ourselves and work to conquer our attachments to material desires."

Baptiste thought for a moment. Had he ever wanted things? Ever envied anyone for his possessions? "I don't think I have any material desires," he said.

"Then your spiritual journey will be easy," the bishop replied smoothly. "In any case, you need not take vows. You could join us as a lay brother and be just as useful to the world."

Baptiste clenched and unclenched his fists. DuBourg seemed determined to snare him. He would fight fire with fire. "I believe that the Church Fathers made a fundamental error, sir," he said.

The bishop laughed. "Well! And what is this error that you have detected?"

"They separated good from evil. Christ was good and Satan bad. But this is a false idea. Every man is both good *and* evil. You cannot simply cast the bad parts out."

There was a long silence.

"I was told that you were baptized," DuBourg said quietly.

"I was, yes."

"The result is the remission of the sin of Adam. You are endowed with free will. You may decide to run to Christ or to Satan. It will be up to you."

"I cannot agree, Excellency. Everyone, it seems to me, is a mixture. For example, General Clark is as good to his family as a man can be. But he whips his slaves and deceives the Indians," Baptiste said woodenly. His face burned. It had been an impertinent and disrespectful thing to say.

DuBourg's eyes widened briefly, but the rest of his face was impassive. His fingers drummed for a moment on his desk. Then he said, "Baptiste, you have a sharp mind. But it is undisciplined. You malign your patron. And you contradict the Church."

Baptiste held the bishop's gaze.

"Any statement must be either true or false. It cannot be some mixture of the two," DuBourg added.

Baptiste decided to refrain from further contradiction. DuBourg studied him for a moment, then said, "Occasional questioning is to be expected from a clever youth. What pains my heart is your rejection of a way of life that would allow you to flourish under God's loving protection." His eyes softened. "But if I cannot persuade you to join us . . . so be it. Go your way; make a mark in the world if you can. But be on guard. Worldly power is held by men who believe it is their birthright and is not yours."

Closing the door behind him, Baptiste felt a flood of relief that nearly buckled his knees. He let out a great sigh. He was free to go wherever his destiny beckoned. How could the world not receive him? He was young, strong, and well schooled. The last thing he wanted to be was "on guard."

ONE DAY, WHILE he was counting blankets in the back of the store, Cadet asked Baptiste if he'd been invited to General Clark's wedding. "No?" Cadet said when Baptiste was clearly taken by surprise. "Well, he is to be united again in matrimony in a Presbyterian ceremony at James Kennerly's house." He added that the bride was a widow and first cousin to the late Julia Clark. She was bringing more children to the Clark household, in addition to the five already there.

"The general leaves you to yourself, then," Cadet observed.

"He often sends for me. He wants to know how I'm doing in school," Baptiste said defensively. It was what he wished, not what was true.

"Ah, well, school. If I were you, I'd polish my wilderness skills. Don't let them decay. The Americans try to 'civilize' Indians and French-Indians. It only makes them unfit for employment in the wild country. When two mixed-blood boys are presented to me and one has been twice as long at the mission school, it means he is twice as good for nothing." He gazed at Baptiste for a moment. "You don't want to be educated only to be useless."

"That is certainly not what I want!" Baptiste said hotly. "And I'm not at a mission school."

"Of course not," Cadet conceded.

On the long walk back to Honoré's house that evening, Baptiste fumed with anger at Cadet, who had insulted him. He had proven himself to Cadet over and over, and yet the man still underestimated him. What must he do to make people see him for what he was? Cadet had also suggested that he was not as important to General Clark as he thought. If so, he didn't know what he could do about it.

Sometimes he would squint and imagine Lucretius's atoms dancing before him. One would suddenly swerve. He had always thought his destiny waited at the end of a rutted trail, like the ones immigrants' wagons cut in the prairie. But what if his path swerved out of the rut? What if his future depended only on chance?

Clark must still blame him for his loss of the election. And he had so many people to look after! Kinship was as important to him as it was to Indians—or métis or French, for that matter. Where, in the crowd of Clark dependents, did he have a place?

These tormented musings were interrupted by loud hoofbeats and the yapping of dogs. A horseman was approaching the corner at high speed. Baptiste barely got out of the way. He recognized Colonel William Ashley, a slight figure on a huge white mare, trailed by a pack of foxhounds. The colorful soldier and trader had been living in St. Louis only a short while, but his Virginia cavalier's bravado quickly captured people's imaginations. Baptiste stared after him. The fellow could surely sit a horse—and what a horse!

The next Saturday morning, Jim's forceful voice, in counterpoint to Honoré's feebly protesting one, rang up the stairs. From what Baptiste could make out from his bed, M. Honoré was trying to prevent his visitor from charging up to Baptiste's room. A minute later, though, Jim was there, brandishing a newspaper. Baptiste had never seen his imperturbable friend so stirred up.

"B'tiste!" he cried. "Did you see today's *Gazette?*"

"Not yet. I was sleeping!"

Jim punched at a boxed text on the page. "Read it!"

To enterprising men

The subscriber wishes to engage ONE HUNDRED MEN, to ascend the river Missouri to its sources, there to be employed for one, two, or three years—For particulars, enquire of Major Andrew Henry, near the Lead Mines, in the County of Washington (who will ascend with and command the party) or to the subscriber at St. Louis.

WM. H. ASHLEY

"The blacksmith told me about this. I got a copy so you could see for yourself. People say Ashley will do business in a whole new way," Jim said when Baptiste had finished reading. "They say men will go to stay in the wild country and take beaver themselves. They say they'll bypass the Indians altogether." He was hopping with excitement.

"But that's illegal. And why would you stand in freezing water and club beaver if Indian trappers will do it?" Baptiste fell back on his pillow.

"That's the beauty of it, B'tiste. They're going to use castoreum bait and steel traps, not clubs. Ashley pays men to go to the mountains, where they do the trapping instead of trading with Indians for furs. Ashley collects a share of the pelts. There's no limit to how much money can be made by all parties. I'm signing on."

Baptiste felt a stab of pain in his chest. "You are?"

"Well, of course I am!"

"Who else is going, do you know?"

"Only bully men! Those ready to hightail it to the wild country. It's farewell to the tepid life here in St. Louis!"

This was more than Baptiste could bear.

"I'll sign up too!" he cried.

"Yes, do! We'll be wilderness comrades." Jim made an owl-eyed face. "And we're going to be rich!"

Baptiste couldn't resist him. How could he bear being left behind while Jim went on an adventure like this? A man's adventure! But barely an hour passed before Baptiste realized he would have to get General Clark's permission to sign up. He was supposed to be in school. His tuition was paid in advance. So he raced over to the Indian agency, still in a state of almost delirious excitement.

"WHAT IS IT, Pomp? You look unhinged," Clark said when Baptiste burst into the office.

Clark was smiling. Baptiste suddenly remembered that he was to blame for the election loss. But Clark looked happy to see him, no hint of anger on his ruddy face.

"Sir, the election . . . ," Baptiste said tentatively.

"You needn't be concerned on my behalf," Clark said. "Life has blessed me more than I have been buffeted by it."

"There was a rumor . . ."

"You came to tell me there are false rumors abroad?" He chuckled indulgently.

Baptiste felt limp with relief. He'd carried such a burden of guilt for so long. Suddenly, it was lifted! The way was clear to join Jim!

"Sir, Colonel Ashley has advertised—"

"Yes, I know," Clark interrupted, setting his papers down. "Some think that independent trappers will harm our relations with the Indians. I hope that Colonel Ashley intends to cultivate their friendship."

"I want to join up!"

Clark smiled. "Any warm-blooded young man desires to test his manhood, Pomp. But I have extended your education because you excel at it. It is important that you finish your present course of study."

"But, sir, I'm nearly eighteen. I've been in school longer than most of the other boys."

"It would be folly to go."

Baptiste had thrust himself forward with all conviction, only to hit a wall. A wave of anger swept over him. Clark had been toying with him almost from the time he'd come to St. Louis as a little child. Now, at eighteen, must he turn down the greatest opportunity ever offered in the West?

"Sir," he blurted, conscious that his voice was rising in volume, but unable to stop himself, "Ashley's expedition will change the fur trade."

Clark's blue eyes were icy. "It may not change it for the better. When Missouri was a territory, we took the wise counsel of our French partners. Their blood was mixed with the Indians, along with their enterprises. Everyone prospered together. But I fear the French and the Indians alike may be losers if Ashley succeeds."

"But the Chouteaus are the richest men in the territory," Baptiste protested.

Clark ignored him. "Men in business no longer equate their own well-being with the well-being of the whole nation, as my generation did. They care only for their own self-interest."

Baptiste was hopping with impatience. Clark had strayed from the subject. He was an old man who'd gone soft and lost his influence! "What about me?" he shouted. His words hung in the air. Clark looked at him in surprise.

"I haven't paid your tuition all of these years for you to go off on a daredevil enterprise that may end in disaster. Ashley has assembled a batch of illiterates and inebriates. They were recruited from the grog shops and other sinks of degradation. The crew is beneath you, Pomp."

"You are mistaken, sir! My best friend is among those men. He is the finest fellow I've known—"

Clark spat out his reply. "I don't think you are yet a judge of men. You must stay in school. If you are not educated, a world predicated on self-interest will never treat you fairly. The current advantage is with white men of narrow vision. I regret it, but it is true."

"You may not insult my friend!" Baptiste shouted. Clark recoiled slightly, but said nothing.

After a moment, Baptiste asked, "What am I being educated for? Where will I ever belong? Not in your house. Not with my mother's people. Not with my father's people...and not with yours!"

"You will decide what kind of man you want to be in due time. Be patient."

"Patient? Damn patience! Patience didn't send you on the expedition!"

"Captain Lewis and I were experienced men," Clark retorted.

"But how will I gain experience? You have controlled my life since I was a baby! I thought you would raise me as your own son! Isn't that what you told my mother? But you betrayed me! What am I to you?"

Clark's face had turned bright pink. He reached reflexively for Baptiste, who took a step back. "Baptiste, my boy," he said softly. "I couldn't leave you in the Mandan Villages to suffer their fate. I wanted your mother to see you thrive and to come into your promise. I did this for her as well as for you. But you are not my son. I cannot rule your life. Think of your mother. She was the mirror of patience. Don't throw away what I have given you and dishonor her memory."

Baptiste was just barely holding back tears. Mention of Sakakawea only made him feel more alone. His fists beat on his thighs while he struggled for words. "You hold me back! I am your captive! Other boys learn a trade at fifteen and I am well past that. I have been waiting and waiting! What am I waiting for?"

"Continue your studies," Clark said.

Baptiste gulped air. Was this all that Clark could say? Merely the old saw about school? It was humiliating!

He turned and fled the room.

WHAT HAD HE done? Now he had to live with his outburst. Had he freed himself from Clark's clutches? Should he slink back and beg pardon? He weighed going to Ashley and pleading for a place on the expedition, then berated himself for a coward when he didn't do it. Some sense that he must not defy fate held him back. Or it might have been habitual obedience to Clark's authority.

SEVENTY YOUNG MEN responded to Ashley's advertisement, all of them stout fellows. As the one being left behind, Baptiste realized he would miss Jim terribly, but Jim would be having too many adventures ever to think of him!

The leave-taking on the wharf a few weeks later was colorfully chaotic. Ashley issued commands from his noble horse. His recruits and their well-wishers whooped and backslapped and speculated about how successful and how filled with memorable incident this first foray would be. Baptiste recognized the rapscallion river pilot Mike Fink and sober Jed Smith. Jim's face, as he stood between Tom Fitzpatrick and Jim Beckwourth, was flushed with the fever of adventure. He was going off to be a man among men! When he saw Baptiste, he pushed his way through the crowd of hearty bucks to pump his hand.

"I wish you were coming, my friend!" he cried.

"So do I," Baptiste replied. For a long moment, neither knew what more to say. Then Jim made a harrumph sound, turned on his heel, and sprang aboard one of the boats. He looked back and waved.

Baptiste lingered until they had pushed off. Then he trudged back into town feeling hollowed out. It was the second time he had watched as someone he loved left without him. What a hopeless feeling it was!

He straightened his back and muttered an oath. He had turned on Clark, and gained nothing by it. What kind of man *did* he want to be?"

BAPTISTE'S FRIENDS WOULD all be leaving school at the end of the term, Taillez and Pelagie to go into business with their fathers. Wilkerson's situation was closest to Baptiste's, as his father was dead and no one had come forward to offer him a position. He finally made up his mind to join the United States Army and began strutting around like an officer. He was accordingly teased, and stopped.

Baptiste also endured some friendly ridicule after a letter from DuBourg informed him that he had attained first place in the class. He still had no idea what he was to do next. He imagined brandishing the document in Clark's office and asking what place in the world he had earned by learning its rules and customs so thoroughly. Presumably, as his guardian, the general received a copy.

Then, one day, Cadet sent for him. They met, not at the store but at the French fur company's well-appointed office near the courthouse. Cadet's lean frame was draped over a chair upholstered in silk, presumably imported from France. A desk was piled high with orders, receipts, letters, and account books and above it hung an engraving of a battle during the Napoleonic wars. A dusty, stuffed beaver perched on a shelf.

Cadet beckoned at Baptiste to sit. "Will you take some cider? No? All right. I'll get to it, then. We have new opportunities here in Missouri. Statehood has invigorated trade for everyone. But there are upstarts who threaten to destroy the peaceful relations our family has built for generations with the Osage and their neighbors." He paused, eyeing Baptiste keenly. "One upstart is particularly reckless."

Baptiste maintained an impassive expression. *Ashley.*

Cadet continued. "I need intelligent, sober men who can act as go-betweens. My brother François and his wife are newly established on the Kaw River, at Chouteau's Post. It will be a lively community. Nice for a young man."

"I am interested," Baptiste said carefully. "But, as you know, General Clark—"

"Oh, this was his idea."

Baptiste could only gape at the man. "Well, then, I accept," he said finally. Clark was still playing him like a marionette. But why object, when this would give him a foothold in the fur trade! A new post founded by the Chouteaus was sure to succeed. He hadn't realized it, but he was bitterly anxious to be free of swarming St. Louis, with its odors of sewage, offal, and smoke. He would go up the river again! The idea thrilled him.

THE ACADEMY FACULTY announced a Commencement Exercise to usher its first class of graduates into the world.

"Tradition is the *vinculum*, the fastening, of any institution of learning," Father Gregoire intoned. "To inaugurate our own, we will follow the examples of the most venerable universities." He and Father Francis wrote out a program for the occasion. Each of the dozen scholars was to declaim briefly in Latin. Baptiste, as valedictorian, would deliver a short speech on a subject of his own choosing (appropriate to the occasion!) to the audience of relatives and dignitaries.

The boys joked about this assignment, but every one of them was soon poring over ancient texts and dictionaries and committing lines to their slates, from there to be memorized.

Baptiste knew at once which ancient text he should use. His life so far had been ruled by chance—the luck of being born at the right moment in the right place (to the right woman!), of being chosen by Clark. He was heading toward his destiny, but it could not be predicted. A series of choices, and chance, would lead him there. As he made his way, he would accumulate experience and the choices would be wiser. At least, this was his hope. Such were his reflections, lying in his bed, a copy of Lucretius's poem in his hand, while the moon shone in his window.

THE COMMENCEMENT WASN'T a culmination—its very name said that. It was more like a hurdle to cross, before he could do anything important. But he must cross gracefully. It was a ritual and he knew the importance of ritual.

He woke out of a dream on the morning of the Commencement, instantly tingling with nerves. Invitations had been sent to parents and dignitaries, but he didn't know whether the general, who lived most of the time at his country seat, planned to attend. His son and nephew were in a lower class and wouldn't graduate for three years. Baptiste washed and dressed distractedly, rehearsing his talk and then forgetting the pages and having to go back for them.

The weather was mild and a breeze scented with sweet spring flowers was a balm to his nerves. He found his classmates milling around a big, old hickory tree that would be the backdrop for the ceremony. They had all been given black robes to wear, which led to some mild horseplay until Brother Lucien appeared, carrying a giant mace. The boys all jumped to attention. It was a lethal-looking object.

"Who's going to get it on the noggin with that?" Wilkerson cracked, out of the corner of his mouth.

Relatives and city officials were arriving, chatting in small groups, men and women together, an unusual sight, their voices jubilant. Baptiste stood apart, silently rehearsing his speech. Out of the corner of his eye, he spied Clark jovially shaking hands with the bishop, then greeting several of the faculty. He was wearing his black suit with a scarlet scarf at his waist and he looked enormous. He was indeed Jovial. Baptiste felt a little surge of pride in his patron. The boys were told to line up and Clark looked over at him, nodded and smiled, as if they had never hurled angry words at each other.

A drummer and a horn player began to play. The faculty formed an avenue for the scholars to walk through while Lucien waved his mace. Each graduate was handed a diploma by the bishop before he delivered his brief Latin oration (or, in Taillez's case, a Greek one). Baptiste felt a wave of fondness for his friends, each one so different from the others.

"Baptiste," Father Gregoire prompted softly.

He gathered himself and stepped forward.

"I must begin with thanks to General Clark, who brought me to this city, has educated me, and today is here to witness my commencement." Clark's face reddened. He looked very pleased.

Baptiste told the gathering what Lucretius had written about atoms so long ago in his poem *On the Nature of Things*. He concluded by saying, "Lucretius said men can never triumph by waging war, and cannot conquer nature. There is only brief life given to us, to be lived in harmony with all nature. Lucretius spoke of the pursuit of happiness, and so did our founders. Here, all men are born with equal rights to pursue happiness, thanks to them."

He looked out at the faces arrayed before him. Clark's was still flushed, but not disapproving; a few others were uncomprehending. One or two priests looked guarded. Lucretius had never been assigned. But Baptiste didn't seem to have offended anyone.

He bowed slightly and walked back to the line of scholars. The little audience clapped weakly. Taillez smirked and stuck out his hand to shake Baptiste's. "That was over my head, friend," he murmured. "It must have been profound."

Suddenly, Clark was beside him. He draped a long arm over Baptiste's shoulders. "Well done, my boy," he said. "Mr. Jefferson owns five copies of Lucretius's poem. He was most certainly inspired by it when he wrote our Declaration. You have had a brilliant insight."

"Thank you, sir. I was given the book by Dr. Saugrain. I did not, at first, understand that its ideas could apply to us."

"Well, America is a hybrid creation. We have borrowed wherever we could." They were briefly silent. Remembering their last meeting, Baptiste felt his neck heat up. He had wanted to pursue happiness with the Ashley crew and Jim. Clark had stood in his way.

"I suspect that you are yet smarting from disappointment," Clark said, as if reading his mind. "You have a young man's lust for adventure. And you will find it soon enough." His eyes twinkled. "With much less danger. Hearing you today I cannot regret my insistence that you remain in school. Like you, I have tried to honor your mother's wishes. She would be very happy today!"

CHAPTER ELEVEN

At the Chouteau Post

That summer, Baptiste lay along the prow of a keelboat on the Missouri, idly dragging a fishing line. The current was swift and they made rapid progress. He had completed this loop, between St. Louis and the post at Chouteau Landing at the junction with the Kansas River, three times now, carrying messages for Cadet. This time he was in charge of a load of valuable furs. He would stay in St. Louis long enough to collect pay owed the French-Indian métis at the post. The money bag was proof of Cadet's trust in him. The work was easy, everyone knew him now—he was still called little Baptiste. But people uttered it respectfully. Cadet had promised a promotion.

Ironically, while his tedious job required no education, it was bearable because he had time to lose himself in books. Sadly, Madame was dead. But Reverend Peck had given him a Bible, along with Plutarch, Tacitus, and, with a wink because they were frivolous stories, the novels of Sir Walter Scott. Baptiste had to admit that he was living the life of a literate river rat. Was Clark keeping track of him, and was he disappointed?

While he made the same round trip week after week, America was stretching out across the prairies, each new wave of settlers sucking another into its wake. Land agents, lawyers, bankers, dry goods brokers, and owners of lead mines were all reaping the rewards. Baptiste remembered his talk with Benoit Chouteau at Cadet's ball. He had thought the other boy's future was too narrow, limited to the family enterprise so entwined with tribal life. He, Baptiste, wanted a future in the wide world! He smiled ruefully.

The Chouteau fortune continued to grow, thanks to furs and the familial connections so carefully cultivated. Not far from his little Kaw Post on the Kansas, young François Chouteau and his bride, Berenice, the daughter of the governor of Illinois, were building a fine new home. Berenice was a queenly little thing, surrounding herself with courtiers who danced their nights away.

Baptiste's post consisted of a few wooden cabins, managed by Cyrus Curtis and Andrew Wood and a crew of mixed bloods and Indians. Curtis's wife was a shy woman he seldom saw. But most of the women were far bolder than any of the females he'd observed in the city. Mrs. Wood had taken a shine to Baptiste and mothered him, planting kisses on his cheeks and preparing special sweets for him. The post employees made uproarious sport over it. Sometimes, when someone was playing a fiddle, Baptiste grabbed Mrs. Wood by the waist and launched her into a vigorous dance, to much hooting and hollering.

There wasn't anyone on the post who knew how to read or was inclined to introspection. Baptiste had no one to talk to. He saw the same faces every day and traveled the same route. When would he see more of the world? he wondered.

Profound boredom was a new experience for him. He often thought of the adventures Jim must be having, although it worried him a little that no one had heard from the group. He was carrying a copy of the *Iliad*. He was struck by a speech of Achilles: *"I carry two sorts of destiny towards the day of my death. If I stay here and fight beside the city of the Trojans, I shall not return home, but my glory shall be everlasting; whereas if I return home to the beloved land of my father, my glory will be gone, but there will be long life left for me."*

He had returned to the land of his father. But was long life, rather than fame, truly his destiny? He had been schooled for something very different.

There was more than the usual harborside commotion when he arrived at the wharf in St. Louis. The steamship *Cincinnati* had apparently just docked and a throng of citizens was hoping for a glimpse of the visitors who had come to the outermost edge of civilization. Baptiste didn't hang around but went straight to the Chouteau mansion to make his report. There were more than three hundred homes in the city now, and quite a few of them were made of brick.

Two weeks later, he was headed back upriver, guarding a pouch full of US currency. It was a big responsibility. But he was needed for neither his education nor his gifts.

BY LATE JUNE, the heat on the river bluffs was intense, nearly one hundred degrees in the shade of the tall cottonwoods. To find relief from the baking yard of the trading post, Baptiste hiked along the bluffs and cut into deep woods. He walked for several miles with an eye out for deer, but none showed themselves. Nor did he encounter any Kansa. He might as well be alone in the world. There wasn't even any birdsong. He cut back to the river.

Suddenly, the sultry air was rent by loud cursing in Creole French. He heard the clap of a rifle shot, followed by splashes and more angry cries. Trouble. Baptiste crept closer. On the deck of a pirogue, two swarthy men in buckskins were pummeling each other. Both fighters were bleeding profusely. A third man tugged on a line, trying to free the boat from a tangle of roots and branches at the edge of the river.

Baptiste had witnessed such scenes before and he knew better than to get involved. The third man looked markedly different from the others. He was about twenty-five years old, well taken care of, with pale skin. He wore a lush, close-cut jacket, and a broad-brimmed hat with a feather in its band. One of the other men suddenly brandished a gun and fired it wildly. This could end very badly!

Baptiste crouched, gathered his strength, leapt over the gap to the deck of the pirogue, and tackled the armed man's legs, toppling him. The fellow flashed him a wild look and scrambled over the side. The rifle flew into the air and splashed into the water. The second ruffian threw a punch at Baptiste, which he easily ducked, causing his opponent to tumble forward. The well-dressed man, who had been watching with a look of amazement, moved in and pinned his assailant to the deck. He and Baptiste exchanged a glance, then lifted the man together and heaved him into the water, where his mate was still thrashing desperately. Neither seemed to pose further danger as they grabbed at roots in an attempt to reach dry land.

"What Sir Paladin are you?" exclaimed Baptiste's new ally, breathing heavily. He spoke French with an accent. German, perhaps.

"I am Baptiste Charbonneau. At your service."

The man looked at him appraisingly. "Aha! You are the son of Toussaint Charbonneau and Sakakawea! You have saved my life today! In the manner of your courageous and resourceful mother, from the story I was told."

"It was my privilege," Baptiste replied, amazed that the man knew his story.

"Bishop DuBourg spoke of you" came the answer. "We traveled together on the *Cincinnati* to St. Louis from France. When I obtained my permits from General William Clark, your name was mentioned again. And, come to remember, M. Auguste Chouteau, who received me at his country estate, also spoke of you. . . ."

"He is my godfather." Clark must have intended him to meet this fellow . . . but why?

"Well, encountering you in the flesh, I am not disappointed," the stranger declared. He gave Baptiste's shoulder a light thump. "This nation constantly reminds me that it is not birth but education that determines the moral development of a man. And I find that moral development can often be read in a face."

"What do you mean, sir?" Baptiste asked, startled.

"Why, you are a mixed blood, a métis, as they say. So were my erstwhile boatmen. And nearly every other reprobate I've encountered on this continent. You distinguish yourself from them by most obviously having been enlightened at school." He occupied himself for a moment with brushing dirt from his garments and pressing out their wrinkles with his palms.

Baptiste held his tongue. Here was yet another white man with disdain for "mixed bloods." He decided not to bother with niceties.

"I have identified myself. Who are you?"

"Forgive me!" the other said, laughing. "I am Paul, Duke of Württemberg, come to America for the purpose of scientific study."

"I see," Baptiste replied. European royalty. A worthless lot, holding back the future. America had rid itself of them.

"The scene you witnessed has been tiresomely repeated since I left St. Louis. My crew has mutinied, been dismissed and replaced several times. They drink their allotment of whiskey and then gamble for everyone else's share. Finally, they go after mine. I sent my valet, Schlape, and our large boat to the trading post where I am to rendezvous with him. I do hope Schlape is all right. How far is the post?"

Baptiste answered that the post was an hour away by water.

"I can guide you there, if you like. Mr. Wood and Mr. Curtis are not at home . . . Your Highness," he added. "But Mrs. Woods is there."

The duke clapped him on the back. "You speak English," he observed, when he heard the names pronounced. "But French is your first tongue." Baptiste nodded. "I will ask you not to burden me with *highnesses*. I have been traveling incognito to avoid such nonsense. It is hardly proper in your republic. By the way, do you feel as pinched in the nether regions as I do? My buckskins are rapidly shrinking, after our dousing in the river. I see that yours are too. We make a comical pair."

"I have a solution for that," Baptiste promised. The fellow's high spirits were hard to resist.

THEY POLED THE pirogue upstream. The duke continued to exude good cheer, declaring he felt fortunate to have found

someone to whom he could confide the bizarre and at times farci-
cal particulars of his journey into the backcountry! "You grasp the
indignities of it—and the humor, I daresay!"

He kept up a steady patter, remarking on the river, the wretched
settlers' huts he'd seen, the sorry horseflesh he'd found in St. Louis
and elsewhere, the hospitable Irish sisters near St. Charles who
had offered to let him sleep in their bed—*with them*, the lawless
scalawags who had made fun of his European clothes and firearm
and challenged him to a shooting match. (He had pretended to
be a greenhorn and stunned them with his skill.) He chattered
about the unpredictable river, numberless plant and animal species
that were new to him, geography, climate, and the weather.

Paul even discoursed on various Indian dialects and their ori-
gins. All the while, he trained his keen gaze on the passing scene.
Occasionally, he posed a question to Baptiste, who answered, but
Paul already had a scientist's knowledge of the region. The duke
clearly liked Baptiste and was favoring him with his most candid
thoughts. His mind was a hive of curiosity and information.
Baptiste realized how starved he had been for companionship.
And what a stimulating companion this fellow was!

After a while, the duke took out a pocket notebook and began
to write and sketch in it. When Baptiste said they were nearing
their destination, Paul closed the book with a look of satisfaction
and gave him another hearty clap on the back. "Well done, my
friend!" he said. "Now I'm starved. Can Mrs. Woods cook?"

MRS. WOODS WAS delighted to see them and served up a
porcupine stew, hog jerky, and corn bread, which the duke made
a show of praising. Having never been cajoled with honeyed

phrases, she made a flustered exit, bowing and backing into the doorframe.

"I wish I could offer you finer fare," Baptiste said when she had gone.

"Oh, well, fine fare is decidedly the exception in the new world, except in New Orleans. Poor Schlape is disgusted by the American diet." He wiped his mouth with his neck scarf and pushed his chair back. "Tomorrow, let's go hunting!"

Before dawn, Baptiste took their shrunken buckskin trousers outside and tied their bottoms to the side of the cabin. Then he pulled as hard as he could, until the legs were again their proper length. He went back inside, smiling to himself. The duke would be pleased!

"Excellent!" Paul cried, drawing on his pants.

Baptiste organized a party consisting of himself, the duke, and a pair of hunters employed by the post. They rode in a single line along the sheer, sandy bluffs of the Kansas. Where these leveled off, a sandbar ran into the water, opposite wooded hills, which Paul paused to admire for their loveliness. Baptiste was struck by how often his visitor saw beauty in the landscape. He'd never heard anyone else remark on it. Most men assessed the terrain as treacherous, hospitable, navigable, full of game, empty of game, and so on, but never as beautiful. He had kept his own admiration to himself.

"Look at that tanager," Paul exclaimed. "Surely the most exquisite of North American birds. Our German birds are quite plain."

"We have many brilliantly plumed creatures," Baptiste said. "When you see the parrots of the region, you can decide which you prefer."

After sunset, the temperature fell and they passed a comfortable night unmolested by mosquitoes. But at daybreak, a south wind brought swarm after swarm of them. A brisk walk along the shore was tolerable, but when the men entered the woods, the buzzing was so loud and the air was so thick they could see only a dozen paces in front of them. "We won't get any whitetail at this rate," Baptiste remarked. "They have the sense to stay hidden."

Duke Paul, batting at his ears, nodded grimly. One of the hunters cupped his hands around his mouth and made the mewling sound of a fawn calling its mother. Paul leaned toward Baptiste. "Hunters in Germany also call deer," he said in an undertone. "It is extremely unsporting." Baptiste was thankful that he hadn't performed this trick for the duke.

The hunter went on mewling, hoping to attract a doe that would be an easy target. Suddenly, a huge black bear crashed out of a thicket. Expecting to find a tasty fawn, it advanced on the hunter, who froze in terror. Baptiste instantly fired his gun. The ball struck the bear in the head, stunning it. A second shot killed the huge beast. The hunter exhaled, looked at Baptiste, and laughed with maniacal relief. Paul raised his eyebrows. "You are quick, Baptiste. It is an invaluable trait. Often the difference between life and death."

"Indians disdain the meat. It can be tasty enough. See what you think," Baptiste said casually. Inwardly, he was very pleased with himself. He had wanted to impress the duke and had succeeded, thanks to the unfortunate bear.

They spent a few hours butchering it and carried some steaks back to the sandbar. Baptiste noticed several holes filled with large turkey eggs and collected a few of them to complete their meal.

He volunteered to do the cooking and they enjoyed a delicious supper. The hunters huddled by themselves with scarcely a glance in Paul's direction.

Paul and Baptiste conversed in English. The duke said he planned to continue up the Missouri to Fort Atkinson and then on to the Yellowstone, gathering plant and animal specimens and visiting various tribes. This was his first foray into North America, a paradise for an intrepid European scientist like himself. He would return to Germany in the fall, but planned future trips to the New World. There was so much to see and to catalog! He was modeling his career on that of his idol, Alexander von Humboldt. "His heroic efforts to chart the unity in nature's diversity are my great inspiration," he said. " 'All forces of nature are interlaced and interwoven,' Humboldt said. 'Everything is interaction and reciprocal.' He understands that when avarice leads men to try to conquer nature, the result is catastrophe. Cutting down forests, irrigating deserts, importing alien species, all disrupt nature's order."

Baptiste said, "I have read his book. He has made me want to see South America."

Paul gave him a wry look. "Perhaps you shall," he said. "For my part, I am keen to see the Sioux, Oto, and Pawnee Nations."

"The tribes of the upper Missouri may preserve their customs, I suppose," Baptiste said. "Those who live and trade closer to St. Louis are losing them. But city living doesn't offer anything to sustain them."

"Americans misunderstand Indians. Mr. Jefferson paid his compliments to their dignity, but he too saw just one standard of 'civilization.' The Indians have their own and it is different."

Baptiste said, "Almost no one here understands that. Americans see only people with what they consider primitive customs and are determined to move them out of their way."

The duke gave Baptiste an appraising look. "I notice that you speak of Americans, as if you were not one."

Baptiste thought for a moment. "I grew up in St. Louis, among Spaniards, French, Germans, Osage, Delaware, Sioux, Shawnee, Kickapoo, Patawatomi, mixed bloods like me—and whites. There was much intermingling, to the benefit of all. The Anglo-Saxons were the minority, but their numbers are increasing. They call themselves Americans and claim god-given rights and privileges. Progress itself is Anglo-Saxon, they say."

Paul laughed. "That sounds like the place I come from, minus the progress. Surely, Americans are building a future for all men to prosper if they try."

Baptiste thought of Jim. In the old fur business, the Chouteaus and Lisa were the ones who got rich. Ashley was supposedly changing things so that the workers prospered. Maybe Jim was making his fortune already! He made up his mind to find out, the next time he went to St. Louis, how he could join them.

At dusk, great numbers of deer and turkeys emerged from the forest to cool off by the river. "What a splendid sight," Paul remarked companionably. The hunters picked up their rifles, but Paul waved them away. "We have had our hunt. Leave these wild creatures in peace."

But soon the idyll was banished by darkness. This time, mosquitoes hounded them all night. "They are unendurable," Paul exclaimed. "Let us retreat to the post." If Herr Schlape and his boat had arrived, he said, they would continue up the Missouri without delay. He could forsake this place; there were so many others he intended to explore.

The craft was waiting for them. Schlape was upbraiding several men who were indifferently moving provisions from the store. Baptiste pitched in to help. Duke Paul was wonderful company, unpredictable, intelligent, and clearly a man of character. Paul didn't hide his noble origins. And yet they posed no barrier to friendship. He had brightened Baptiste's dreary existence, but now their acquaintance would be cut short.

When all was ready for their departure, Duke Paul beckoned to him. Baptiste steeled himself for a last farewell.

"I have a proposition for you, my friend," Paul said. "You needn't decide the matter now. But give it your best thought while I am gone." Baptiste held his breath. "I want you to come with me to Germany in a few months' time." Paul paused, grinning, to let the surprising idea sink in.

Baptiste was stunned. "I am honored," he said. "I don't know . . ."

Paul said, "When you have considered it well, you will see its great virtues. Your education will be further extended. For me, the advantage is in your company. You will make an ideal hunting companion. I will have your fresh point of view on the Old World. But truly, Baptiste, we will have a wonderful time!"

What had he heard of Germany? There were a few Germans in St. Louis, hearty fellows, hardworking, if rather grim. The duke, in contrast, was exuberant, extravagant in his enthusiasms and warm in his affections. Baptiste tried to conjure scenes of Europe. He had little to go by, but Candide had lived in a German castle for a while. . . .

"I will think very hard on it," he said carefully. Was this going to be his version of Lucretius's swerve? If he accepted, it would carry him far off any course he'd ever imagined for himself.

"I look forward to your 'yes,' Baptiste," Paul said. He turned with a salute and bounded onto his boat. The crew threw their backs into poling the loaded vessel against the river's onerous currents. The sky had darkened; a thunderstorm was near. They were in for quite a trip, Baptiste thought.

The next day, a boatman arrived in the wake of the storm. He had seen Paul's party in passing and given them distressing news: "The 'Ricas attacked William Ashley's men! At least a dozen died!"

Baptiste cried "Jim!" aloud. Had his friend been killed or wounded? The man didn't know the names of any of the fallen.

"Ashley bought nineteen horses from the 'Ricas and went to his camp, intending to leave in the morning. Sometime after midnight, there was a wild outcry. Seems a couple of Ashley's trappers had slipped into the Indian village looking for women. One of them was caught. The Indians gouged out his eyes before cutting off his head. At dawn, 'Ricas started shooting at the Ashley camp. Killed scores of men and wounded more."

"You heard nothing at all of Jim Bridger?" Baptiste asked again.

"I seen quite a few men drifting down the river in canoes. Casks of whiskey got loose when their keelboats capsized in the battle. Most of the men were drunk as skunks. I didn't know any of them."

Baptiste thought, *That wouldn't be Jim. Maybe he had escaped, then.*

"Did the duke's party turn back?" he asked.

"Hell, no! That man has no fear! He is heading right on into the 'Rica village to say howdy!"

Paul's bravado had charmed Baptiste. But now it seemed absurdly foolhardy. Maybe there would be no trip to Germany after all. If Paul was so headstrong, he wasn't likely to survive his journey. And Jim? His best friend in the world! Funny, mild, good-natured, hardworking Jim . . . There would be no joining the Ashley enterprise either. Baptiste spent the following weeks anxiously bargaining with the spirits for Jim's safety.

A month later, Mr. Curtis returned from Fort Atkinson, where he had seen many of the wounded from Ashley's crew. Baptiste confronted him before he was off the boat.

"Did you see Jim Bridger, then?"

"I don't believe I did. But I wasn't taken to meet each man. They were poleaxed, all of them. Ben O'Fallon chewed them out good for leaving the Arikara to mangle fourteen of their comrades. They meekly took it."

Baptiste shuddered.

"O'Fallon wants vengeance, calls the Arikara attack 'the most shocking outrage ever witnessed by civilized men,'" Curtis went on. "Talk like that is going to bring us a war."

"They were provoked by those men who invaded their village," Baptiste said. Curtis waggled his eyebrows in disgusted agreement.

Soon afterward, a messenger carrying letters to Clark in St. Louis stopped at the post to say that the Indian war had already commenced. US Army Colonel Leavenworth had taken the Sixth Infantry Regiment and two cannon out of Fort Atkinson to retaliate against the Arikara village. A number of trappers and Sioux fighters hostile to the Arikara had joined them.

"Leavenworth ought to be court-martialed," Curtis said.

Baptiste was chilled. "I wanted to sign on with Colonel Ashley," he said. "General Clark wouldn't let me."

"Well, he showed some care for your hide, son," Curtis replied. "But Clark granted Ashley a license. He surely knew they intended to trap, not to trade. Trade in pelts is all the 'Ricas have to live on. They are going to stay angry a long time. Firing cannon at them won't help. From now on, trappers will have to go far away from the river, into the mountains. It will be a lonesome and dangerous enterprise."

Terrible events were altering Baptiste's prospects, along with those of the fur business. There was nothing he could do about any of them.

CHAPTER TWELVE

With Duke Paul

Clark's nephew Ben O'Fallon himself stopped at the post with an entourage of militia officers on their way back to St. Louis. With his lip curled in disgust, he reported that Colonel Leavenworth had launched his assault on the Arikara village, then promptly called a cease-fire so that he could negotiate a truce. The remaining Arikara had fled.

"Leavenworth acted the coward, in the name of the United States." His eye fell on Baptiste, who was waiting for a private moment to ask about Jim. "He dispatched your old pa with a note inviting them to come back to their village in peace," Ben went on contemptuously.

Toussaint. Baptiste was startled to hear of him. But of course the old man was always upriver, shuttling between the tribes, just beyond Baptiste's awareness.

"What about Ashley's men? Did you see anything of Jim Bridger?" he asked.

"I don't recall the name," said O'Fallon vaguely.

"And Duke Paul?"

"Oh, we couldn't miss *him*," O'Fallon said. "He went all the way to Fort Recovery. The duke insisted on continuing to the Mandan Villages, but he was ordered to turn back or face certain

death. He was angry as tarnation. The man is wanton and abso-
lutely fearless."

Curtis and Woods put the trading post on high alert, fearing that
the Arikara might inspire other tribes to launch attacks. They grumbled that Ashley had jeopardized the entire fur business with his plan
to trap, rather than trade with Indians for their pelts. The Indians
were likely to take their business to the British company instead.

"The best we can do is hunker down," said Woods. "War is in
the air."

In the meantime, what had happened to Paul? Baptiste did not
consider himself superstitious. But one thought crowded everything else out of his mind: If he decided yes to Europe, would that
doom the duke?

FINALLY, IN OCTOBER, a new boat bound from Fort
Atkinson for St. Louis tied up at the dock. And there was Duke Paul,
the first to disembark, fairly charging down the gangplank with a
broad grin. He signaled to Baptiste to stand by while formalities
were observed. After conferring for a few minutes with Mr. Woods,
he took Baptiste aside and delivered a brisk account of himself.

"I have had interesting encounters, my friend. I could not
ascend to the Mandan, and so did not see where you were born.
But I met your father. He was sent to fetch me to the factory at
Grand Detour. I gave him my news of you."

"I haven't seen him for years," Baptiste said, still feeling shaken,
but incredibly relieved.

"He presumed that your life in St. Louis has made you 'soft.'
I explained to him that soft and refined are two very different
qualities."

"No one would call him either," Baptiste replied.

Paul laughed. "Indeed! The old goat had recently taken an Assiniboine bride of fourteen years. The hunters at the fort gave him a splendid chariveree, drums, pans, kettles, and guns firing. In return, Toussaint gave a feast and glasses of grog to all the men. Then he went to bed with his young wife, vowing to do his best."

Suddenly, Baptiste wondered if he had half brothers and sisters in the wilderness—neglected relations he didn't want. How was it he had never considered that possibility before? Paul was looking at him questioningly. "I have upset you," he said quietly.

Baptiste composed himself. "No, you haven't. We heard that you were warned to turn back after the Arikara attack. But we heard nothing of your whereabouts afterward." Paul's pride would be hurt if he said he'd been worried about him.

"I spent several profitable weeks among the Omaha, Oto, various Sioux and Pawnee," Paul said heartily. "They all welcomed me. Colonel Leavenworth has been wrongly criticized for calling off his attack on the Arikara. Benjamin O'Fallon urged a bloodbath, but it would have been an act of madness to risk so many lives. Leavenworth was sure to be repulsed and his wounded troops cruelly treated by the Arikara. American fur trade is suspended because of this incident. You will be frittering your time away if you stay here." Paul looked intently into Baptiste's eyes. "Will you come with me to Germany, Baptiste?"

Why not?

"Yes!" he heard himself say. "I gratefully accept your invitation. If I see more of the world, I will be better able to find my proper place in it."

"Well put. I agree!" Paul exclaimed.

"My mother undertook that long journey to the Pacific. It is my turn to cross the Atlantic."

"Bravo! We'll start as soon as the fog lifts. The autumnal storms are expected and much of the prairie is already on fire. At night, the spectacle defies description. But smoke is thick everywhere. The trip will be dangerous and we must not delay."

Some enterprising Kansa Indians sold Paul a large black bear they had killed. "I thought our bear tasted like the best wild boar," Paul said. "Due to the creature's vegetable diet." He also collected persimmons to add to a store he'd been keeping. "I believe these will grow in southern Germany," he said. "They are delicious."

As they descended the river toward St. Louis, Paul described his experiences along the northern Missouri. He had spent several weeks with the Sioux. One of their chiefs had swum across a river to declare his loyalty to the United States. Paul had seen brave warriors nursing their wounds after the Arikara battles. He had galloped against the wind through a prairie fire and been served a nauseating meal of dog meat, cooked in a filthy pot by a woman with grimy fingers. (Paul was open to any experience, Baptiste thought, but very fastidious.) He had met Pawnee covered entirely with tattoos. "And look at this," he crowed, pulling a scalp with luxurious long hair from his satchel and shaking it. "A gift for my collection."

Baptiste recoiled, in spite of himself. Whose was it? "You were welcomed everywhere?" he asked.

"Usually, yes. I was made welcome and even received their confidences." He recalled a Sioux chief who told him privately that he deeply regretted signing treaties with General Clark. "He was visibly moved. His eyes welled with tears."

"I have seen the same profound sadness," Baptiste said.

"Yet he had no choice," Paul added. "And all parties, whites and Indians alike, are at the mercy of quarrelsome and drunken interpreters who try to trick them out of goods and animals. I have had to deal with that sort at every turn. Unfortunately, the fur companies must rely on these depraved individuals to conduct their negotiations." Baptiste's face must have betrayed his discomfort. "You have escaped depravity, my friend," Paul hastened to add.

Paul opened his notebook and began to write. Baptiste was left with the fear that had it not been for his education, Paul might never have chosen him.

But he *had*, and now they were embarked on a great adventure!

THE TRAVELERS WERE low on provisions, so they laid by at the first sizable settlement, called Blufftown. Paul called at several houses to interview its citizens. Baptiste marveled at the duke's impersonation of a common man as he chatted with worshippers freshly returned from a camp meeting. Back on the boat, Paul had much to say about the proliferation of religious sects in the New World.

"This is a wide-open society, every man in business for himself. Even the religious faiths compete for customers in the open market! It is because the government takes no role in religion. I have long meant to ask you, Baptiste, what faith you profess."

Baptiste hesitated. He hadn't thought about the subject since he rejected Bishop DuBourg's offer. "I guess I am a pantheist, like Mr. Jefferson," he said, trying out the idea. "I put my faith in nature. The world's superstitions have caused so much war and suffering."

Paul laughed. "Indeed! We are fortunate men, to be alive during the flowering of the scientific age, Baptiste."

The trees were turning their fall colors. "Exceedingly picturesque," Paul called them. The river was low, exposing a number of
small islands with large flocks of white geese and pelicans preparing to migrate, resembling, from a distance, drifts of snow.

Hard winds had begun to blow, buffeting and slowing their
craft. Paul was anxious to reach St. Louis in time to catch a steamship for New Orleans. He ordered the captain to tie up so that
their party could disembark and continue their journey by wagon.
Baptiste reflected that no one he knew was so concerned with
timeliness—or was able to command instant obedience from
people the way Paul habitually did. The duke was frustrated when
they weren't able to cross an ice-clogged river on a horse boat.
He didn't spare the pilot his fury.

The delay meant they had only a few hours to spare in
St. Louis. Baptiste had intended to offer his resignation to Cadet
Chouteau in person. There was time only to call on General Clark.
He was eager to see the expression on the man's face when he
delivered his news. He and Paul went together to the office.

Clark received them warmly. Baptiste quickly made his speech.

"Sir, Duke Paul has invited me to accompany him to Germany.
I am here to ask for your blessing."

Clark extended his hand. "You have it, my boy! This is an
enterprise worthy of your gifts and your intelligence. And a
chance to emulate your mother's wide travel." He smiled. "She
had the fortitude to meet any challenge. Seeing Europe firsthand
will enlarge your understanding—and so will seeing America
from afar."

"Baptiste is every bit as charming and bright as you predicted," Paul added. Baptiste was startled. Had they conspired to send him on this journey, he wondered. Paul smiled and said, "Of course, I had to see for myself what sort of companion you would make."

"You will have much to tell me when I see you next," Clark said as they parted.

THE STEAMSHIP THEY boarded was named *Mandan*. Baptiste smiled to himself at the coincidence. Paul's mountains of baggage were overseen by Schlape. The valet spoke only German, so Baptiste communicated with him with gestures and grimaces. Paul was very amused, but Schlape could never be induced even to smile.

As the boat pushed off, Baptiste let his eyes wander over the city spread out before them. How different it was from when he'd first glimpsed it, thirteen years earlier. What he had seen with the eyes of a small boy had spread and multiplied, become far more complex, even as it became familiar. He couldn't count the houses and factories that had not been there then. And how different he was! He felt proud of himself. He had learned so much and now he was ready for whatever lay ahead. He trusted Paul—and that trust was a feature of his own hard-won self-confidence.

"Good-bye, St. Louis, crucible of my self," he said softly.

FARTHER DOWN THE river, Baptiste saw his first palm trees, yuccas, Spanish moss, cotton fields, and sugar cane. Slaves on the levees paused to follow the boat with their eyes.

Watching them, Paul grimaced and said, "Slavery weakens the republic and makes it vulnerable to its enemies. You may not realize it here in Louisiana Territory, but Spain, Britain, and France are all eager to increase their hold on this continent. They will exploit weaknesses."

"They claim here that commerce depends on slavery," Baptiste said.

"That is the shortsighted view. But the practice offers no incentive to the whites to work. If the United States are to be strong in the long run, mutual hatred between the races must end. The history of all ages and nations offers ample proof that the solution is intermarriage. In time, it will lead to peace between the races."

Baptiste had never heard that opinion expressed, not even by Reverend Peck. It was shocking. But Paul had a way of stating his ideas that precluded debate.

"I suppose you may be right," Baptiste said. "I believe that General Clark is cruel to his slaves because he sees them as less than human. They have complained to me about it."

"There was an excellent black man on your famous expedition," Paul said. "I believe he was the general's childhood companion. What has become of him?"

"I was told that York was sent away in disgrace because he asked permission to live with his wife."

Paul emitted a snort of disapproval. "It pains me to hear it," he said. "But once the races are more widely intermingled, an equality of humanity will be acknowledged by everyone. Alexander von Humboldt has said it very well: 'All of the human species are in like degree designed for freedom.'"

Paul brought an open mind to everything he saw. Now that Baptiste was on his way to Europe, he must do the same!

✽   ✽   ✽

IN NEW ORLEANS, the duke arranged to have his collection of birds, animals, and plants packed for shipment to Württemberg. As they hustled through the crowded streets, Baptiste gaped at the houses with their curlicue iron balconies, the colorful crowds, stands selling exotic fruits and vegetables, and especially the stylish people of color. The streets contained a great variety of people—even more than in St. Louis. Paul noted with amusement that women often stared brazenly at Baptiste. At first, he lowered his eyes in embarrassment. But he soon found that it was very amusing to stare boldly back, which elicited even saucier looks from them.

Paul led him to a tailor's shop. Over the course of an afternoon, Baptiste was measured and fitted for a suit of such sumptuous fabric that he complained, at first, that he would be too constrained by it to conduct himself normally.

"Nonsense, my friend," Paul said. "We are merely aligning the quality of your outside with that of your inside."

Within a few hours of donning his new silken breeches, quilted vest, silk shirt, and blue jacket, Baptiste was carrying himself with more élan. A fine garment was not a disguise—one rose to its character!

One afternoon, Paul went into a shop and emerged with a small leather-bound book, which he presented to Baptiste. "You will want to keep a history of so momentous a journey," he said. Baptiste, having watched Paul write down everything he saw, was seized by a powerful feeling of insufficiency. Observing was one thing; committing thoughts to paper was quite another.

"Don't worry—it's not to be read by anyone else," Paul said, his eyes twinkling. "The first marks you make on the page will be the hardest."

"Thank you." Baptiste carefully fingered the crisp, blank pages. The leather cover was supple in his hand. He would begin the record of his life that evening.

A notice in the newspaper announced the imminent departure for France of the brig *Smyrna*. Paul booked passage and they departed on December 24, 1823. The duke and Baptiste shared a passenger cabin, and Schlape bunked with the other servants. Paul's patience was soon tested. They drifted for days on the motionless Mississippi, helpless prey to mosquitoes. Baptiste was startled when he looked over the side one day and spotted the impertinent heads of several alligators poking out of the mud. At once, marksmen went to work killing them. One wounded creature was hauled on board and put into a spare cask. Its captor tended it for the rest of the voyage. Baptiste kept watch over it too.

We are two curiosities taken out of our natural habitat and across the ocean to Europe, he wrote in his book, adding a sketch of the creature, then a self-portrait. Keeping a journal was easier than he had thought. He had only to keep his eyes open and describe the sights!

FINALLY, THEY WERE towed to the mouth of the Mississippi and put out to sea. Navigating the competing currents of fresh and sea waters proved difficult. As the duke watched the coast gradually vanish, he turned to Baptiste. "We are leaving a promising nation behind," he said soberly, "a noble enterprise. I only hope that the ideals of Franklin and Hamilton are honored by their successors—the rule of law, freedom of trade, and a peaceful and honest policy toward the rest of the world. They were wise men!"

To Baptiste, those men and their ideals felt distant, pulled out of a book. "I read about the founders in school and General Clark

is well acquainted with Mr. Jefferson. But it didn't make me feel
that I am an American."

"And you are the protégé of General Clark, are you not?"

Baptiste said, "He altered the course of my life. I owe that to
him, not to his country."

"I imagine you are preparing your mind for Europe," Paul
said, smiling. "You are separating yourself from your past."

"Perhaps."

They were now on open water. Paul was silent for a few minutes, gazing at the horizon. Then he said, "You will be able to
choose where you belong. The world is becoming more and more
fluid. But to my mind, you could not choose more wisely than to
come back here. If this bold experiment succeeds, it may lead all
other nations to follow suit."

Baptiste wasn't so sure. The United States was a country bent
on getting rich. Political power belonged to the elite, which had
become Anglo-Saxon during his years in St. Louis. He would
never be part of it. Paul was giving him the second great opportunity of his life by taking him to Europe. He felt buoyant. Destiny
beckoned.

The weather was fine and the waves of the Gulf were like
mirrors. The first sunset turned the sky a brilliant scarlet.
Dorados, bonitas, dolphins, and flying fish skittered and leapt and
gamboled on all sides. Gannets and gulls soared overhead. Paul
particularly admired a frigate bird, which he expertly shot and
stuffed for his collection.

They dined with the captain, a sturdy, bearded Dutchman, his
grinning Cypriot mate, and the four other passengers. Everyone,
even the jolly captain, deferred to Paul because of his noble rank,

and the conversation was his to direct. Paul began by making introductions all around.

"Mr. Jean Baptiste Charbonneau," he said, gesturing grandly, "my companion on the Missouri, hunter extraordinaire. He was born among the Mandan, the son of the Shoshone woman who guided Lewis and Clark. He was educated in St. Louis." He added wryly, "I offer his impressive history because I know how modest he is and how reluctant to trumpet his own virtues." Everyone smiled and examined Baptiste with interest. The other passengers were a pair of New Orleans bons vivants with commercial ventures in Europe, and two garrulous sisters going to visit relatives in France.

One of the ladies asked Baptiste about his mother and expelled a little gasp of dismay upon learning that she had died "so young!" The businessmen had not been north of New Orleans and had many questions for Paul about what he had seen. He obliged with encyclopedic descriptions of plant, animal, and aboriginal life along the Missouri.

The captain cleared his throat and asked, "Did you find the yellow fever anywhere on your travels?"

Paul said yes, he had. "In Cuba. Mr. de Lilly has an excellent method for treating his patients. It differs greatly from the routine employed in most American cities, which leads to certain death."

"Gracious!" cried one of the ladies, her hand clutching delicately at her throat. "What is that routine?"

"Excessive amounts of mercury are prescribed," said Paul. "Indeed, it is recommended for nearly every complaint, the lamentable consequence being a poisoning of the system, or at the least, the loss of some teeth."

Baptiste remembered reading of jalap in the journals of Lewis and Clark. "I was sick and nearly died on the journey to the Pacific," he said. "My mother was as well. The captains must have given us jalap and calomel—it contains mercury, I think."

"It does, indeed. The favorite prescription of Dr. Rush," Paul declared. Baptiste smiled. The duke might well pass as a physician himself! The breadth and depth of his knowledge seemed boundless.

The mate spoke up then. He had sailed on a Spanish ship and met neither with yellow fever nor with scurvy.

"It is true," Paul confirmed. "The Spanish and the English impose rigid discipline and give their men excellent nourishment. I might add that their hospitals are models of cleanliness and orderliness too. This cannot be said of the Dutch." He flashed a look at the captain.

"I profited from Dr. Saugrain's vaccination," Baptiste said, and was rewarded with a ring of expectant expressions. He told them about being pricked and falling ill, along with the other boys.

I am going to see the world too, he thought. *Soon, I will know the kinds of things that Paul knows.*

AFTER THREE WEEKS of balmy days and calm nights, Baptiste endured a time that he would remember with horror for the rest of his life.

The skies turned black and the sea erupted in fretful swells that soared to huge heights and rolled the ship violently from side to side. Parts of the railing were shattered by the force of the water. Barrels and other gear flew overboard. The thermometer plummeted to below zero. Baptiste lay retching and moaning on the floor of the cabin. The duke looked in from time to time to deliver enthusiastic reports on the latitude and longitude points of their position. The cause of Baptiste's acute suffering, he averred, were the effects of the Bank of Newfoundland on the wild ocean. It was not surprising that a man born in the middle of a large continent was susceptible to seasickness.

That was no comfort! Baptiste lost all sense of time. He barely heard Paul tell him that lightning and thunder mixed with snow and hail were pummeling the little brig. The captain and crew were barely in control of it. Water poured under the cabin door and the unearthly noise of the creaking masts and the whistling rigging pierced his brain. Paul shouted over the racket that he thought the storm was finally abating. But after he left, it seemed to intensify. Days passed. Paul brought him some broth to sip but he couldn't keep it down.

Finally, the winds withdrew, nearly as suddenly as they had arisen, leaving the brig enshrouded in dense fog. "We are nearing the Channel," Paul said. He consulted his notebook to verify the latitude. Baptiste had put his own book in a cupboard to protect it from the reeking flood. He hadn't been able to write a single word.

They entered the English Channel in fair weather and Baptiste ventured warily to the deck. Paul pointed to the high rocky coast of France, and to his surprise, Baptiste's heart lifted. He was relieved to find that emotion hadn't been beaten out of him by the voyage. A pilot arrived to guide them into Havre de Grace.

With sublime relief, Baptiste staggered down the gangplank and felt solid ground at last. For a moment, he wobbled. Steadying himself against the harbor pilot's cabin, he silently called on his

Charbonneau forebears to bless his arrival in France. Then he added the Chouteau and Berthold ancestors and, for good measure, the great Lafayette, who, he remembered, was expected shortly in America to receive its thanks for his part in the War of Independence.

CHAPTER THIRTEEN

In the Old World

Baptiste had never ridden in a coach. Clark and his family traveled all the way to Washington in theirs. Now, crossing France, he discovered how uncomfortable such a journey was. He and Paul were squeezed into springless boxes that heaved, bounced, rattled, groaned, tilted, and shuddered almost without respite. Many of their fellow passengers chattered incessantly over the racket; others blew their noses on their sleeves, coughed, snored, ate portable meals that spattered on their neighbors' overcoats, and loudly complained, which elicited only insults from the coachmen.

Baptiste was newly conscious of his own appearance; he was the stranger, the one with darker skin. He glanced warily at his fellow passengers, but surprisingly, only one or two seemed wary of him. There was no shortage of people who resembled him in St. Louis. Here, he was unique. He would have to see what that meant.

Women passengers sat with their enormous hats on their laps. The men kept their beaver hats on their heads. The first time he saw one, Baptiste leaned closer and said, "Your hat once lived in Louisiana." The man looked started.

"You Americans don't wait for introductions," he sniffed.

Baptiste laughed. Back home, he was métis. As a consequence of leaving the United States, he had become an American!

"You may be surprised to learn that although I am from there, sir," he said, "I have never held a beaver hat."

The man took off the hat and handed it to Baptiste. The fine fur was luxuriously soft. The great vogue for such hats in Europe underpinned the economy of St. Louis. The fortunes of the Chouteaus, Manuel Lisa, and William Clark depended on beavers. Remarkable to think of it!

"Thank you," he said, returning the hat to its owner.

Every ten miles or so, they stopped to water and rest the animals. The innkeepers anticipated Paul's arrival; elaborate meals had already been prepared for him. A clutch of travelers who were denied service until the royal guest had eaten his fill stood humbly by. Such a group of Americans would have been bitterly complaining, even storming the dining room, Baptiste thought. After dinner, Paul was given a bed of his own, but Baptiste shared a straw "tick" with a sweaty, snoring stranger.

Everywhere they went, the people were white-skinned. How odd it was, after the vari-colored palette of St. Louis! And the distinction between servants and laborers and their betters was marked. Back home, it was often hard to tell them apart, and a boatman or a voyageur would never grovel before an official.

The pace of the coach was too slow for the always impatient Paul. After a few days, he hired horses for Baptiste and himself, which resulted in their having repeatedly to wait, after they'd sped over the landscape, for the coach and their luggage to catch up to them at their nightly destination. But it was glorious to fly along on a good horse.

One night, he reached into his satchel and his fingers touched the journal Paul had given him. He had neglected it for too long!

This countryside differs greatly from the one I know. The vistas lack the stark grandeur and severity of Missouri but are lushly beautiful in an intimate way. Everything has been shaped, cultivated, and lovingly tended for centuries. Even the lowliest peasant's cottage is cared for and embellished, quite unlike the slipshod shacks that have been thrown up along our rivers and their tributaries. Centuries of human ingenuity and artistry have been at work here. The Hand of Man is everywhere evident.

BAPTISTE AND PAUL cantered through quaint villages of half-timbered houses, onion spires, great cathedrals, meandering rivers, cliffs and ravines, ancient forests, sleeping farmland and vineyards, crystal lakes, mountains, crumbling hilltop fortresses, cloisters, and ruined castles.

Europe still bears the scars of Napoleon's conquests. He waged a total war. Ordinary citizens were forced to fight and their families suffered along with the armies. We pass impoverished parents and children standing woefully by their cottages, hoping for . . . what? Paul's grandfather permitted Bonaparte to march across Württemberg and received a king's crown in return. Half of Germany cringed before the Little Emperor and the other half was crushed by his armies. In his wake, the Old Monarchies have reestablished themselves.

Napoleon had a name for Paul's grandfather: "The Great Belly," and said of him, "God created him to see how far the human skin could be stretched without breaking." He was seven feet tall and weighed more than four hundred pounds.

So Paul informs me.

At long last, near Ludwigsburg, a pale edifice gradually rose above the horizon, its splendor dazzling in the brilliant sunlight. Baptiste stared at it in awe. Seeing this, Paul was quick to offer a corrective: "My ancestor Carl Eugen exhibited even greater hubris than my grandfather did," he drawled. "Carl's motto was *I am the*

Fatherland. He set out to create a second Versailles—and there you see it. Taxes were collected at gunpoint to pay for his bloated and decadent amusements. It is still a gilded cage. I invited you here to help me escape its constraints. We will seize some liberty for ourselves, you and I."

BUT THAT DIDN'T happen for some time. Life in the palace was both regimented and stunningly boring. Everything happened according to schedule, but everyone waited endlessly for things to happen. Nothing could be done, it seemed, until the king wanted it done.

Baptiste's window looked over a vast garden planted in flat geometric beds, bordered by hedges whimsically trimmed in the shapes of exotic animals. Farther still lay more garden beds, meadows, and dense groves.

He had to climb a stepladder to get into his canopy bed, whose cool, slippery sheets were startling to his skin, and slipped beneath billowing comforters like ocean waves, next to fat, faintly fragrant pillows. Baptiste stretched and lolled, a pampered cat.

Then there were the clothes. Paul put away his buckskins, and Schlape resumed his duties as personal valet, dressing his master in military regalia. Baptiste was given the prince's livery, which, to his surprise, was red, white, and blue, but with enough gold embroidery to mark it as regal. What did this mean? Until now, he had traveled as Paul's companion; they'd been almost on equal footing.

"Why have you outfitted me as a servant?" he asked, hearing petulance in his tone. But he was bothered, and with reason.

"You know, we both have to make concessions here in the palace," Paul said carelessly. "Think nothing of it. A mere accommodation to custom that cannot be changed. By the way, I want you to wear your American leather when you are presented to the king."

ON THAT OCCASION, Baptiste stood with his back stiff, his eyes on the middle distance, his expression neutral, while Paul introduced him:

"Sire, I give you my young American friend Jean Baptiste Charbonneau, hunter extraordinaire. As an infant, he crossed the North American continent and afterward was educated in St. Louis by order of General Sir William Clark. He will welcome all questions you have about the New World." Baptiste suppressed a smile.

Applause from the courtiers echoed hollowly. The king, who was wearing a civilian tailcoat, acknowledged his exotic guest by almost imperceptibly tipping his head. He had no immediate questions.

"His lack of curiosity always stuns me," Paul muttered. "It foretells an imminent decline for the monarchy." Baptiste was relieved to have been let off so easily.

He was marched down gilded corridors on floors gleaming like gemstones, past rows and rows of statues. Whole rooms were made of marble. Chandeliers sparkled, towering curtains parted to reveal vast parkland, sculpted greenery, endless extensions of the building, or a parade ground.

Paul was always surrounded by attendants and Baptiste also had an escort. For a long time he hardly said a word to the man, who, because everything was unfamiliar, reversed custom and walked ahead of Baptiste as a guide. Trailing the self-important fellow, Baptiste strutted and pranced in imitation and was occasionally caught doing it by some shocked courtier. Neither he nor Paul was ever left alone, except to sleep. Even then, his minder was posted just outside his door.

Women in brilliantly colored gowns, with high, cinched waists and puffed sleeves, their hair adorned with feathers, jewels, stuffed birds, and flowers and twinkling jewels, stared at him with open curiosity. He joined scores of diners at a table of almost comical length. A staggering amount of food was ladled onto his plate by a relay of waiters, beginning with soup, continuing with spiced meat pies, roasts, jellies, cakes. He easily identified the little charred bodies of songbirds and the larger joints of cow or mutton or venison. But much else was slathered in unfamiliar sauces. Women on his right and left pestered him for conversation.

"Do you find Germany to your taste, monsieur?"

After replying politely that he did, and finding that she seemed to expect more from him, he held up a forkful of meat and asked, "Is this a traditional dish, madame?" Madame warmed to the question, gave his arm a squeeze, and repeated it to her other neighbor. "I suppose it is, young man. For as long as anyone remembers."

The woman on his other side was complaining about the blinding gas lamps that were proliferating in German cities. And what of the high rate of road accidents due to speeding carriages. The plump faces around him, glowing in the candlelight, looked briefly concerned. A man called across the table that, indeed, life was accelerating even as the times cried out for deliberate, thoughtful solutions to the rising plethora of problems presented by modern life.

Baptiste remembered the words of a wise Osage chief who spoke of the white man's warm houses, gardens, and machines. "White man possesses the power of subduing almost every animal that he uses. He is served by slaves. Everything around him is in chains." He had paused, then added, "And so he is in chains himself."

The Indian tribes had been free of material desires, and from what the Anglo-Saxons called Progress.

AFTER DINNER, THE men retired to a book-lined room to smoke or take snuff. Figurines of horses and growling lions, stags, bears, and boars perched on every surface. Baptiste joined a group of youths wearing white shirts that billowed from high, open collars. They affected airs of nonchalance, discussing Lord Byron's part in the Greek insurrection. Byron had been Wilkerson's favorite poet.

"I find it overly theatrical," one drawled. "Why on earth should an Englishman fight for Greek independence?"

"*Bien sûr*," came a reply. "Byron plays the hero. He sees history as a romance."

Baptiste supposed that this pampered courtier must not really know Byron's heart. Wasn't poetry composed with sincerity?

"Independence is a great cause," Baptiste asserted. "Lafayette fought selflessly for it in America. So did your General von Steuben."

"They were adventurers. Much like Byron. Our Prince Karl sent troops to fight on the side of the English," said a long-nosed young man. He grinned. "The cause doesn't matter, the adventure does. Of course, he chose the wrong side."

"Byron was hounded out of England," another said smugly. "His escapades are meant to obscure his affair with his sister. . . ." The young men all smirked.

One had been studying Baptiste's face. "And where were you educated, monsieur?" he suddenly asked.

"St. Louis Academy," replied Baptiste proudly. The bishop would be amazed to see him now.

"Have you heard that your Mr. Jefferson and Mr. Adams have died, and on the same day?"

After a moment, Baptiste said, "How small the world has become. As I have been traveling, I did not hear the news. It is a great loss to the United States. Mr. Jefferson sent my . . ."—he faltered, looking for the word—"my *patron*, General Clark, to find the way to the Pacific. He will be very sad indeed."

"They were irreplaceable men! Who will lead America now?" the man continued. "They say freedom is the great struggle of our time. Will it be lost in America?"

"Well," said another before Baptiste could respond, "we are told that Americans are not just free, but wild and unruly." This fellow's eyes gleamed insolently. "No man bows to another man there, is that not so?"

Baptiste felt another flash of annoyance. "Democracy replaces its leaders from the citizenry," he said. "The nation will not collapse because its founders have died."

"No nation has tried democracy since the time of Pericles. In America 'the people' is the mob. A mob has no brain! However do they maintain order?"

Baptiste mastered his irritation. He even smiled. It was amusing, if ironic, to find himself the representative of American

democracy! "We are a nation of laws. Those who don't obey them
are punished by the courts. Just as they are here, I presume."

"Ah." His questioner arched an eyebrow and exchanged glances
with his friends. "Well, here is another question. Professor Hegel
tells us that progress is the result of conflict between opposites.
But your savages have clashed with Europeans for many years
and yet no progress has come."

Baptiste maintained his neutral expression. He had never heard
of this Hegel or his theory of opposites. It sounded ridiculous.
And here was the word *savages* again, uttered mindlessly by a man
who considered himself "civilized."

"Indians are being forced to cede their lands, their hunting
grounds, their trade routes and gardens. These actions don't bring
improvement," he said evenly. "It is not a clash of opposites, but
oppression of the weaker. . . ."

"Weaker? Aren't they depraved, beyond the reach of reason?
We hear horrific tales of brutal murders, settlements burned,
women raped, and children kidnapped. . . ."

"There is what you call savagery on both sides—"

Suddenly, Paul was at his side. "Baptiste is fatigued, as am I,"
he said, draping an arm over Baptiste's shoulders. He steered them
toward the door. "I thought I had to rescue you. Some of that lot
are obnoxious. They talk of revolution because they have nothing
to do, and are bored to stupefaction."

"I thought they were trying to make me out a fool," Baptiste
said. "They did know a little of America. Am I to be the spokesman for that country?"

Paul raised his eyebrows. "Speak your mind. You are an
ambassador of sorts. Don't let them intimidate you."

✳   ✳   ✳

IN PREPARATION FOR writing a book about his American travels, Paul began to catalog his specimens, review his notes, and confer with colleagues. Scientists from the German provinces and beyond came to hear firsthand about the trip, and he wanted Baptiste by his side. Baptiste patiently answered questions about Indian tribes, the mineral resources around St. Louis, and, most frequently, General Clark. Except on the latter subject, he always had less to say than Paul did. The scientists had read accounts published by the Corps of Discovery and Major Stephen Long. They ascribed a sacred purity to the vast, little-known "wilderness." Baptiste was amused by this sentimental attitude. Didn't they realize that Indian civilizations had occupied the continent for thousands of years?

A German professor of anthropology came to study Paul's collection of New World plants and animals. "Most intriguing," he kept saying. "Buffon was mistaken when he predicted that anything transplanted to the New World—even men—would in time be degraded because plants and animals there are smaller than they are in Europe."

"Indeed, the opposite is usually true," Paul said.

The professor had a new theory he called "race." He had studied a variety of human skulls to determine how many kinds of people there were in the world.

Paul observed that it was a novel idea.

The professor said, "I have concluded that there are five human races. Of these, the Caucasian is superior to all others."

Baptiste smiled. "Perhaps it is only the most fortunate."

The professor bowed. "I do not mean to cast you as inferior, Monsieur Baptiste. Exceptions prove the rule, do you not agree?" He added, "One day we will have the means to improve the human condition by eliminating the inferior races, or at least their defects."

Baptiste reflected that such views were already being put into practice in America. The government was forcing Indian tribes to give up the lands that sustained them. They pretended it was for their own good. But were they not being slowly starved out of existence? He kept his thoughts to himself, but he was certain that when they were alone, Paul would agree with him.

Everyone had an opinion too about President Monroe's doctrine forbidding any further colonization of North and South America by European powers. Would such a ban imperil the future of scientific investigation? It worried them.

"The United States is still young and must protect itself— but not from scientists," Baptiste said. "Science flourishes when men are free. Mr. Jefferson believed that above all. I am sure that other presidents will as well."

"You make a fine spokesman for America," one of the courtiers said. "As soon as you open your mouth, one forgets that you are part savage."

Baptiste was struck dumb for a moment. Then he said, very quietly and firmly, "You betray your ignorance, sir."

"Oh, pray, pay no attention to him," another hastened to say.

"Forgive me," the courtier murmured.

✳   ✳   ✳

MOST OF BAPTISTE'S days were filled with scientific study
and the normal demands of palace routine, but sometimes Paul
would burst into Baptiste's room crying, "Today we are free!" It
meant they would ride, pushing the magnificent royal horses
to their utmost. Paul said that horses loved to work, and to race.
A horse would run itself to death if its master commanded it. But
he would never do that, of course. Rather, he pampered his mounts,
something rarely seen either in St. Louis or on the plains.

In foul weather, the pair went to an indoor riding school for
the Royal Guards, which Paul had joined at the age of nine. At
sixteen he had been made commander. Soon after that, he begged
his uncle to let him resign his commission so that he could dedi-
cate his life to science. "My father was apoplectic. I was betraying
my royal duty. But I had an ally in my uncle. He founded the Royal
Academy of Science. It is admired all over Europe."

At other times, Baptiste was neither required in Paul's study
nor asked to go riding, and on those days he cherished his independence. Except, of course, for his footman, who shadowed
him everywhere, much to Baptiste's annoyance. After a word to
Paul, the footman was dismissed.

Untethered, Baptiste wandered contentedly, making sketches
in his journal and trying to find words that captured the super-
abundance of cultivation and display. Armies of gardeners were at
work everywhere. Baptiste strolled through acres of formal beds,
discovering orchards and vegetable plots, and even a glass house
that contained trees laden with oranges. He picked one and bit
through its thick rind. Sweet juice flooded his mouth: delicious!
One day he walked for hours across meadows and into dense woods.

He breathed deeply of the fragrant air and marveled that even a forest in Germany looked tended.

He came to a clearing. At its center was a hut. A man was mending its turf roof. Baptiste hailed him, using the little German he had picked up. The man quickly descended.

"Have you lost your way?" he asked. He struck a pose outside the door of the cottage and Baptiste realized he must be defending it from a dark-skinned intruder.

"No, I have simply been wandering your beautiful forest. I am American, here for an indefinite stay."

At this, the man relaxed and introduced himself. His name was Rudolf. "Will you come inside for some refreshment?"

Had he been a larger man, Baptiste would have felt quite cramped in the homely little room. But as it was, he experienced an odd nostalgia, as if he had been there before, possibly in a dream. A plump young woman with cheeks as red as Rudolf's sat mending a garment. She greeted him shyly. Two little girls were playing by the hearth with wooden dolls. They stared openmouthed at him.

Rudolf offered Baptiste the remaining stool. He looked around. The room's walls were whitewashed, the floor made of neatly fitted stones. Lace curtains lifted gently at the pair of windows.

"We enjoy visitors," Rudolf said. "Ramblers sometimes come and interrupt our solitude."

"I am living in the palace," Baptiste explained. His words had an immediate unfortunate effect on the couple. They both started, exchanging looks of distress.

Rudolf said, "You are not a courtier, sir."

"No, I am not. I have come from America with Prince Paul."

"America!" Rudolf cried eagerly. "We hope to immigrate to Pennsylvania." He stood and lifted a wooden box from the mantel and shook it. It seemed to be filled with coins. His wife frowned at him. *Don't show a stranger our treasure!* But Rudolf ignored her. "Do you know that region?"

"No," Baptiste said. He tried to think of something he knew about it. "I believe that the journals kept by Lewis and Clark were published in Philadelphia. It is part of Pennsylvania."

Rudolf nodded. He considered for a moment, then said, "I must tell you that we live here under the protection of the royal family, like every peasant. But my political views are not pleasing to them."

"Oh, some of those people like to challenge my views too," Baptiste replied carelessly. "They are blind to any ideas not their own. I don't take them very seriously."

Rudolf shook his head grimly. "As their guest, you may be able to disagree with them, but my opinions are considered insurrectionary. Failure of crops and lack of employment have caused great suffering here," he said. "And because of that, I believe the monarchy is doomed. But for us, in the present, the news from countrymen who settled along the Hudson River and in Pennsylvania gives hope. Land there is wonderfully fertile."

"I have no doubt that it is," Baptiste said. "I know nothing of farming, only of the fur trade in the West."

Rudolf nearly leapt from his stool. "Do you know John Jacob Astor?"

"I have certainly heard of him," Baptiste replied. "He controls the fur trade in the Great Lakes."

"He was born not far from here," Rudolf said with pride. "He has prospered in America," he added unnecessarily.

THAT NIGHT, BAPTISTE recorded the encounter in his journal. *Rudolf and his little family live a simple, virtuous life in the shadow of a palace stuffed with spoiled poseurs. They are called "nobles." But it is Rudolf the honest laborer who has nobility. He will contribute much to the United States if he manages to emigrate. It seems that many Germans already have.*

The next time he went to visit, Baptiste pocketed some oranges and presented them to Rudolf's girls. They sat on his knees, smiling shyly. He was surprised by how contented it made him feel. He invented a story about a fox and a badger, using comical voices. The girls laughed and clapped their hands. Then their mother sent them outside, each with a curtsy to their guest.

"The girls are already fond of you," Rudolf said. "They will expect to see you regularly."

Baptiste blushed. "If it pleases you, I will come as often as I can. They are delightful," he said.

Rudolf smiled. "Come walk with me for a while. I would like to talk," he said.

They left the clearing and followed a narrow path that snaked through magnificent oaks whose branches formed a dense canopy. "You know, my great-grandfather died—was killed—while working for Paul's great-grandfather, Duke Carl Eugen. He was one of thousands of peasants forced to do work that was dangerous and exhausting. They cut down acres of forest, excavated the great lakes you see now, and hauled the stones that built the palace. Many perished in this effort." He paused, staring into the distance. "Württemberg's Versailles, he called his new home. Armies of serfs carried hundreds of torches to light the forests and the lakes. Why was this?" Rudolf paused for effect. "So that Eugen and his guests could watch satyrs and nymphs spring out of artificial grottoes and perform water ballets."

"It sounds like a Roman orgy," Baptiste commented.

Rudolf nodded. "This orgy should have ended long ago, with the French Revolution. When that didn't happen, Napoleon should have ended it. But instead the monarchy renewed its power." His eyes gleamed, and though he leaned closer, his voice rose. "Now a new wave of rebellion is cresting. Germans are getting ready to throw off our oppressors and unite as a nation. America's experiment is our inspiration. One day it will happen here as well. The people will rise up and cry 'enough!' "

Baptiste was stunned by Rudolf's version of Württemberg history. Paul had carelessly ridiculed his forebears' vanity and display. But he said nothing of the peoples' resistance. And he went on living in a palace built upon the backs of workers little better off than slaves. Was the world the same everywhere?

CHAPTER FOURTEEN

A Hunt

Baptiste sought out Rudolf whenever he could. One day, he rode a horse to the hut in the forest, pulling a second one on a lead. Paul had given him free run of the stables and he took gleeful pleasure in sharing the palace privileges. Rudolf was incredulous. "You want me to ride with you on one of the royal mounts? Do you know that I am a peasant?"

"I do. You shall be our guide. I was born in the company of explorers. It's embarrassing that I have hardly penetrated your country at all. Please. Show me."

Rudolf whistled softly, gave Baptiste a half smile, and swung himself onto the horse. They set out over meadow and low brush. For a long while, the only sounds were the thudding and jingling of their horses and the occasional call of a falcon. They cantered through a shady ravine shut in by rocky hills, and picked their way along the banks of a murmuring stream. Entering a grove of arcing trees, seemingly without end, Rudolf called over his shoulder that they were in the Black Forest. Twice they came upon half-timbered cottages whose occupants were busy carving cuckoo clocks, the local industry, Rudolf said. As the sun sank in the sky, sending yellow shafts through silhouetted branches, they entered a village.

There was a small inn. They stopped in the forecourt for coffee. Before long, a line of ragged men and women hiding their faces in their sleeves snaked along the high street. There were small children in the line as well, all singing. Their plaintive voices sounded immeasurably sad.

"They're beggars," Rudolf said. "Twice a year they must be exposed to their neighbors' contempt to atone for their idleness."

"But surely they don't choose to be idle," Baptiste exclaimed.

"Of course not. It is one of our cruel traditions," Rudolf said. "I will not find it in America"—he raised his eyebrows—"will I?"

"I have not seen it there," Baptiste said. He was thinking how he would miss Rudolf.

Suddenly, Rudolf pushed back his chair and pulled his jacket up over his face. Baptiste, startled, looked around to see what had brought about his friend's action. A roughly dressed man had entered nearly in a crouch, a long sack slung over his shoulder. He cast anxious glances right and left. Baptiste glanced at Rudolf, who nodded.

The innkeeper signaled from a shadowed doorway and the man disappeared with his sack. Rudolf let his face show. "It would not be well for him to see me here with you," he whispered. "He would inform the palace." He made a move to leave.

Baptiste nodded, left a coin on the table, and followed Rudolf outside. They rode back in silence. Baptiste was wishing that he and his friend were free! That was the word that flew into his mind. Free to spend time openly together. But there was still much about German life that he didn't understand. And, to his surprise, he had no intention of asking Paul to explain.

✧   ✧   ✧

A WEEK LATER, as Baptiste descended the palace's great marble stair, a clear soprano voice called out, "M. Baptiste, *l'Américain.*" It was a pretty young cousin of Paul's. She consorted with the long-haired poets; he'd forgotten her name.

"Princess Louisa," she reminded him archly. She wore a toga-like shift with little puffed sleeves and a band tied in the Grecian style around her forehead. With golden curls, opaline eyes, and alabaster skin, she was a confection spun of sugar, he thought.

"Come with me. I have something to show you," she trilled, and, with a toss of her head, skipped off down the corridor. Without a thought, he followed. Her flimsy garment fluttered, giving him startling glimpses of pale, slender legs. She flounced over to a servant who was dozing in a chair, gave him a poke, and laughed at his surprise. Suddenly, she was gone down a corridor.

He found her in a large, dark, wood-paneled room. She flopped onto a chaise and flung her arms wide.

"You see? Grandpapa's treasures," she said. "He had to buy these from great kings because he had no painters of his own. We are poor, that way, in Württemberg. Grandpapa taxed the people until they rose up in protest and had to be put down by the soldiers. Aren't they amazing?"

Baptiste assumed she meant the paintings. Here was another chapter in the tale Rudolf had begun! His eyes slowly adjusted to the dim light and he saw that the walls were hung from top to bottom with canvases. He turned slowly, looking. There were Bible subjects, classical myths, landscapes, battles, portraits.

"And what do you think of our little collection, M. Noble Savage?"

Baptiste turned sharply and couldn't hide a look of displeasure. "Please do not call me that, Your Highness," he said.

Louisa looked surprised. "I love the idea," she exclaimed. "The *bon sauvage*, the good wild man, lives in a state of nature, not yet corrupted by our wicked ways. He is pure, don't you see . . . ?" She was looking intently into his eyes. When he gave nothing back, she turned away and sighed.

"In America the term *savage* is ugly and cruel," he said. "I have not been living in a state of nature, as you say," he added huffily. "I have been going to school, reading books. Voltaire, for instance . . ."

"Voltaire wrote about fools and knaves," she piped up.

"And isn't the world filled with them? In any case, I am not a savage."

She laughed. "I know that! I am teasing you. Forgive me! It is a habit learned at this stifling court to keep from being fossilized. Has Paul told you about fossils?" She stopped to gulp some air, then hurtled on. "Paul has brought you here because he respects your intelligence. 'Noble Savage' is a poetic notion. You must admit that you are an exotic creature here in our little kingdom . . . and so very handsome." She flashed him a sweet smile. "In fact, I want to paint your portrait. I will capture you."

Should he be insulted? She saw him as a subject rather than a person. But perhaps if he let her study him at length, she would see him truly. At any rate, she was beautiful.

"If you like, mademoiselle."

She curtsied. "The light is good in the conservatory."

They set off down shimmering hallways. Footmen and a steward looked up and turned quickly away as they passed. The conservatory was awash in sunlight. She narrowed her eyes and arranged him so that a shaft of light fell on his right side. She took his head in her hands and set it at an angle. He couldn't help laughing.

"You don't take me seriously," she protested. "Where did you get that superior air?" She thrust her chin out at him.

"I am not used to posing," he protested. "No one has ever asked."

"I warn you, I will make of you whatever I wish," she declared. "The artist will follow her impulse. But I promise to honor your beauty." She gave him a sidelong glance. "Plato says that beauty is divine." Baptiste felt blood rush to his cheeks. Louisa laughed. "Do you read Byron?" she asked. "Everyone does. You look like a Byronic hero sprung from the New World."

Baptiste suppressed a smile. People here were forever making observations drawn from some book. Did experience itself affect them?

She began sketching in pencil, frowning and biting her lip. "Tell me what to put in the background. A river, mounds, trees, Indian dwellings like the ones the duke spoke of?"

Baptiste closed his eyes. He described the landscape he had left behind when he took the keelboat down the river to St. Louis the first time. The Mandan Villages sat on the high frozen bank and the muddy Missouri churned beneath its scrim of ice. What a long time ago that was! He had been five. Now he was nineteen. For a moment, he was overcome with amazement at what had happened to him. What a mystery life was.

He had spoken with intense feeling, but Louisa chose to ignore it.

"But our rivers run crystal clear!" she cried. "I will not make a brown river!"

He was supposed to remain still, so he composed himself. He had been surprised, after all, by the depth of his emotion.

Louisa worked with extravagant concentration for a long time, stopping only to chide him when he scratched his cheek. Her eyes flew to him, then rested on the paper, flew back and left him again. It was a strange experience. He might have been just a chair, not a man sitting in a chair.

"I have copied your face," she said. "That's enough for today." Her own face was slightly flushed. Was she embarrassed? Excited? He leaned over to look at the picture, but she blocked his view. "Not until I am finished!"

OVER THE NEXT weeks, Baptiste worked every day with Paul. And nearly every day when they put aside Paul's notes, Louisa was ready with her brush. When, after a few hours, she tired of painting, she proposed that they walk outside. She had foiled her chaperone so often her mother finally dismissed the woman. Louisa was free to go where she liked, to consort with anyone.

LOUISA PUZZLED BAPTISTE. She was giddy and whimsical. Yet she had spoken with eminent scholars and was related to every crowned head in Europe. Sometimes, she was even becomingly down-to-earth.

"You would find my uncles and cousins tedious. Life at court is the same everywhere: There is nothing more boring than courtiers who bow and scrape while scheming to outmaneuver their rivals. How is it in America? Do the people rule the court?" she

asked one day, as they strolled along a garden path that he already
knew by heart.

"I haven't been to Washington City, so I can't say what our
'court' might be like, if we even have one. I suppose my patron,
General Clark, held a kind of court for Indian chiefs. They came
sometimes to ask for favors from the white man's government, but
usually to protest its treatment of them. And the general offered
them treaty terms. He had the power, like a king's, I suppose." He
paused. Louisa was asking about democracy. "Americans are fickle.
They don't hold their betters in high esteem. A man may hold
power one day and lose it the next. Just recently, there was an election and the general lost, even though he had served his country
heroically. His opponents resorted to lies and tricks to ensure his
defeat."

"Where the custom is every man for himself, the best may not
rise to the top, then?"

"Not always."

She looked thoughtful. "But you admire M. Clark? Would
you follow anywhere he led?"

"I am on my own singular path. I have always been," he answered,
aware that he was embroidering—even inventing—the truth.

"You are here at Paul's invitation. You are the human specimen in his cabinet of curiosities."

He was silenced by that. Was Paul only displaying him to the
curious? Louisa must think he had no other purpose in life. Then
he saw that she was suppressing a smile. He was being teased. "And
am I not a fine specimen?" he tossed back.

Louisa raised a gloved hand to her mouth in feigned shock.
"Jean Baptiste, you already sound like a born courtier." Her eyes

dropped to the toes of her dainty shoes. "But I suppose this singular path of yours . . . it will take you back to America, won't it? There is nothing to keep you here. . . ."

"I have no plan to leave," he said hastily. "I am Duke Paul's guest for as long as he will have me."

"But you are free! You are an American! What do you want for yourself? Money? Position?"

He considered. Was he free? In all of his life, he had not felt free. He had believed he must live up to Clark's expectations and his mother's example. Louisa was asking him to say what he himself wanted. He couldn't answer at first.

"I want to be worthy in men's eyes," he said finally.

"What do you mean, 'worthy in men's eyes'?"

"My mother was a good woman who was never rewarded for her brave service."

"You wish to vindicate her—and all the Indians!" Louisa cried, her eyes bright. "That is a noble ambition!"

"That's not what I meant," he answered. "I am Sakakawea's son, but I am not Shoshone. I am my father's son, but I am not French." He paused for a moment before finishing the thought. "And so, I belong nowhere, and to no one."

He hadn't quite articulated that truth to himself before and it startled him. But he concealed his surprise by holding her gaze before turning back to the path in front of them.

After a brief silence, Louisa said quietly, "But if you belong nowhere and to no one, you may make anything you like of your life." There was an edge in her voice. "Nothing is expected of you. You have neither duties nor obligations."

Baptiste shot her a glance. "But you say this as if you were not also free. After all, your family rules this land. Every day, you may follow your whim, walk with me, paint my portrait. You have no cares and look . . ."—he flung his arm wide—"there is not even a chaperone lurking to constrain you."

Louisa's expression hardened. "I will not be free to amble about with you forever, monsieur." She cast her eyes toward the dark forest beyond the garden wall. "You Americans hold your destiny in your own hands. And that is most refreshing in this airless place." But her bitter tone belied the words.

Baptiste was shocked. "Louisa . . ."

"Look, the sun has fallen below the trees. It's chilly." She turned back toward the palace, walking quickly.

Baptiste was confused. What had upset her? He had spoken honestly. But he felt rebuked by her sudden change of heart.

"Baptiste! Are you coming?" she called.

He hurried after her.

LOUISA HAD PLANTED a disturbing idea: Paul thought of him as a specimen in his cabinet of curiosities. She belonged to the court and must know. He began to take stock of his time with the duke. Yes, he was often on exhibit. He felt most on display when he and Paul went hunting.

"You will be astonished by my friend's prowess," Paul would crow to visiting sportsmen. "He is as skilled as the Plains peoples, for whom farming and making things are women's work, whereas hunting is worthy of a man. The Mandan or Sioux male cherishes the hunt as only a German aristocrat can. Truly, it is in the forests of the New World that the noble rituals of the hunt endure. Our German forests are sacred to us, the source of the people's strength. It was Germans garbed in tree bark and fur who resisted the Roman incursions, with their corrupting luxuries." Here, Paul would pause and smile ironically. "Forests like ours are sacred to American aborigines too. Tragically, the Anglo-Saxon settlers are cutting them to the ground."

There was truth in what he said, Baptiste thought. But he could not agree with the romantic comparison of Indians to German aristocrats. And every Missouri youth was skilled at hunting.

"Baptiste is able to think like his prey, to feel its beauty and, like it, become one with the landscape. With us, hunting is blood sport and enflames the passions. But it brings out the utmost self-control in him," Paul continued pompously.

The greatest difference between Württemberg and Indians in Missouri was that no one in Württemberg hunted in order to eat. Prey became trophies; the meat was often discarded. The heads of dozens of animals slain by royal hunters were mounted above the palace's gigantic fireplaces. The practice offended Baptiste. Americans were treating the bison herds in the same way, killing for the sake of killing. Still, this German hunt offered a chance to ride at top speed through the lush landscape and test his skill to its extremes. He kept his objections to himself.

ONE BRILLIANT MORNING, hunters gathered in the stable yard. Horses nickered, raising and lowering their heads, flicking their ears and scraping the ground. Paul idly fed chunks of apple to his mount while he chatted with courtiers. A few women were sitting sidesaddle, backs straight, hats at rakish angles, tendrils of hair falling coquettishly over their cheeks. Their grooms grinned up at them. A priest circulated, joking as he went. He had earlier blessed the hounds. They were a blur of black and brown, yelping and straining at their leashes, eager to be first on the scent.

The horns were blown, echoing over the countryside—and alerting every animal within miles, Baptiste thought. This was not how he had learned to track prey. The pack took off in full cry, divided in two, then merged again. Baptiste hung back. The bunched hunters crossed the long meadows, then broke up into trios and pairs and came together again. Beaters were stationed on the perimeter of the woods. When the stags were flushed out, riders would chase them until they were exhausted. Then the nobles would come in for the kill.

Baptiste spurred his mount to a gallop, relishing the speed and power beneath him. The landscape was a peripheral blur. He heard a shout from behind him—the dogs had scented a stag who was poised, head high, every fiber of its powerful body alert before it turned and plunged into a thicket, the baying pack in hot pursuit.

"We've let it slip!" cried Paul. Other riders pulled hard on their reins and whirled to turn into the forest. Baptiste didn't follow but continued over gullies, through a rippling stream, into a glade of thick oaks. Sweat flew from his horse's flanks. A couple of hounds were tearing ahead through the brush. He had seen a faint trail in the grass. And there was the stag, just as he had expected.

Baptiste had a clear shot. He took it, and the stag fell. He pulled up beside the body and dismounted. The bullet had entered exactly between the creature's eyes. Baptiste murmured thanks. Surely the animal spirits reigned here too.

He waited until two grooms arrived to carry the animal back to the palace. Then he retraced his route, looking for Paul. "I thought my dogs had cornered him," the duke said when they met. "But we erred. When will I learn to stick by your side?" He gave Baptiste a wry glance. "But no one can stick by your side. You are a lone rider."

They hunted for a few more hours, taking two well-antlered stags and a boar. On the way back to the lodge, Paul and Baptiste came upon a group of agitated hunters, some of whom had dismounted and gathered around Paul's cousin Friedrich, who remained seated on his mount. Baptiste had never met him, but he'd heard that pigeons Friedrich raised ate the seeds peasants planted in the fields. When they complained, he only mocked them.

"What has happened?" Paul asked.

"We've captured a poacher," said Friedrich. A groom shoved a man forward, causing him to stumble and fall. His hands were tied behind his back and his jacket was slashed. He had been whipped.

"State your name," Friedrich commanded. The man raised his head with a defiant glare. His face was bloody and grimy. Even so, Baptiste recognized him. *Rudolf!*

"He lives here. Why is he a poacher?" Baptiste asked Paul urgently.

"He has stolen game that belongs to the king," Paul muttered. "Every creature that roams our kingdom belongs to my family."

Baptiste was stunned. Such a crime was unknown in Missouri. Nobody owned the game that roamed the vast forests and plains.

"You know the penalty," Friedrich said casually.

Rudolf's eyes blazed. "My family will starve," he said, unintimidated. "They are already hungry."

Friedrich ignored him. "The penalty for poaching is death by hanging," he said.

"NO!" Baptiste cried. "Let him go!" He had startled his horse, sending a restless wave through the other mounts. Rudolf looked at him with amazement.

Friedrich said coldly, "This is of no concern to you. You do not belong here."

Baptiste felt Paul's hand on his arm. "Baptiste, do you know this man?" he asked under his breath. Baptiste nodded.

"My dear cousin," Paul said. "Baptiste speaks as an American. While I was there, I took prey wherever it roamed. We ought to leaven our justice with mercy, don't you agree? To serve the peoples' needs."

Friedrich glared at him. "You will live to regret this," he muttered. "The peasants will not conclude that we are merciful, only that we are meek."

But he gestured to the groom who was standing over Rudolf. "Release him." To Rudolf he said, "You and your family are banished from this kingdom." Friedrich gave his horse a vicious kick and galloped off.

"Well," said Paul. "I intended that you would enliven our hunt, Baptiste. Now it seems that you function as its conscience."

Baptiste said, "He is a good man. I happened across his home in the forest and have had many enlightening conversations with him."

"I have no doubt of that. You would catch the scent of a good man. It is fortunate that you were here to intercede on his behalf. On another day, he would not have been so lucky."

Baptiste was not comforted. "Thousands of acres of forest and a starving family cannot take game?"

"We live in close quarters here, Baptiste. It is not the American wilderness."

"Without your protection, that might have been me," Baptiste added.

Paul looked startled and opened his mouth to object, then thought better of it.

"You are right."

With a sinking heart, Baptiste went looking for Rudolf the next day. As he had feared, the hut was empty, the family gone.

CHAPTER FIFTEEN

———◆———◆———

Thinking about the Future

One evening, the young courtiers introduced a new dance called the waltz, which paired a man and a woman in an embrace and sent them flying about the room to a hectic beat. To Baptiste it was stirringly romantic. Their elders stood about lamenting the fading popularity of the minuet, in which dancers moved together in a stately walk, punctuated by bows and curtsies. "It is the dance of kings and the queen of dances," one of them told Baptiste with a sad shake of his head.

A composer of waltzes had been brought to the palace to play. He filled the room with sound, throwing his body up and down the keyboard. When he invited onlookers to try the dance, Baptiste boldly took Louisa in his arms and swept her in wide circles over the floor.

"Baptiste, you're brilliant! My mother is shocked—look at her expression!" Louisa whispered. Baptiste nodded to the woman, who was indeed glaring at him. Louisa's scent made him light-headed. He fancied he could feel the beating of her heart through his coat. His was thundering. He breathed thanks to old Signor Lagonia, who had made a confident dancer of him. A fie on Louisa's mother! He didn't care what she thought!

✦   ✦   ✦

THEN, FOR DAYS on end, he saw nothing of Louisa. It was so strange—he realized he'd grown accustomed to her companionship. He waylaid one of her servants, who said she had gone to visit a cousin in Baden-Baden. Why hadn't she told him she was going? He went over every one of their exchanges but could not explain it.

A week later, there was a timid knock on the door of his bedroom. Louisa was there.

"Let me in. Quickly!" she said, throwing a glance up and down the corridor.

"Where have you been?" he asked.

"Mama...I was taken to see a distant cousin....He is my intended."

"Your *intended*?" He stared at her.

"My life was planned when I was born, Baptiste." She pursed her lips and sighed. "You are a man. Your life is yours to make. You are American....You will go where you choose and do what you wish. I am a woman and a princess. My duty is to marry the man they choose for me."

"My mother was forced to marry my father. I watched him beat her. I think she died an early death because of him."

"I will not suffer," she said gently. "I will have children and serve my master. He will surround me with such luxuries as he can afford. I will link my family to his and enrich them both. One day, one of our sons will sit on a throne."

"You are a princess! Can't you—"

"German princesses are as common as wildflowers in a field," she said lightly. "I will have no importance whatsoever except as a maker of babies."

"But that's the way of the past! You're sacrificing your happiness to further a dynasty." He clapped his forehead.

"My dear! I must do my duty. You are so handsome, so intelligent. There is no one in the whole world like you!"

She touched his cheek, opened the door, and slipped out. When he stepped into the hallway, she was gone.

IT WAS A second loss. Baptiste had found friendship in Europe with Rudolf and with Louisa, only to have it snatched away by stupid customs and cruel masters. He spent days wandering out of the palace and long minutes later finding himself in the orangerie or in the arbor, with no memory of having set out for either place. If he took his journal, he jotted down a few sentences. Sadness turned to anger. Louisa's passivity infuriated him. But it was nothing compared to the injustice suffered by Rudolf and his family. Baptiste's eyes filled and his sentences veered over the page. Rudolf had been a real friend—he had trusted him. Was there anyone now to trust? Was Paul truly his friend?

In the mornings, he was expected to organize Paul's notes. He sat in a sunny corner of the room that housed the collection, writings and drawings arrayed before him. An hour or two would pass, and he'd have accomplished nothing.

Paul's tolerance was quickly exhausted. One day, he said, "I am going to Mergentheim. You will come along."

Baptiste answered tonelessly, "Will I? And if I prefer to stay here?"

"I say this for your own good. You are melancholy. I know it is quite fashionable these days. But your feelings will lift in a different setting."

"My feelings are quite appropriate!" Baptiste muttered.

Paul's expression softened. "Of course. Your emotions rise from deep within you. You are my American and always have been." Baptiste flinched at his condescension. How could he have thought he was Paul's companion? He was his trophy.

"Not everyone overlooks race, as you know, even in Germany," Paul added more sharply.

"Rudolf did."

"You know full well that he broke the law. Come to Mergentheim. You will find that pleasure is a powerful antidote to loss."

THE SPA AT Mergentheim had been built after a shepherd stumbled over some steaming hot springs. Their sulfur content was especially high—the highest in Europe, people claimed, and especially effective against disorders of the digestive tract. If only that were his complaint, Baptiste thought. Paul's entourage took the waters and enjoyed diversions such as the new game of roulette and the still scandalous waltz. Baptiste refused to dance, disappointing those who had seen him perform at the palace, but gradually, his mood began to improve in spite of himself.

After a few weeks, the royal party traveled on to Bad Carlsruhe, Paul's birthplace, where the magnificent hunting lodge was surrounded by streets laid out like a fan. The change of scene hardly mattered for the hunting party, who took their quotas of stags, boars, and pheasants and then sated themselves at lavish banquets.

AFTER SEVERAL MORE weeks, Paul announced that the entourage was about to pull up stakes again, this time to travel to

St. Petersburg for the funeral of his cousin the czar. Baptiste thought that this endless, extravagant pilgrimage was absurd. He was accumulating remarkable experiences of no value at all, moving over the map of Europe like a sleepwalker.

"St. Petersburg is a young city, created by Peter the Great, a visionary ruler who deserved his title," Paul, ever the teacher, told Baptiste. "Württemberg is a mere gilded duchy, while Russia is a great state whose immense power has created awe-inspiring opulence protected by ruthless secret police and all-powerful censors. We have them too, but on a modest scale."

The czar's funeral had drawn delegations from all over Europe. Alexander was both mourned and reviled. He had instituted democratic reforms early in his reign but then revoked them. "I hear that members of the officers' corps are planning a coup to seize the throne," Paul reported. "There are two royal heirs battling to succeed the czar."

Indeed, the city was an armed camp. The harbor was filled with gunboats, and soldiers lined every avenue and canal. At a reception, Baptiste was introduced to the British ambassador and he spoke English for the first time in three years. The Englishman was bubbling with a gossip's self-importance. He claimed to know that the czar had not died at all. "His Majesty was seen only yesterday boarding a ship to go into exile. He has found a monastery that will take him in."

"Is there a chance that reformers will seize the throne?" Paul asked.

"It is possible. The American infection is overspreading Europe," the diplomat replied with relish. "The fires of revolution have been lit again." He urged Baptiste and Paul to pay a visit to

London, where another of the Württemberg cousins was king of England as well as of the German province of Hanover. Paul remarked that few observers found any redeeming qualities in the man. Indeed, he might be the worst monarch ever. He was long estranged from his wife and had fathered children with a bevy of mistresses. He ate and drank to excess and was even more obese than Paul's own grandfather, "The Great Belly," had been.

A battle over succession would be waged there as well. Despite the odor of reform he detected in the air, Paul said he had no interest in who the next English monarch would be. But he was very eager to attend a meeting of the Royal Society in London. When Baptiste looked puzzled, he explained that it was the foremost scientific organization in the world, although a German one was rapidly catching up.

And so their whirlwind tour continued. To get to England, Baptiste endured a short but brutal crossing over turbulent, metallic seas. Their little boat was tossed like a leaf. He wasn't quite as sick as he had been on the Atlantic, but guarding constantly against the possibility that things would get worse left him exhausted, when they finally landed at the base of a rocky cliff. They climbed a long stair to the top and rode in a creaking coach.

A railway had been laid between Darlington and Stockton, and Paul said he must see it. George Stephenson's engines were being tested, generating outraged objections from every quarter. Gentry protested routes that crossed their estates, farmers claimed cows in the vicinity of trains would quit giving milk, and there was general fear that trains would make women miscarry their babies. Even women not with child had no business on trains, gentlemen said.

They took a test ride, sitting with Stephenson himself on the bench of the engine, facing the stove and behind a barrel of water. Crowds lined the tracks, heedless of danger, to cheer as they chugged along. Its speed was hardly greater than that of an aged horse. The engine was unequal to climbing hills, so they often rolled along below ground level or on a bridge that had been thrown from cliff to cliff. Paul was almost deliriously excited. He kept saying to everyone they met that the promise of rail travel was without limit.

"It is the dawning of a new age," Paul said.

"Didn't the steamboat already mark its dawn?" Baptiste asked, flaunting his own experience of Progress.

"The steam railroad will affect far greater numbers," said Paul. "It is a juggernaut! More amazing technologies will follow in its wake. Every man will have his personal steam-driven vehicle and be free to go wherever he fancies. Think of it! Mankind's dominion over the earth will be complete. Individual liberty is all but guaranteed."

A young woman rode with them in the open engine, clutching her hat. She exclaimed that now she knew how a bird felt flying through the air. In the passenger cars, people coughed and choked on the smoke. But the sense of the railroad's power to go and go, without ever tiring, was exciting. And the smoke was white, unlike that of the steamboat, which blackened the sky.

But what will happen, Baptiste wondered, to horses and carriages and stagecoaches and all the men who drive them? And how will all the traffic be managed?

Paul was thinking along similar lines, but with his customary optimism. "Such problems will be solved by the same ingenuity that breeds all innovation. Since trains can outrun any method we have to send messages," he mused, "it will be crucial to keep accurate time and to set schedules, or else calamitous wrecks will ensue. The problems will all be solved by standard clocks and schedules."

IN LONDON, PAUL decided they would stay in a hotel rather than guest quarters at the palace. He chose a Quaker establishment.

At breakfast, he frowningly poked around the table, then called to the innkeeper, "Sir, why is there no sugar?"

"We are boycotting it, Your Highness" was the host's reply. "The sugar trade finances the slave trade. We aim to do away with it. When sugar goes, slavery will follow, is our hope."

"Good for you," said Paul. "Perhaps my companion and I could have some honey."

"I hope your boycott succeeds," Baptiste said.

"I believe that in the end, right shall triumph," said the innkeeper.

"I wonder if such a campaign could be effective in America," Baptiste said.

"It must be tried," said Paul, "or the country will be split asunder. We have agreed that there is not a superior race nor an inferior one."

The innkeeper turned to Baptiste. "We have news from our brother in Philadelphia," he said. "Thou may be interested to know that General Jackson is campaigning energetically for the presidency. He asserts that the election was stolen from him in '24 and many agree."

Paul, not to be left out of a political exchange, interjected, "Jackson strikes me as an American Bonaparte."

"Not at all," the innkeeper said. "He stands for giving every man a vote, even those without property. He is a democrat."

"Property or no property, if the electorate isn't educated, the great experiment will end in mob rule," Paul observed.

Baptiste said, "Candidates and their handlers seek votes in many different ways. Elections can't be driven in a single direction. Americans love competition." He was wondering if it was possible that the new universal suffrage law would award him a vote if he went back.

"We have been disappointed that Mr. Jackson is curiously unmoved by the struggle of the Indians to survive," the Quaker observed.

"That will greatly mar his rule, if so," said Paul.

When the innkeeper had withdrawn, Baptiste confronted Paul. "I thought you championed equality. Why do you talk about mob rule?"

"I am the devil's advocate," Paul said evenly. "But I have always said that it is education that breeds responsibility. And democracy demands responsibility of its citizens. If there is not universal education, it will not work."

Thinking about America from a vantage in Europe is like viewing the panorama in the square in St. Louis. Unlike Europe, America is constantly unfurling. Life is bound to be very different when I go back——. But am I going back? When?

BAPTISTE AND PAUL admired the many new parks and squares being laid out around London. They were sylvan refuges for the new class of men made suddenly rich by mechanized factories. As they strolled through Regent's Park, Paul remarked, "You know, Napoleon planned to escape from his exile to America. He imagined that if he got a fit of the blues, he could jump on a horse, ride like the wind, and never meet another soul. It seemed like a dream of heaven to him, after the wars and intrigues of his life."

"It's true. A gallop over the plains liberates a man," Baptiste said.

"And any man may take that ride, be he a deposed emperor or Osage warrior," Paul added.

A well-heeled aristocrat passed them in a carriage with a driver and mounted footman. "Here in England, life seems to be strictly hierarchical," Baptiste observed. "Where a king sits at the top of the heap, everyone below him must also have someone to reign over."

Paul laughed. "Monarchies will disappear in my lifetime, and with them, the hierarchy of classes. In my old age I expect to be just a simple citizen."

But he needs money to finance his expeditions, and that comes from the king's coffers, Baptiste thought.

AT THE ROYAL SOCIETY, Baptiste listened to Michael Faraday lecture on the effects of temperature on the intensity of magnetic forces. His announcement of a successful generator using alternating electric current caused the man next to Baptiste to utter an exclamation. "This is the end of our age of steam! Behold the age of electricity!" he said, rising from his seat. Baptiste thought the age of steam had been remarkably brief.

The next evening, Paul took the podium to deliver a colorful account of his trip up the Missouri. He described the tribes he had met, the varieties of plants and animals he had collected for his museum in Württemberg, and the founding and operation of trading and army posts by the government. As arranged, he pointed to Baptiste, who sat in the back, and asked him to stand. The members turned to ogle him and he bowed.

"Mr. Charbonneau is a man of many parts. He has graciously agreed to answer your questions when I have finished," Paul told them. "My subject is vast. I cannot hope to be comprehensive."

The members of the Royal Society plied them both with a great many questions and the meeting didn't break up until after midnight. On their way out of the building, two members solicited confidential advice from Paul about investing in American railroads. *Why am I still here?* Baptiste asked himself. *Other men see the future in America.*

THE NEXT DAY, they called at Buckingham Palace, and Baptiste waited in a gallery while Paul met with the king. Two portraits of American Indians wearing the ruffles and silks of English courtiers hung among the dozens of paintings crowding the walls. The men must have been brought to England just as he had been brought to Germany and been assimilated or at least appropriately costumed. Their appearance had been captured by painters and was on display for generations to judge. How had they felt, he wondered. Did taking them from their native culture rob them of vital qualities? Or had they gained some? Their expressions gave no hint of an answer.

He remembered Louisa asking him what he wanted from life. He decided to put the question a little differently to Paul when they were alone.

"What are the rewards of a well-lived life, would you say?"

Paul took a few moments to consider. "Surely, it is the esteem and admiration of others." He held up a finger while he thought further. "Hunger for the esteem of others is as natural as hunger for food. Conversely, the contempt of the world—or even its neglect—hurts like a kidney stone."

Baptiste reflected that he had said almost the same thing to Louisa. "Isn't it odd, then, that human history is so filled with men who commit evil acts?" he said.

Paul laughed. "Not every man esteems virtue," he said. "Many are governed by beastly impulses. Now tell me, you have seen much of Europe these last months. Where would you go next, if you had your choice?"

Baptiste remembered Caesar and all the other emperors whose names he had memorized in school. It seemed so long ago. He felt a rush of affection for Reverend Peck. What ancient site would Peck want him to visit? He couldn't decide. Place-names without much meaning tumbled about his brain. Then one shone with clarity above the others. "I would like to see where General Pompey died," he exclaimed.

Paul's eyes widened. He opened his mouth to say something, seemed to think better of it, smiled to himself, and said, "An interesting choice. But for now, let us go home! We have been away more than a year. I have family business to attend to. And I believe that your malaise has been addressed, has it not?"

Baptiste merely nodded. Paul always did what he pleased. Paul hadn't thought to ask him what the rewards of the well-lived life were and he had no desire to tell him his own opinion. He had served at the pleasure of Duke Paul for over four years. He must not put off becoming his own master much longer.

CHAPTER SIXTEEN

The Pillar

Soon after they arrived at Ludwigsburg, Baptiste told a courtier he wished to see Louisa.

"She is in Schloss Restatt" was the reply. "With her husband, the duke of Baden-Baden."

He had known it would happen and yet the news upset him.

He found her watercolor portrait of him propped on a chair in his room. She had left no note.

"Girls do have to marry," one of the poets told him that evening. "It is always arranged by others. Soon she will be a stout matron with babies tumbling about her and you will have no more interest in her."

"Get on a horse," another advised, more sympathetically. "Feel the wind on your face."

Baptiste took the advice, riding for hours every afternoon. Of course, that reminded him of Rudolf. He convinced himself that his friend and his family were in Pennsylvania, breaking ground for their first planting.

One day, passing through a village, Baptiste heard a man's sonorous voice issuing from a beer garden. Intrigued, he tied his horse to the post and went inside. The man was reading from a book to an audience of peasants and burghers. Baptiste took a seat and listened. The text began to sound familiar. Then it dawned on him: It described events set in America.

Other men took turns reading, and when it was over, Baptiste pushed through the crowd to ask the work's title.

"*The Last of the Mohicans,*" he was told. "We gather regularly to read the works of James Fenimore Cooper. This is his latest."

"Really! A society for reading American novels!"

"He is very popular! We love anything from America, but Cooper especially. There are Cooper Societies all over Germany." The man's eyes sparkled. "May I ask, without offense, sir, does Indian blood run in your veins?"

"My mother was Shoshone," Baptiste said. His questioner's eyes brightened.

"How do you come to be here?"

"I am the guest of Prince Paul."

"The explorer! We are told he is writing a book about his American journey."

Others crowded around to listen. Baptiste received a barrage of eager questions: "What is the condition of banks in America?" "Why are there so many religions there?" "Is it true there are no taxes?" "No compulsory service in the army? No secret police?" "Can a man really buy land for one dollar and twenty-five cents an acre, and have years to pay?" "They say men easily achieve wealth and power in your country—and yet dine with their inferiors by choice...."

Another man brandished a letter sent from America by his brother-in-law. "Listen, here is what he says:

"*Dear Brother-in-law and Sisters-in-law: One beholds here how the farmer lives without worries. In Germany no one knows how to appreciate the liberty to which every human being is entitled by birth, only here in America can he experience it. Here the farmer may speak as freely as the nobleman and the scholar, everyone may express his opinion in accordance with his knowledge and judgment, for all the laws depend upon the people, and all the officials as well; that is, the people get together and elect them the way the burgomasters are elected in Germany, and they receive no more remuneration than they need for a reasonably good living. There is a tremendous difference, here the officials and priests are dependent upon the people, and in Germany the people are dependent upon the officials and priests. . . ."*

The man thrust his chin at Baptiste, waiting for corroboration of the writer's assertions.

"What he says is probably true. I cannot say. I lived in a town, and then at a trading post. My people are not farmers. America is a big country. Here, you all know what your place is. In America, every man must carve out his place—and often push someone else aside to occupy it." This didn't seem to discourage any of the men.

BAPTISTE LEFT THE place feeling sick at heart. His little speech had forced him to admit again that for over five years, he had been supported by an immensely wealthy man only so that he was available at all times for hunting and other diversions. It had made him soft, dulled by luxury and a pampered routine! He'd left America at eighteen, before he found resources of his own and done so little to find them here.

He could not return to America unless Paul helped him. And so he raised the matter again.

"Paul, I think my usefulness to you has reached an end," he said. "I want to go back to Missouri. It is time to begin my life—"

To his surprise, Paul replied before he could finish his sentence. "We have become entirely too settled, I agree! I am ready to mount another expedition. We will return to the New World together."

Baptiste was immensely relieved and instantly forgiving of Paul. "Will you resume your journey to the western mountains?" he asked.

"First, I propose that we have one last adventure together."

Baptiste looked disbelieving.

"You will not regret it," Paul promised.

He was taking them to Africa. There was a week of preparations and the week after that found them in Spain. The crossing from its southernmost port to the "Dark Continent" was mercifully short. To Baptiste's relief, these waters were calm and the air deliciously balmy. Their party consisted of six: themselves, Schlape the valet, a sketch artist to record the highlights of the trip, and a baggage handler. Paul hired an Arab guide in Tangier.

The utter strangeness of Tangier's sights and smells brought out Paul's playful side. "I have a surprise for you, Baptiste," he said, pausing for effect. "I'll tell you when we get to Alexandria. Five thousand years of history is concentrated in Egypt."

"And Egypt is where Pompey died!" Baptiste said, pleased to find something to look forward to on this unwelcome detour.

"Indeed!" Paul went back to his maps.

Baptiste wandered the jumbled, labyrinthine passages of the ochre medina until he arrived at the stone-vaulted souk. The smells of incense, smoke, and cloves, and other scents he couldn't identify, were intoxicating. Merchants beckoned from every side with carpets, fabrics, pipes, and potions, and called out to him in several languages. Sometimes, as he rounded a corner or climbed a stair, an Ottoman soldier in Turkish dress would suddenly loom. He felt completely at liberty in these mazes. But that was an illusion: They were heavily patrolled.

Paul was eager to gain admittance to a harem. "One sees paintings of such sensual scenes in Europe. But they are only works of the imagination. No Western men have been permitted to go inside. With a few coins and the right gatekeeper, though, I think we will have a unique experience." He lifted his eyebrows.

Baptiste said nothing—all he knew of harems came from *Candide*, and he had a feeling that was a fanciful depiction. Paul was accustomed to getting what he wanted, but in this case, success was unlikely. Indeed, Paul conducted only one or two negotiations before he had to give up.

"It seems that the tales I have heard of concubines and their eunuchs entertaining visitors are mere romances," he admitted. "Apparently, no man may lay eyes on another man's harem." It soured his mood for a while.

Paul perked up when they were invited to dine with a sheik and his male entourage. It was a lavish experience, with strange music, exotic flavors, and seemingly sincere expressions of friendship.

Baptiste summed up the visit in his journal:

Europe and America are changing the pace of the world with their bourgeois insistence on business. In the Arab world, it is leisure that brings satisfaction in life. I was more drunk on it than alcohol ever could make me. All of my senses were stimulated by this place. My only regret is that I have no Arabic and so cannot appreciate the poetry, which Paul says is magnificent. He tells me the hospitality shown us by the sheik is a cardinal Arab virtue.

Paul is fascinated by politics, as always—the British and French are vying for dominance on this continent that is so blessed with mineral wealth. Napoleon's invasion made Europe aware of Egypt and now everyone wants a slice. The same fate may lie in store for other African states below the Sahara. Exotic places raise ravenous appetites in the white man.

At last, the travelers set off for Alexandria, where Paul would reveal his surprise. Old Alexandria lay a few miles from the modern city. It was a ruin of houses with the remnants of walled gardens, laid along regular streets. All that was left of Cleopatra's palace were a few marble walls. It was a sobering scene, proof that magnificence and power were as transitory as all else in life.

They stood on the site of the fabulous Alexandrine library. It was in this city, Paul said, that Euclid developed geometry, Archimedes accurately calculated the value of pi, Eratosthenes estimated the circumference of the earth, Galen gained his understanding of medicine and anatomy. It was here the length of the year was first calculated to be 365 and 1/4 days. All of that in Alexandria! Baptiste allowed himself to feel the layers and layers of learning embedded in this place. He thought of the Mounds in Missouri that were supposed to contain ghosts of an ancient civilization. But no one was studying or even trying to preserve them. He supposed that such places were always looted, wherever they were.

The next day the scholars and dignitaries who were their hosts led them through the Muslim and Jewish neighborhoods of the new city. Most of the houses supported gardens on their flat roofs. The city was thriving, they were told, because of a recently completed canal that linked the Mediterranean harbor to a river, for the transport of Egypt's principal product, cotton.

"Ours is the century of canals," Paul remarked.

Baptiste shot him an amused glance. "Surely of steam," he suggested. "And electricity." Paul ignored him.

"You must see where the Pharos lighthouse once stood in the old harbor, one of the Seven Wonders of the Ancient World," said a bearded old man in their party.

"Yes," Paul replied. "And the climax of our visit . . ." He whispered into the man's ear and was rewarded with a giggle. The fellow beamed benevolently at Baptiste.

What could this surprise be?

To find out, they traveled three miles over the desert on donkeys, for only Muslims were permitted to ride horses. Baptiste was very amused and called out, "A fine figure you cut!" to Paul, who gave him a dismissive wave.

Their objective was a massive red granite tower that rose cumbrously in three parts to the sky and was crowned by a Corinthian capital. Alongside it crouched a carved sphinx. Baptiste regarded the lofty structure with polite interest. Why had Paul been so eager to show him this? The answer soon came.

"Here we are at last: Pompey's Pillar," Paul declared, giving a magician's flourish, very pleased with himself. "When Captain Clark carved his name on that huge rock, he named it for this ancient monument."

Baptiste gasped, and thought instantly of his mother. How moved she would have been, had she lived long enough to know he had come to this place! She had gone bravely into the unknown and strived to understand what she saw. Now so had he. For a moment, emotion made him tremble. If only she had lived! And

Clark: If only he were here to see it! The experience felt momentous. His eye fell on the sphinx, which stared imperturbably ahead. How fortuitous that this keeper of mysteries should be here too! But she had to be prompted to reveal her secrets. What should he ask her?

Instead, a question for Paul popped into his mind. "Are you truly intending to return to America?"

"Of course I am," Paul said carelessly. "I have more than one lifetime of exploring to do. The continent is a paradise for the scientist. I will certainly write more books about my journeys."

Baptiste said, "I am very glad to hear this. I want to go back." His voice cracked with emotion.

Paul laughed and put his arm over Baptiste's shoulders. "I need some time to prepare," he said. "I wanted you to see Pompey's Pillar first." As they walked, he added, "I daresay you'll be missed at the palace more than I. You're a popular fellow."

They went arm in arm along the causeway. It was only later that evening, as Baptiste recorded the conversation in his journal, that he realized he had forgotten to ask the sphinx a question. How could he have missed such an opportunity?

CHAPTER SEVENTEEN

◆————————◆

Becoming a Man

Paul could not be hurried, so Baptiste decided to immerse himself in German literature while he waited. He began with Goethe, Hegel, and other thinkers of the day. He read all the rest of Humbolt's *Travels* with amazement. To him, the earth was not disconnected entities. Everything was linked. What happened in nature in one place affected places everywhere.

The great explorer had recently returned to Berlin from his residence in Paris to serve as tutor to the crown prince. Paul deplored this "waste," as he put it, of Humboldt's genius. "He'll have a hard time espousing liberty at the Prussian court," he said drily.

Baptiste said nothing. Berlin was only a few days away by coach. Why couldn't he go there? It made him feel childish to think that he would have to ask Paul for permission—and for funds.

A few days later, fate seemed to demand that he go. One of Paul's fellow naturalists arrived. He had no sooner thrown off his cloak when he cried, "Baron von Humboldt has been giving remarkable talks in Berlin. He's attempting to explain science to ordinary folk." He laughed. "You don't believe me! But hundreds have flocked to hear him! There are shopkeepers, bricklayers, delivery boys, weavers, clerks, housemaids. . . ."

"And do they comprehend?" Paul asked.

"Seemingly!"

"Can anyone attend, then?" Baptiste asked.

"That seems to be the idea," said the man. "He speaks nearly every night, and from only his usual hodgepodge of notes that fly every which way, no proper text at all. Of course, we all know he is nonpareil."

Baptiste looked at Paul, who seemed to consider, then said, "He is the most famous and admired man in the world. This is an opportunity you must take. I wish I could go with you, but there are matters here that claim me." Baptiste was too excited to ask what those matters might be. Paul arranged for Baptiste to ride as far as Leipzig in a private coach belonging to a local woman of means. From there, he would buy himself a ticket on an *eilwagen*, a kind of diligence.

Germany, he was reminded, was many little countries. He had to produce his passport at nearly every border. Some of the towns and cities they passed through locked their gates at dusk and travelers could enter or leave only if they paid a toll that increased by the hour.

They crossed the final flat plain from Leipzig to Berlin in twenty hours. The *eilwagen* driver proudly referred to the beautifully macadamized highway as a *Kunst Strasse*, or art road, so well made was it. The plump English tourists packed into his coach kept boredom at bay by singing. The weather was cold, but the hot exhalations of his carousing companions steamed the windows. Finally, the merry matron squeezed against Baptiste's right flank asked why he was visiting Berlin. His answer instantly sobered the whole group. "Baron von Humboldt, the Traveler . . ." "We must go!" "Can we hope that he'll express himself in English?" Baptiste said he was afraid not, and they all shook their heads sadly at this chance opportunity so cruelly withdrawn.

There was no more singing and they passed the rest of the journey in pleasant conversation. They passed through the magnificent Brandenburg Gate and along Unter den Linden, whose palaces evoked the ghosts of Greece and Rome. He noticed with a start that legions of soldiers lolled about the empty avenues and suddenly the noble city looked like an armed camp.

The *eilwagen* discharged its passengers. After bidding them farewell, Baptiste asked a soldier for directions. Surprisingly, the man knew all about Humboldt's lecture. It would commence in three hours and he had better show up at the Singakademie two hours early if he wanted a seat. Did he know that Baron von Humboldt had traveled more than six thousand miles in South America?

Outside the hall, mounted police were already herding a milling crush of people of every age, every class, and every line of work. There were even women eagerly awaiting scientific enlightenment. Some enthusiasts had attended previous lectures and promised that no one would be disppointed. And while the baron's ideas might be well received in Paris, how brave he was to declare them in Berlin! He might have the king's favor, but even in the palace, enemies of his liberalism abounded.

Finally, the crowd was funneled into the hall. There was a call for silence. The only sound thereafter, save for an occasional cough or the scraping of a chair leg, was that of Humboldt's clear, gentle voice. He roved the stage, gray-haired and shabbily dressed in an outmoded coat and knee breeches, trailing scraps of notes like autumn leaves. With powerful fluency he invoked the vast canvas of the universe and the laws that knit it together. To illustrate, he described fossils, mosses, northern lights, nebulae, ocean depths, magnetism, temperature zones, the migration of peoples over the globe—in short, Nature, as he had experienced and understood it. All Nature was knitted together, and when men disrupted it, the effects could be felt not just in that place, but everywhere.

Human cultures and economies were inseparable from nature. He told his listeners the so-called New World was not "savage" or "degenerate," as Buffon had claimed, but as ancient and rich as their own. The democracy being tried out there would eventually spread over the world, to all peoples, because it was right and just.

He acknowledged that many thinkers disputed his ideas. He welcomed it. "Without a diversity of opinion, the discovery of truth is impossible."

Diversity of life, diversity of thought—his ideas were tied together by the uncanny force of his intellect and imagination, the poetry of his language, and, Baptiste felt, by the soulful comprehension of his listeners. All were rapt, he most of all. In fact, Humboldt's words often seemed addressed directly to him. The baron referred to himself as "half-American." While in America, on the peaks of mountains and volcanoes, he had looked out over the world and perceived a unified, living organism, a great chain of cause and effect, death and renewal.

John Locke had said that in the beginning, the world was America. Humboldt hoped the future would be America, the world united under Nature and with human rights for all peoples equally.

He called for the study of science. "It is in undertaking these researches that we prepare ourselves for an intellectual delight, a moral freedom that strengthens us against the blows of destiny, and which no external power can possibly destroy."

BAPTISTE WAS SO stirred by these words that he stumbled out of the hall barely conscious of the chattering throng. The brisk winter air cleared his head as a cheer rose. He turned and saw a knot of people surrounding a slight figure emerging from the building—Humboldt!

The people's adulation threatened to topple him, but Humboldt attended to every question and gave each a thoughtful answer. Baptiste hovered at a distance, with no hope of attracting the great man's attention. He felt fortunate just to witness the scene. He thought of Lucretius and his idea that all the material world was made up of swirling atoms. The truth of unity in both men's vision of the universe awed him.

Suddenly, Humboldt's eyes met his. He held Baptiste's gaze and then beckoned. People around Baptiste looked curious and made way for him. They were about the same height. That made it easier to overcome his shyness.

"Sir, it has been the great honor of my life to hear you speak," he said.

"You are a North American," Humboldt said with a smile. "You stand out in this crowd."

"My mother was Shoshone, my father born in Montreal," Baptiste said. Prodded by Humboldt, he quickly summarized his life story. Humboldt was astounded. He had met with President Jefferson just after the purchase of Louisiana and learned of the

plan to send Meriwether Lewis to explore the vast territory! What
a beguiling coincidence—what had brought Baptiste to Berlin
at this moment?

Baptiste began to explain, very aware again of the press of curious faces surrounding them, and then of a pair of towering men in
uniforms adorned with the Prussian black eagle who were making
clear their intention to remove Humboldt from the scene. The baron
nodded curtly to them and placed his hands on Baptiste's shoulders.

"I am glad we have met," he said quietly. "My most fervent
wish was for a life in wild nature. I believe you will live that life."

And then his escort took him away.

Baptiste lingered in Berlin until his money ran out, except for
the coach fare in his boot. There were no more lectures that week.
The return journey gave him plenty of time to think about
Humboldt's hopes for America—and for mankind. Who would
protect the native peoples and their cultures, free the slaves, halt
the evils of empire and its exploitation of nature? What man would
choose not to fell a forest or dam a river if profit were involved?
Weren't greed and the human instinct for enterprise too powerful
to be contained? Jefferson and Clark expected commerce to solve
American problems. How could it? Had Humboldt uttered a
prophecy? Was that what the sphinx might have told him?

Paul asked to hear about Humboldt's talk, but he was clearly
preoccupied, tapping his fingers on the table and periodically
clearing his throat. He let Baptiste finish and then said, with false
nonchalance, "A matter has been decided while you were gone."
Baptiste braced himself.

"I am to be married in a few weeks. Our trip must be put off
for a while." Paul smiled ruefully.

Baptiste was stunned. Instead of offering congratulations, he blurted, "But to whom? I haven't seen you with—"

"It's an arranged match," Paul said evenly. "My wings are being clipped. My bride is a duchess of Thurn and Taxis. Her father owns several breweries and has an income from the postal service. That is recommendation enough, isn't it?" Paul grinned impishly. "Her name is Maria Sophia," he added.

"And so you will stay in Germany," Baptiste said.

"For the moment. I'm being given Schloss Mergentheim. I will install my museum of natural history there. The hunting is exceptional, as you know. We will be free of my uncle and his court. Finally, I escape the burden of family—by starting one of my own!" He laughed.

"A family," Baptiste repeated stupidly.

"Babies are expected of husbands. Don't look so unhappy! You will enjoy the hunting, truly, Baptiste."

Baptiste took a deep breath to calm down. His reaction was selfish. He owed Paul his good wishes, at the least. "I am sorry. It is such a surprise," he said. "I wish you both well."

"That's my good man," Paul said.

BAPTISTE WAS A speck in the crowd at Paul's wedding less than six weeks later. Peasants lined the streets to cheer the royal procession. Baptiste wondered if they'd been forced to attend. The wedding party entered the palace through the garden, under a triumphal arch festooned with flowers. Paul wore full military regalia, the red, white, and blue of the Württemberg ruling family. The bride's gown gleamed white and a veil blurred her face. A dozen bridesmaids bore her train. There were heralds with trumpets, and monarchs from the German provinces and many countries.

A bishop joined the couple in matrimony. The royal family was Protestant, while most of their subjects were Catholic. Baptiste marveled at the passivity of the people. But they were well accustomed to obeying the pope and despising their rulers.

After the ceremony, the newlyweds received their well-wishers. Baptiste had heard nothing from Paul except the secondhand order to wear his "American garments." He was, after all, the embodiment of Paul's work.

"Baptiste! My dear companion! Sophie, here is my hunter extraordinaire!" Paul gave Baptiste a hearty clap on the back. His bride held out her little hand to be kissed. She had flung back her veil, exposing blond curls, milky skin, and a frosty civility. She evinced not the slightest interest in him.

He sat at a long table, far from the happy couple and the extraordinary centerpiece of sugar, resin, and chalk that depicted a garden with hunters, hounds, stags, and Adam and Eve lurking in a glade. A choir of children serenaded the happy couple. Baptiste allowed himself to wallow in gloom. All hope that Paul would return to America, and he with him, was gone.

PAUL AND HIS bride took up residence at Mergentheim Castle with her retinue and his household from Stuttgart. The buildings and grounds dated to medieval times, with numerous improvements and additions made over the centuries. The newlyweds had separate apartments.

When he resumed work on his book, Paul mentioned that Mergentheim had only lately been acquired by his family.

"Napoleon seized the property and gave it to Württemberg. My grandfather sent troops to take possession. The local peasants resisted. They managed to disarm the royal army and tear down the Württemberg escutcheon. There was a bloody battle, which we won, naturally. It left strong resentment in the town, though. That was less than twenty years ago."

Baptiste only half heard him. Paul had a wife, and he had no one. He had lost his friends and Paul didn't even appreciate his own good fortune.

A FEW DAYS later, Baptiste wandered into the nearby village. He wondered if its inhabitants still resented their royal neighbors, as Paul had implied they did. A poster advertising passage to America hung in the window of a beer garden. He went in and listened for a while as a man read from a guidebook describing the astoundingly fertile land that waited to be claimed in the Ohio and Mississippi Valleys. When the audience was invited to come forward and sign a paper of intent, many rushed to do so.

So many Germans are desperate to start their lives over in the New World. I am ready to start mine too, but I'm anchored to Paul. Marriage for him is an arrangement for the distribution of power and wealth. Affection plays little part. Clark and Cadet loved their wives. But love must be rare among kings and princes . . . because dynasties depend on solid foundations and love is like quicksand.

America came into being to overturn the Old World custom that confines men to the class they were born into for the rest of their lives and the lives of their descendants. In Europe, only a duke has the freedom to do and go wherever he likes.

PAUL BEGAN TALKING about another expedition, but wouldn't say when it might take place. "In a few months," he said evasively. Baptiste had no choice but to be patient. They worked side by side every day. Many evenings, he dined with Paul and Sophia, who barely spoke to each other. Paul was pleasant enough, but he displayed no particular affection for his bride. Still, after a few weeks, there was an announcement: Sophia was to have a child.

The shared dinners ceased after that. Baptiste seldom saw her. But twice, as he passed her living quarters, he heard her high, sharp, hectoring voice, followed by Paul's low, placating one. Perhaps he could feel some sympathy for his friend after all.

WHEN HE PASSED the tavern in the village, sounds of laughter and fiddle music made him sad. He recognized it as self-pity, but made no effort to cast it off. One evening, a few soldiers of the military guard were standing outside. "Come on, have a drink with us," one of them cried. He paused. Why shouldn't he try to have a little pleasure?

Inside the tap room, a drinking contest was under way. Some men were already stumbling about, and everyone was talking at a high volume. The air reeked of beer and sweat. He was surprised to see that the group was not entirely male. A pair of young women were parrying the attentions of several grinning troopers. Baptiste shook his head when he was offered a stein of beer.

"What's this?" cried his host, roughly seizing Baptiste's shoulder. "Come now, you're a man among men. The duke gives his pet permission to drink!" This brought an explosion of merriment from his mates. The situation seemed dangerous, but Baptiste realized he liked the danger. These imbeciles were in for a surprise.

One of the girls, the blonde, pushed a man away when he tried to nuzzle her neck. She was watching to see what Baptiste would do.

"You think me a pet, do you?" he asked the group.

"Barbara, what do you think?" the soldier asked. The blond girl looked Baptiste up and down.

"I think he's more man than all of you fellows together," she said, and turned away as if her opinion settled the matter. Baptiste accepted his stein and drank deeply.

"All? All?" the men shouted, laughing. They were beside themselves now. Barbara winked at Baptiste. She didn't appear to belong to any one of the men. Her friend was letting a husky buck wrap his arms around her.

"Let's see who's the best man!" cried an officer with an excessive mustache. He pulled a fistful of darts from a wooden box on the bar.

"D'you throw darts in America?" one of them asked, in a provoking tone.

"I don't know," he said. "Maybe." As a boy in the Mandan Villages, he and his friends hurled spears at a ring. He had competed in St. Louis and at Lisa's fur-trading fort.

"The American plays for Barbara!" declared the mustache.

Baptiste glanced at Barbara. She raised her chin and grinned.

Baptiste remembered that Paul had pretended to Missouri yokels that he didn't know how to shoot. "All right," he said. "I don't know how, but I'll try."

A dozen men stepped up to take turns. Baptiste was to go last. Each man selected his dart, raised it with a flourish, bowed to the company, took a long draft of beer, bowed again, stepped to a line cut along the floor, and took careful aim. *THUNK!* Cheering and boasting followed.

This took a long time. Barbara's friend disappeared with her soldier.

When Baptiste finally picked up his first dart, there was a forest of feathers near the center of the board but the bull's-eye was
still empty.

"Throw true!" Barbara called out. He smiled at her and she
winked. He threw. Bull's-eye!

Silence fell over the company. "He's won," someone said after
a moment. "Claim your prize, sir," said the sergeant.

He went to Barbara and put an arm around her waist.

"You've won me," she said huskily. For a moment, he was uncertain what to do. The men's expectant faces, flushed, damp, leering,
crowded around them. In another instant, Barbara pulled him away
from the bar and into a back room. The men began to whoop.

In St. Louis, some of the older boys used to return from summers
in their mothers' villages bragging of conquests or simply of having
dispensed with the necessary business of ending their virginity.

It made him terribly sad to cross this meridian so thoughtlessly.

AFTER THAT, BAPTISTE stayed away from the town. Once
he nearly crossed paths with one of the officers on the palace
grounds but spotted him in time to duck behind a wall. He wasn't
proud of such behavior. Gradually, Barbara faded from his mind.

Paul finally began to plan his American expedition. He had
studied the accounts of other explorers who had penetrated the
Upper Missouri and the Rockies, and the prospect of blazing his
own trail put him in high spirits.

"Come, Baptiste," he might say, putting his work aside,
"I challenge you to a race!" Off they would go on horseback, Paul
making up the rules of the contest as they went along and calling
the winner.

"I was first," Baptiste might protest.

"No matter! I was ahead most of the way! Now we will see if you are any better at shooting than you were last year."

Paul's buoyant good humor made it hard to stay angry. And the silly games made time pass more quickly. "It's so tedious, isn't it, waiting for an heir to be born," Paul would complain.

"It must be tedious for you. You can't crack your whip and hurry her up."

"Her maid tells me she's impossible—full of cravings and complaints. Thank heavens I'm here with you and not with her in Regensburg."

"So you say," Baptiste said drily. What a compliment!

THE MONTHS CREPT by. Late in August, his wife's family summoned Paul to Regensburg. The happy news that he was the father of a son preceded his return from there. The atmosphere in the palace brightened. Everyone Baptiste passed was smiling. At dinner, many toasts were given to the health of the little heir. Finally, four days later, Paul himself returned, playing proud papa to the hilt.

"Congratulations," Baptiste said when they met in Paul's study.

"Fatherhood is more gratifying than I imagined," Paul replied, beaming. "Had Sophie given me a girl, I would naturally have been disappointed. But this male child is a spark!" He chuckled. "I feel years younger."

The royal pair had done their duty.

A FEW MONTHS later, on the second of March, 1829, Paul sent for Baptiste. He was in a very different frame of mind.

"It seems that an infant has been born to the daughter of one of my guards, and it is yours," he said icily.

Baptiste was stunned.

"Do you deny it?"

"A child," Baptiste repeated woodenly.

"This is the first I have learned of your involvement with the woman."

Baptiste barely heard him. How would he support a child? He didn't know how he was going to make his own way in America. Where in that rough-and-tumble world would Barbara and their bastard fit? *Bastard?* What was the matter with him, using that term? He would have to marry Barbara.

"The girl has had many partners. But no one who sees the child can doubt that you are its father."

"I will to take them to America."

Paul barked out a cruel laugh. "That is out of the question, Baptiste."

"But it cannot be!"

"I imagine Sergeant Major Fries had a scheme to extort money from you—or, rather, from me."

"I haven't even spoken to him—"

"That's fortunate. He is a hothead."

"I must do the right thing for her."

"You know nothing of our customs or laws. No court will permit you to marry the woman. You are an indigent. You don't have a guild license and you are a foreigner."

"Can't you vouch for me?"

To that, Paul curled his lip. "I cannot blame you for your naïveté, I suppose. These restrictions apply to all Germans as well as to yourself. It has become very difficult for young people to marry. The result is a tide of illegitimate babies. Fortunately, we are addressing the problem with suitable orphanages."

Voices rose in the corridor outside the room. A door shut loudly.

Baptiste was in a panic. But Paul seemed to have offered a lifeline. "Then it is no disgrace for a baby to be born out of wedlock?" he asked.

This caused the duke to explode. "Baptiste, my patience is limited! You will not marry this girl. And under no circumstances will she accompany us to America. I have made all necessary arrangements with Sergeant Fries. The unfortunate episode is closed."

Baptiste would never forget the pattern of carpet beneath his boots. What could he do? He had fathered a child! He was to simply abandon it—and its mother?

"It is time for you to grow up, my friend. You do not live in a storybook," Paul said, turning to his work with a final sneer.

Baptiste was transfixed for a moment, gazing at his patron's back.

His anguish was tempered in only a matter of days, when an officer quietly told him that Barbara Fries's child had died. The infant was born frail and could not thrive, the man added.

Baptiste felt pity for Barbara, relief for himself, and then a wave of crippling guilt. In the end, relief triumphed over guilt. It seemed that a perverse god was watching over him after all, one who didn't hesitate to cause unnecessary suffering before offering a way out. Perhaps it was for the best. He must get on with his life—or, as Paul put it, *grow up.*

CHAPTER EIGHTEEN

America

*"Prince Paul William of Württemberg, a nephew of the
king of England, arrived at New Orleans from Europe in
pursuit of knowledge. About six years ago, he spent some
time exploring the upper regions of the Missouri but
business requiring his return to Europe . . . he has revisited
this American hemisphere and will in the prosecution of his
former plan cross the Rocky Mountains and visit the
continent on the Pacific. He is in his thirty-third year."*

—New Orleans *Times-Picayune*, January 29, 1830

As soon as they set sail from Bordeaux, Paul was as carefree as a
freed prisoner. He and Sophie had been formally separated; she
would live thereafter at Regensburg, while he maintained his
domain at Mergentheim. While Paul had a reprieve from his marriage, this trip to America was underwritten by his wife's family's
fortune. When their child was older, he would send for him and
oversee his formal education. Sophie would not protest; she had no
legal right to keep her son. Baptiste thought bitterly that the

arrangement was reminiscent of Clark's agreement with Sakakawea. The mother lost any say in what became of her child. But would the father pay more attention to his son than Clark had to him?

Baptiste was unpacking his belongings when the boatswain rapped on the door of his cabin.

"Will you be bringing the master's supper to him, or will he eat with the captain?" the man asked.

"I am not his valet," Baptiste said coldly. "I am his companion." The man's eyes bugged and he backed into the corridor. At dinner, Baptiste gave him another malignant stare and the fellow was sullenly deferential for the remainder of the voyage.

Resentment continued to prick at Baptiste during the weeks it took to reach New Orleans via Santo Domingo, and then on to St. Louis. The duke had paid no price at all for his marriage and its failure, while he, Baptiste, was locked in the prison of his mind, reviewing, over and over, his missteps.

I must look on the positive side of the ledger and count the ways Paul has enhanced my education by bringing me to Europe. I speak English, French, German, and Spanish. I am well read in history, philosophy, and natural science. I now have the habit of bathing every other day. I can fight with a saber. My palate is discriminating (and may no longer be satisfied by frontier fare). I am seven years older, stronger, and, thank heavens, wiser.

It is said that being in the mountains cleanses a man's mind. May they cleanse mine!

WHEN ST. LOUIS came into view—sprawling, smoking, and cacophonous, affection for the familiar swelled Baptiste's heart. Home! He nearly gasped aloud. He knew this place better than any other; it was where he had been formed. He gazed over the city, transfixed. But his mind protested that it was not home. He had changed and so had St. Louis. His gaze drifted off toward the forests receding to the west and he was calm.

Boats of all sizes clogged the port, including one that looked like a giant hotel and was powered by steam. The whistles, levee songs, and shouts of the roustabouts, the clanking of wagons and machinery, made a deafening racket. Passengers, merchants, hangers-on, and all their conveyances added their discordant notes. Drays loaded with bales of cotton and hemp, barrels of molasses and sugar, rumbled up the cobbled hill and away into the narrow city streets.

America! Headlong, forward-thrusting, go-ahead land of opportunity! How unlike Europe it was, never still, ever changing, almost before his eyes.

"We have more steamboat traffic than on the whole of the Atlantic seaboard. From here, goods are shipped to New York, Constantinople, St. Petersburg, and Canton," their porter bragged. "There's been a land rush, gentlemen. Tracts you could buy for a barrel of whiskey a few years ago now command half a million dollars."

This was what they yearned for in Europe, Baptiste thought. To throw off their chains and, with drive and cunning, conquer a continent! But who was the land taken from?

A short stroll through town took him past dozens of new buildings: mills, breweries, manufactories, foundries, dwellings. He hardly recognized anything, or, more accurately, now and then he glimpsed vestiges of the town he had known, but they only increased his wonder.

Newspaper headlines trumpeted the passage of the Indian Removal Act. The Eastern tribes were to be force-marched to land west of the Mississippi. President Jackson had boasted that his government would pay their travel expenses, as if it were a holiday. "How many thousands of our own people would gladly embrace the opportunity of removing to the West?" he asked. Had Clark acquiesced in this? Baptiste wondered. During all those years as Indian Agent, Clark had tried to enforce Jefferson's ideas and "persuade" the tribes to submit to American society. Could that ever happen now?

His first errand in St. Louis was to be outfitted for the wilderness. He went to the expanded Chouteau-Berthold store, but neither partner was on the premises.

"Ain't you the dandy," observed the clerk. "And who's yer barber?"

Baptiste laughed. He would let his hair grow, of course. His silk tailcoat and stock also set him apart from the local men. He needed some American clothes.

The clerk filled him in on developments in the fur trade. "Cadet's the partner of John Jacob Astor, no less," he said, "heading the Western Division of the American Fur Company. You might find him at his counting house."

"What happened to Ashley's crew?" Baptiste asked, still hoping that Jim Bridger had survived.

The man looked blank.

"The Enterprising Men he advertised for in '23," Baptiste prompted.

"Ah. After early failures, they have met with success! Colonel Ashley's gone to Congress. His best men are in business for themselves."

"Who are his best men?"

"Old Gabe. Tom Fitzpatrick. Jim Beckwourth. Robert Campbell. Astor undertakes to drive them out of the mountains, but they're putting up a hard fight."

Baptiste felt limp. The hope he had carried for so long was finally dashed for good. He turned away. But then, just to be sure, he asked, "Jim Bridger has no part in this enterprise?"

"Why, that's Gabe," said the clerk. "He's an owner of the company. We call them the Opposition, as they're opposed to Astor."

Jim was still out there! He would find him. Cadet would be able to help.

BAPTISTE'S NEXT ERRAND was to deliver the report of his time abroad that, seven years before, Clark had said he would expect. He rented a horse from a livery stable and rode to Marais Castor, Clark's country home.

The orchards and vineyards surrounding the plantation had grown to maturity but were still in winter's grasp. It was a fitting estate for such a man, Baptiste thought—rough-hewn, compared to its European counterpart, but vigorously productive.

Clark met him at his front door. He sported a fringed brown hunting shirt bound at the waist by a long scarlet sash. Though he was white-haired and past sixty, he still looked virile.

"Pomp!" Clark exclaimed. "My dear boy. You look the picture of suavity. I am so pleased to see you."

Baptiste realized he was smiling broadly. Affection pooled in his breast.

THE SECOND MRS. CLARK ordered tea and punch and they sat drinking it in the parlor. Baptiste asked politely about events in

America over the seven years of his absence. It produced a litany of vexing changes.

"Our republic has become unruly," Clark concluded. "Liberty was our first ideal. This generation claims it is equality. We hear Senator Clay talk of 'the self-made man.' When every man wants to make himself richer than every other man, how are they to be 'equal'? Once raised above their fellows, they cling to their gains and strive mightily to stifle competition. Mr. Astor is the prime example. It is said that his profit from furs was one million dollars this year. He bought the better part of Manhattan Island with it. Mr. Jackson has invented an American myth with his 'Equality of Opportunity.'"

"But that is the magnet that draws men from the Old World," Baptiste said. "People in Germany look to America. I met many who were eager to come here to liberate and also to enrich themselves."

"They will be productive citizens, I suppose. But let me tell you of the president's inauguration in Washington City, which Mrs. Clark and I attended. General Jackson allowed *the People* in. The mob nearly destroyed the President's House, smashed china and glassware, and he himself was almost suffocated against a wall. Finally someone put tubs of punch on the lawn to lure the new democracy out." He shook his head wonderingly.

"You know, sir, in Europe those 'People' would have been thrown into prison and left to rot after such an incident," Baptiste said.

Clark threw him a sharp glance. "Yes, but liberty entails responsibility." He shifted in his chair. "Please, I am eager to hear about your long sojourn away."

"I have made up my mind what to do with my life," Baptiste said.

Clark's eyebrows shot up. "Tell me."

"No one, save Paul, knew me in Europe. I wondered if I could find my place there. Would they see me fresh and judge me on my merits? Then I saw a man nearly killed for hunting on a royal preserve. The guilds were closed to me and so was marriage. I never felt despised for my mixed blood, but I had no business there. And so, I came back to America.

"I find the nation is being made by white men for white men, many of them not even born here, as I was. I cannot be a citizen; I cannot make my voice heard on any public question. I cannot put my education to work for my own or the common good. Thankfully, it will always feed my soul."

Clark's blue gaze bored into him. His lips trembled. But he didn't speak.

"And so, I will go into the mountains," Baptiste continued. "I will seek my fortune with the mountain men. I can follow sign. I am self-reliant. I will not be tied to any one or any place."

Clark said softly, "You left here a boy and have returned a man."

"It is my pursuit of happiness," Baptiste said.

Clark laughed. "I remember. Your Lucretius address."

Baptiste was silent for a moment. He had the approval he'd always sought from Clark. He needed no more. "I am told that Cadet Chouteau is running Astor's Western operation," he said.

"Indeed. They have built Fort Union, with Mr. MacKenzie in charge. It is themselves against their rivals, whom they call the Opposition. They find every way to skirt the law and introduce liquor there. No bargain with Indians is ever made without it."

"Has there been any improvement to the living conditions of the tribes?" Baptiste asked.

"My boy, I wish that I could ease your mind on that score," Clark replied. "The life your mother knew as a girl has been all but erased from the plains."

"To her sorrow, she knew that would happen," Baptiste said.

"We had to weaken the Indians when they were hostile. Now that most of their lands have fallen into our hands, justice and humanity require us to cherish and befriend them," Clark said wearily.

"But their wretched condition seems to stifle any affection for them," Baptiste observed. He was struck by the phrase *fallen into our hands*. How innocent and misleading it sounded!

Clark sighed. "They have come by the hundreds to me for aid and comfort during your absence," he said, his voice rising slightly. He leaned forward. "I fed and housed them and my wife even sewed shirts for them." He added, "Of course I paid her for her labors." He grimaced. "But if I am damned in the hereafter, it will be for the treaties I made with them."

So he did feel guilty.

"Relations are even worse now," Clark went on. "The government assigns an agent to every tribe. Many have never before laid eyes on an Indian. They keep the tribes in continual broils and quarrels for their own profit."

Baptiste decided to try to comfort him. "You tried to stem the tide of history." That prompted a new thought. "Have you heard anything of my father?"

"Oh, yes. From time to time he is hired by some traveler and pretends to guide him. I thought of retaining his services for Duke Paul."

Baptiste laughed. "He is a rascal and Paul likes rascals."

Clark leaned toward him. "Baptiste, I know he left you no legacy," he said. "He taught you nothing of life. You were denied a father's guiding hand. Perhaps I am to blame."

"Sir, do you think for a moment that I would trade the education you provided me for a few lessons in scheming?"

Clark emitted a "Hmmmpf." After a moment, he grinned. "I suppose not, my boy."

A high-pitched scream was heard at that moment. Mrs. Clark leapt to her feet and cried, "*POMPEY!*"

Baptiste sprang up automatically. But she wasn't looking at him; her attention was on the outdoors, a few dozen yards distant. Clark twisted in his chair to peer out the window. "He's all right," he said unconcernedly. "He has taken a little fall." Nevertheless, Mrs. Clark apologized and made her exit.

"He's only five," Clark said. "His mother favors him."

Baptiste sank back into his chair. His heart was pounding.

A new son called Pompey. *He must call every "promising little boy" Pompey*, he thought.

He felt hurt and embarrassed. The name Pompey had been his badge and his mother's pride. It marked him as exceptional! He had carried it on his sleeve forever! But now it seemed that Clark expressed nothing by it but careless affection, distributed among any number of little boys. After a moment, Baptiste wanted to laugh at himself. He had made far too much of a small boy's nickname. There was no need to cling to it now. He had reached manhood. His last illusion, that he had been Clark's one and only Pomp, was now erased, and that was fitting.

✳   ✳   ✳

CLARK WAS SAYING, "While you were gone I listed the whereabouts of all members of the Corps of Discovery. It was a melancholy exercise. So many are dead or missing. Your mother, of course, but it cheered me to write that you were safe in Europe."

"I'm glad to have brought you cheer, sir, but it is time for me to leave safety behind."

Clark gazed appraisingly at him.

"Well, I wish I could help you in your endeavor. Ashley's expedition was fatal to my fur company," Clark replied. "If I were you, I would apply to Cadet. He is a genius of commerce. And he bridges the cultures. The Chouteau name is now stamped on flagpoles and on Indian medals throughout the West. His lobbyists induce the Congress to pass laws favoring the company, and the government does its business with the tribes through him." He chuckled. "And yet he still refuses to conduct his correspondence in English. It annoys a great many Americans."

"I had already decided to consult him."

"*Carpe diem*," Clark said. "I am told that Mr. Astor predicts that beaver hats are going out of fashion, to be replaced by silk."

"Interesting. If so, it will uplift the trade in buffalo hides."

Clark reached for him. "Blazing new trails is fitting for the son of Sakakawea." His eyes twinkled. "And you will be a good capitalist. That will ensure your liberty and, I hope, your prosperity." He wrapped his huge arms around Baptiste, murmuring, "Do not forget me."

"I used to fear that you would forget me," Baptiste responded.

"Never, Pomp. I always looked forward to reports of you—and I hope news of you and the great things you will achieve will continue to find my ear."

AS HE SPURRED his horse, Baptiste turned to look back at the house with its garland of fruit trees. Surely, he would return here before very long, to tell Clark that the strands of his destiny had been knitted together.

CADET CHOUTEAU DIDN'T look much older. He was still raven-haired, wiry, and keen. His eyes glinted in eager expectation of sharp dealing, and his speech and gestures were urgent, as if the stakes were rising every moment. Indeed, they were. Cadet's world throbbed with entrepreneurial energy. He was the sort of man who triumphed in this new United States. He greeted Baptiste with an enthusiasm that seemed only a little ironic.

"So, have you realized that Europe is finished and your future lies with us frontier provincials?" he asked.

"I would never call you a provincial, Cadet. I understand that you luxuriate for months at a time in New York City."

Cadet laughed. "You have caught me out, Baptiste. Yes, I do. Emilie loves to shop in New York. And Mr. Astor's interests overlap my own."

"You manage a vast enterprise, French and German united," Baptist observed.

"American," Cadet corrected. He studied Baptiste for a moment. "We negotiated an Osage treaty a few years ago," he said. "It established reserves for métis. Some provision had to be made for them."

Baptiste waved at him to stop. "I want to enter the fur business."

Cadet's black brows shot up.

"Baptiste, you must know that it is no place for a man of your education...."

"I haven't become a milksop, Cadet."

Cadet smiled. "And in what capacity would you join us, Baptiste?"

"As a free trapper."

Cadet's eyes widened. "Trapping brigades these days are a motley crew who do the trapping themselves and avoid Indians. Our men and the competition gather for the annual 'Rendezvous,' where our company buys their pelts and sells them supplies."

"So I understand. Ashley's expedition changed the way business is done. It is surely the most independent, self-reliant way of life a man can lead today."

"Indeed. And dangerous. We are launching a major offensive to undercut the competing company of Ashley's remnants." Cadet paused to see that Baptiste understood.

"If I were to follow your brigade, it would lead me to the Opposition," he said.

Cadet laughed drily. "It would indeed."

Baptiste was satisfied. The Astor brigade would take him straight to Jim, and he was determined to find his old friend. He was leaving material comforts behind—well, not his books. He could see himself reading aloud to Jim. Years ago, the wise Osage chief had said the secret to personal freedom was to have no artificial wants. Baptiste had found the same idea in the writings

of Seneca and Marcus Aurelius. Even Bishop DuBourg had alluded
to it. Baptiste reckoned it must be true.

BAPTISTE AND PAUL had a last dinner together before the
duke set off on his expedition. Baptiste had composed a valedic-
tory statement. When they had finished their venison steak, he
delivered it:

"Paul, you showed me so much of the world. I became a
man while we were together. Seen from afar, America drew me
back. I would like your blessing, as I seek my own way in the
mountains."

Paul smiled. "I had a hunch about you and I was right. You are
a remarkable student of life. There is no quality more valuable in a
man." He raised his glass and touched it to Baptiste's. Their eyes
were damp. The waiter set puddings before them and they attacked
them. Paul was the first to speak again.

"General Clark has arranged for your father to interpret for
me when I reach Mandan country. Is there anything you would
like me to tell him?"

"It would surprise me to know that he had any interest in me."

"You are his son!"

"Then say that I am going to the mountains and to watch out
for me."

Paul's jaw dropped in surprise as he looked over Baptiste's
shoulder. "There is the devil we speak of now. You can tell him
yourself!"

The old fellow entered in a bent crab-walk, twitching and
grinning. His long gray hair was tied at the nape of his neck

and dressed with feathers. Baptiste barely recognized his deeply scored face. He shot to his feet and stepped forward to meet his father.

Grinning, Toussaint feinted, as if to dodge him. Apparently, it was meant as a comical move, so Baptiste laughed. They stood looking each other up and down.

"B'tiste . . . you put me in mind of your mother."

"I know I do," Baptiste replied.

"You've traveled far, I hear . . . in royal company, to gilded palaces." He cocked his head at Paul.

"Sit down, Toussaint," Paul said.

Toussaint darted to a vacant seat. The sinewy old fellow was surprisingly spry.

"Duke never told me you'd be with the expedition," he said cagily.

Baptiste smiled. "I won't be. I'm heading into the woods with a brigade of Cadet Chouteau's."

"Aha!" cried his father, visibly relieved that he would not be hounded by his educated son. "Robidoux and Fontenelle's bunch. They'll be leading you into war, you know. Old man Astor means to shadow the Rocky Mountain Company 'til they find the choice beaver, then snatch it out from under their noses. By such foul means he aims to drive them out of business."

"The Rocky Mountain men can fend for themselves, from what I hear."

"Oh, yes. They are far superior. That's why Astor has to cheat. But lives will be lost . . . ," said Toussaint. With a thoughtful look he added, "War or no war, life is rough in the mountains."

"You've endured the hardships for a good many years."

"Does my heart good to see you following in my footsteps," Toussaint said slyly.

Baptiste was brought up short. His intention was to follow his mother's footsteps. It was true that Toussaint's marked the territory too. But he would not follow his old man's *example*. The appeal of the mountain man's life lay in its purity, not its barbarity.

He wanted to settle a central question with his father. He'd been nursing it for so long it took an effort to draw it forth.

"Tell me about how she died."

Toussaint seemed confused for a moment. His gaze settled on a spot on the floor that seemed finally to provide him with an answer.

"Childbed fever, I expect. I wasn't there.... A man goes through quite a few women in a lifetime. I just lost one more to the cholera." He fingered his chin whiskers and looked at Baptiste. "How about you, son? Have you got a woman?"

Baptiste choked down his fury. "I'm not asking about *women*, old man. I'm asking about my mother. Did the child live?"

"A short while ... everyone at the fort liked Sakakawea," Toussaint added vaguely.

"She was the angel of the Expedition," Baptiste retorted, his voice rising. "She was better than you or any man. Because of her, the Corps survived their journey. You were useless to them. Her spirit will live in history for all Americans!"

Toussaint looked as if he'd been whacked with a board. Baptiste was breathing hard. He turned away to collect himself.

Paul cleared his throat. "Charbonneau, I will require several men, horses, and two wagons for the first leg of our trip," he said.

While they discussed arrangements, the old man shot uneasy glances at Baptiste. Paul raised his glass for a final toast to their endeavors and to the health of the young republic.

Baptiste had recovered his composure. He embraced Paul, murmuring an apology for imposing his ancient grievance on their last meal. "It was necessary," Paul told him, and with a brisk salute he strode away.

Baptiste confronted his father. "I expect we'll see each other from time to time," he said. "I have said what I needed to say. Let us continue on without rancor."

"That's what we'll do," said Toussaint, and let drop a wad of spittle.

When they'd parted and walked a few yards in separate directions, Toussaint called out, "I believe she spoke your name at the end."

THE OLD REPROBATE meant it as a sop to my grief. But I don't believe he was told any such thing. If what he said about childbed fever is true, I can lay some blame on him for her death. But I should not burden my journey with bitterness.

Although I am cutting my ties to the past, I will always be pulled in two directions, an educated man of Shoshone and French blood, on the outside looking in. Yet am I not more American than any pure-blooded white man? They are ascendant now, but everything changes with time. Maybe one day men like me will be full citizens of the land of the free.

Tomorrow I go into the wilderness that produced me. My mother carried me on her back then. This time I go on my own legs.

Baptiste closed his journal and yawned. Was all that too pretentious? He ought to get a good night's sleep. He had a long way to travel in the morning.

AFTERWORD

Because Jean Baptiste Charbonneau left almost no record of his life, we can only imagine it, and that is what this book has done. He was "adopted" by William Clark, who was smitten by the infant. We know that his godfather was Auguste Chouteau, that he was baptized in the cathedral at St. Louis, and receipts of bills for tuition, books, clothing, firewood, and board paid by Clark show that he stayed in various schools until he was eighteen, finishing at the future St. Louis University, founded by Bishop DuBourg.

We know that he went to work at Andrew Wood and Cyrus Curtis's trading post, owned by the Chouteau family, on the Kansas River, where he met Prince Paul. Paul's American diary gives him just a few sentences, saying that after they met, they were together "ever since." Alas, the diaries Paul kept in Germany were destroyed in World War II.

A death certificate for the baby Baptiste fathered in Württemberg lists him as an American, not an Indian or a "half blood." The baby's mother was a soldier's daughter. A newspaper recorded Paul's return to America and we know that Baptiste was with him.

At that point, his life swerved again. He chose to go into the wilderness to live the strenuous, hardscrabble life of a mountain man. He consorted with Jim Bridger, Kit Carson, and all the others during the war that John Jacob Astor, in partnership with Cadet Chouteau, waged to monopolize the fur trade. Though he was often in the vicinity of his mother's people, the Shoshone, he never visited them.

An outsider, Baptiste found a diverse society with the mountain men, who were polyglot, like him, in every sense. With them, he participated in each phase of what history books call "Westward Expansion." He blazed the trails that immigrants in their wagon trains followed to the West. He was a consummate craftsman: hunter, wrangler, furrier, freighter, tanner, smith, merchant, brawler, guide. He trapped beaver until they were the first resource to be used up. Then he hauled buffalo hides, was a hunter at the great forts—Bent's and Bridger's—where pioneers were resupplied on their way over the mountains. He entertained John C. Fremont, "the Pathfinder," and met tourists and journalists who were always impressed by his learning and personality, not to mention his woodsman's skills.

During the Mexican-American War, which added more territory to the United States than even the Louisiana Purchase had, Baptiste was a hunter and guide for the Mormon Battalion, and led it all the way to San Diego. There, his sagacity and evenhandedness were rewarded with an appointment as a judge at the mission. Accused by the American occupiers of bias toward Indians, he indignantly quit and followed the Mormons who went to Sutter's Mill, just in time for the gold rush. Remarkably, Duke Paul was in California at the same time. He saw an Indian youth at Sutter's Fort who reminded him of the handsome young Baptiste. In California, Baptiste reentered society after all of his lonesome years in the mountains and deserts. He was a popular character, and, surviving so many stirring events, Baptiste was a witness to the making of the United States.

Sixty years after Lewis and Clark marveled at the "untouched" majesty of the West, theirs for the taking, President Lincoln paused his titanic effort to preserve the Union to sign a new law. It made the Yosemite Valley a state park, protecting its wildness forever. For the first time, men would adapt their behavior to the requirements of nature, and not the other way around. Months later, Baptiste died. His adventures had taken him from the audacious Expedition, innocent of any anticipation that the unexploited land could be used up, to an act of government that saved some of it for future generations.

Cast of Characters

Characters listed in quotation marks are fictitious; all others are historical figures.

WILLIAM HENRY ASHLEY (*c. 1778–1838*)—Merchant and mining magnate. He published his advertisement for freelance mountain men February 13, 1822. He was elected to Congress in 1831.

"BARBARA"—Daughter of a Württemberg soldier; mother of Baptiste's child.

"BIJOU"—Trapper and guide; friend to Toussaint Charbonneau.

JIM BRIDGER (*1804–1881*)—Legendary trapper, mountain man, linguist, and storyteller; lifelong illiterate, mediator between Indians and westward-moving whites. Blazed Bridger Pass and Trail.

GEORGE, LORD BYRON (*1788–1824*)—Notorious and beloved English poet and lover; fighter for Greek independence.

TOUSSAINT CHARBONNEAU (*1767–1843*)—Western guide, from the Lewis and Clark Expedition (they found him unreliable) to Prince Maximilian's journeys. He and the prince were painted by Karl Bodmer.

CHOUTEAU FAMILY PATERFAMILIAS AUGUSTE (*1749–1829*)—helped found St. Louis and established a far-flung dynasty that traded in furs, principally with the Osage. Pierre "Cadet" (1789–1865) expanded the family business, partnering with J. J. Astor.

WILLIAM CLARK (*1770–1838*)—Explorer, soldier, administrator of the Louisiana Territory, and superintendent of Indian affairs at St. Louis. Clark tried to implement Jefferson's plan to "civilize" the Indians, using trade and schools. He negotiated numerous treaties with the tribes, ensuring that Indian lands would be transferred to white settlers.

JAMES FENIMORE COOPER (*1789–1851*)—Wrote his first novel on a bet. The series featuring Natty Bumppo, pitting civilization against wilderness, was immensely popular. He was in Europe while Baptiste was there. Upon returning, published an attack on American provincialism.

BISHOP LOUIS DUBOURG (*1766–1833*)—Born in Haiti, educated in France. Fled the French Revolution, ending up in Baltimore. He had been president of two colleges when the Church appointed him to be its presence in the new Louisiana Territory. He founded Saint Louis Academy in 1818.

"FATHER FRANCIS"—Instructor at Saint Louis College.

"FRANÇOIS"—French/Osage boy in school in St. Louis.

ANTON FRIES—Baptiste's baby, born February 20, 1829, and died that spring. Baptiste listed in the birth register as "the American Jean Baptiste Charbonneau of St. Louis."

"HONORÉ"—Elderly French citizen of St. Louis.

ALEXANDER VON HUMBOLDT (*1769–1859*)—Intrepid explorer, principally of South America and Russia. First great nature writer to stress the interconnectedness of the global environment—an ecologist *avant la lettre*. He sought to unify science and culture under the Greek term *kosmos*. Immensely celebrated in his lifetime.

ANDREW JACKSON (1767–1845)—The seventh president of the United States and the first to win on a popular vote. He represented the common man. A brawler, soldier, lawyer, and politician, he rose from the backwoods to Washington, DC, and the White House.

"LAGONIA"—Itinerant dancing master in St. Louis in 1817.

MANUEL LISA (1772–1820)—Crafty and ambitious fur trader. Challenged the Chouteaus and Astor. Was married to both Indian and French wives, sometimes simultaneously.

"LOUISA"—Princess in Württemberg.

JOHN C. LUTTIG—Lisa's clerk, or manager, in the Missouri Fur Company. His journal of 1812–1813 was published.

MOUNTAIN MEN—Jim Bridger, Jed Smith, Tom Fitzpatrick, Jim Beckwourth, and Mike Fink all answered Ashley's call to go into the mountains and trap beaver. They were part of a multicultural group that blazed the trails that the settlers followed to the West and helped invent its enduring mythology of self-reliance and grit.

JOHN O'FALLON (1791–1865) and Ben O'Fallon (1793–1842)—Nephews of William Clark, sent as teenagers to live with him in St. Louis. Clark gave them appointments as Indian agents. John was later given a commission in the US Army and made a fortune as a contractor. Ben's hot temper and stringent dealings with tribes earned him a questionable reputation.

DUKE PAUL OF WÜRTTEMBERG (1797–1860)—Explorer, naturalist, and supporter of American democracy. Heedless of danger, he traveled to America three times, finding the headwaters of the Missouri River and crossing the continent, gathering botanical and anthropological evidence for a museum he founded in Germany. Married **Princess Sophie of Thurn und Taxis** (*1800–1870*) in 1827. They had one son and divorced in 1835.

THE REVEREND JOHN MASON PECK (*1789–1858*)—a Baptist missionary to Indian tribes, educator, antislavery activist. Author of several books. He and **the Reverend James E. Welch** organized the first African sunday school, in 1817.

"PELAGIE," "TAILLEZ," AND "WILKENSON"—Baptiste's fellow students at St. Louis Academy.

PLAINS INDIANS—William Clark's Indian agency and the various fur trading enterprises in St. Louis all had dealings with Osage, Sac, Fox, Sauk, Sioux, Arikara, and Potawatomi tribes. Sakakawea was a Shoshone kidnapped by the Mandans as a child and sold or given to Toussaint Charbonneau.

"PRISCILLA" AND "GILBERT"—Slaves belonging to William Clark. Also **Venus, Scipio, York.**

"RUDOLF"—A German peasant, subject of the Württemberg royal family, who immigrates to Pennsylvania.

SAKAKAWEA (*c. 1788–1812*)—Baptiste's mother. Kidnapped by the Mandans as a child from the Shoshone or Hidatsa. She was an unflappable helpmeet to Lewis and Clark. She died of "putrid fever" at an upper Missouri Fort, after giving birth to a baby named Lisette. The baby's fate is unknown.

For some readers, the spelling Sakakawea will be unfamiliar. Her name is frequently represented elsewhere as Sacagawea and Sakajawea. There are several explanations for these variations. Sakakawea was born into the Lemhi Shoshone nation. At an early age, however, she was captured and enslaved by the

Hidatsa. The Hidatsa say that her name means "bird woman," and Toussaint Charbonneau (her husband) referred to her as the bird woman, as did Clark in his journals. The Hidatsa spelling is Sakakawea.

However, the Shoshone say that her name does not mean "bird woman." They say that her Hidatsa name is a homophone for her Shoshone name, which means "boat launcher" or "boat puller," and is spelled Sacajawea. This is the current preference of the Lemhi Shoshone, and although it's spelled a few different ways on their website (http://www.lemhi-shoshone .com/sacajawea.html), the spelling is discussed and made explicit in a special piece by the *Idaho Statesman* (http://sacajawea.idaho statesman.com/chapter1/page1.htm).

The other spelling is Sacagawea, which is related to Sakakawea in meaning, but reflects a different spelling. In Clark's journals, he used eight different spellings for her name, reflecting the difficulty of transliterating another language— especially one that is oral rather than written. Most of his spellings included the letter *g*. This became the official spelling used by the US government and many other organizations.

Although this debate is far from resolved, we chose to use the spelling embraced by the Three Affiliated Tribes (Mandan, Hidatsa, and Arikara) and which seemed to us to reflect the most current thinking of linguists and indigenous scholars.

DR. ANTOINE SAUGRAIN (*1763–1820*)—Born and educated in France, came to North America bearing a letter of introduction to Ben Franklin. He took part in scientific expeditions in the West and, when the Americans took possession of

Louisiana, was the only doctor in St. Louis. He supplied Lewis and Clark with medicines and later was the first to administer Jenner's smallpox vaccine west of the Mississippi.

TECUMSEH (*1768–1813*)—Charismatic political and military leader of the Shawnee tribe. He and the followers of his visionary brother, known as "the Prophet," fought against the Americans in the War of 1812; Tecumseh was killed in battle.

Bibliography

Sources particularly recommended for young readers are preceded by an asterisk.

*Ambrose, Stephen E. *Undaunted Courage: Meriwether Lewis, Thomas Jefferson, and the Opening of the American West.* New York: Simon & Schuster, 1996.

Anderson, Irving W. "A Charbonneau Family Portrait." *The American West* 17, no. 2 (March/April 1980).

————"J. B. Charbonneau, Son of Sacajawea." *Oregon Historical Quarterly* 71, no. 3 (September 1970); also vol. 72, no. 1 (March 1971).

Bergon, Frank, ed. *The Journals of Lewis and Clark.* New York: Penguin, 1989.

Berkhofer, Robert F., Jr. *The White Man's Indian: Images of the American Indian from Columbus to the Present.* New York: Knopf, 1978.

Billon, Frederick L. *Annals of St. Louis in Its Early Days.* New York: Arno Press, 1971 (reprint).

Bowers, A. W. *Mandan Social and Ceremonial Organization.* Chicago: University of Chicago Press, 1950.

Brackenridge, Henry M. *Journal of a Voyage Up the River Missouri, Performed in 1811.* 2nd ed. Baltimore: Coale and Maxwell, 1816.

Butscher, Louis C. "A Brief Biography of Prince Paul Wilhelm of Württemberg (1797–1860)." *New Mexico Historical Review* 17, no. 3 (July 1942): 180.

*Fenn, Elizabeth A. *Encounters at the Heart of the World: A History of the Mandan People.* New York: Hill & Wang, 2015.

Foley, William E., and C. David Rice *The First Chouteaus: River Barons of Early St. Louis.* Chicago: University of Illinois Press, 1983.

Furtwangler, Albert. *Acts of Discovery: Visions of America in the Lewis and Clark Journals.* Champaign: University of Illinois Press, 1993.

———"Postscript." *Oregon Historical Quarterly* 102, no. 4 (Winter 2001).

———"Sakakawea's Son as a Symbol." *Oregon Historical Quarterly* 102, no. 3 (Fall 2001): 290–315.

Hafen, Ann W. "Jean Baptiste Charbonneau." In *Mountain Men and the Fur Trade of the Far West,* edited by LeRoy R. Hafen. Glendale: Arthur H. Clark, 1966.

*Holmberg, James J., ed. *Dear Brother: Letters of William Clark to Jonathan Clark.* New Haven: Yale University Press, 2002.

Houck, Louis. *A History of Missouri from the Earliest Explorations and Settlements until the Admission of the State into the Union.* New York: Arno Press, 1971 (reprint). First edition 1908, 3 vols.

*Hyde, Anne F. *Empires, Nations and Families: A New History of the North American West, 1800–1860.* New York: Harper Ecco, 2012.

Jones, Landon. *William Clark and the Shaping of the West.* New York: Hill & Wang, 2004.

*Limerick, Patricia Nelson. *The Legacy of Conquest: The Unbroken Past of the American West.* New York: Norton, 1987.

Lottinville, Savoie, ed. *Paul William, Duke of Württemberg: Travels in North America, 1822–1824.* Translated by W. Robert Nitske. Norman: University of Oklahoma, 1973.

Luttig, John C. *Journal of a Fur-Trading Expedition on the Upper Missouri 1812–1813*, edited by Stella M. Drumm. Argosy-Antiquarian, 1964 (reprint; original 1920).

Oglesby, Richard Edward. *Manuel Lisa and the Opening of the Missouri Fur Trade.* Norman: University of Oklahoma Press, 1984.

Porter, Clyde H. "Pioneer Portraits: Jean Baptiste Charbonneau." *Idaho Yesterdays* 5 (Fall 1961): 7–9.

Ronda, James P. *Thomas Jefferson and the Changing West.* Albuquerque: University of New Mexico Press, 1997.

Sachsen-Altenburg, Hans von, and Robert L. Dyer. *Duke Paul of Württemberg on the Missouri Frontier: 1823, 1830, and 1851.* Booneville: Pekitancui Publications, 1998.

Sage, Rufus B. *Rocky Mountain Life.* Boston: Thayer & Eldridge, 1859.

Scharf, J. Thomas. *History of Saint Louis City and County.* 2 vols. Philadelphia: Louis H. Everts, 1883.

Schroer, Blanche. "Sakakawea: The Legend and the Truth." *Wyoming* 10, no. 5 (December-January 1978): 20–44.

Steckel, Richard H., and Jerome C. Rose, eds. *The Backbone of History: Health and Nutrition in the Western Hemisphere.* Cambridge: Cambridge University Press, 2005.

Thorne, Tanis C. *The Many Hands of My Relations: French and Indians on the Lower Missouri.* Columbia: University of Missouri Press, 1996.

Thwaites, Reuben Gold. *Early Western Travels, 1748–1846.* 32 vols. Cleveland: Arthur H. Clark, 1904–1907.

*Tocqueville, Alexis de. *Democracy in America.* Edited by Phillips Bradley. New York: Knopf, 1945.

Trafzer, Clifford E., and Joel R. Hyer. *Exterminate Them! Written Accounts of the Murder, Rape, and Enslavement of Native Americans during* the *California Gold Rush.* East Lansing: Michigan State University Press, 1999.

*Vestel, Stanley. *Jim Bridger, Mountain Man.* New York: William Morrow, 1946.

White, James Haley. "Early Days in St. Louis." *Glimpses of the Past* (Missouri Historical Society) 6, nos. 1–3 (January-March 1939) (offprint).

Acknowledgments

This book began long ago as a picture book. As I learned about the baby born on the Lewis and Clark Expedition, it became clear that his story didn't fit into thirty-two pages. It was set aside for a while. I am most grateful to Arthur Levine for reviving the idea of Baptiste's promising life and turning it into a novel. He paired me with the extraordinarily gifted editor Emily Clement, who wouldn't rest until the manuscript was as good as she thought it could be.

As a work of fiction, this story consists of mostly imagined scenes. But many of Clark's remarks are drawn from his letters and other sources from the period, and Prince Paul's from the journal he kept of his first North American expedition. My hope is that Baptiste's story sheds light on the many factors that contributed to what used to be called "the winning of the West."

Professor David Nasaw's encouragement and help at a crucial moment has made me feel very blessed. Professor Patricia Limerick, Western historian extraordinaire and Director of the Center of the American West, University of Colorado, Boulder, took the time to consider the project and put me in touch with Sam Bock, her wonderful research assistant, who read the manuscript and offered excellent advice. Any remaining errors of fact or judgment are mine.

Thank you, everyone.

This book was designed by Carol Ly. The text was set in Centaur MT, a typeface designed by Nicolas Jenson, Bruce Rogers, and Frederic Warde. The book was printed and bound at R.R. Donnelley in Crawfordsville, Indiana. Production was supervised by Elizabeth Krych and Rebekah Wallin, and manufacturing was supervised by Angelique Browne.